'I don't believe for a moment that you have any interest in me.'

'You're wrong.' He reached out and lowered her hood, brushing his fingertips against her damp cheek. In her eyes he saw the startled shock. 'I find you very interesting indeed, Princess.'

He could see from the look on her face that she wasn't at all looking forward to their union. 'Our marriage can be more than political.'

She turned her face to the window, the melancholy sinking in. 'Sometimes I wish I could live like an ordinary woman, just for a few days. Free to make my own decisions.' Her voice held a note of misery, as though she believed herself a prisoner.

'Is it such a hardship, wearing diamonds and silks?'

'Sometimes,' she admitted. She stared outside the coach and said, 'This isn't the way to my grandfather's lodge.'

'We can't go there,' he admitted. 'If we do, they'll find you within a few hours.'

Her face paled. 'Then you really are abducting me?'

'Yes.' He made no apology for his actions. 'You'll still have your holiday away from the palace,' he reassured her. 'And I'll bring you back within a week.'

As my wife.

AUTHOR NOTE

THE ACCIDENTAL PRINCE is a book I've wanted to write for a long time after completing THE ACCIDENTAL COUNTESS and THE ACCIDENTAL PRINCESS. Fürst Karl von Lohenberg was a character who intrigued me in THE ACCIDENTAL PRINCESS, and I wondered what he would do after losing the kingdom he'd been born to rule. He struck me as a fighter—a man who wouldn't stop until he got what he wanted. And in this case he's determined to marry a princess and reclaim his throne before anyone can stop him.

It's no secret that I love fairytales, and all three books in this series have elements of classic stories such as *Cinderella* (THE ACCIDENTAL COUNTESS), and *The Prince and the Pauper* (THE ACCIDENTAL PRINCESS), and it seemed fitting to do a *Cinderella* reversal with THE ACCIDENTAL PRINCE. I had great fun with this book, and I hope you'll enjoy how Karl and Serena fall in love as an ordinary man and woman.

Many thanks to my editor, Joanne Grant, and to Flo Nicoll for her help with this book. I always appreciate the work that goes into making a story stronger. Thanks also to my agent, Helen Breitwieser, for being such a wonderful supporter. I appreciate all of you so much.

Visit my website at www.michellewillingham.com for a full listing of all my books, excerpts, and behind-the-scenes details. You're welcome to interact with me on Facebook at www.facebook.com/michellewillinghamfans or on Twitter at @michellewilling. I love to hear from readers, and you may e-mail me at michelle@michellewillingham.com or via mail at PO Box 2242 Poquoson, VA 23662 USA.

THE ACCIDENTAL PRINCE

Michelle Willingham

MILLS &
BOON®
TM

First published in Great Britain 2013
by Mills & Boon, an imprint of Harlequin (UK) Limited.
Large Print edition 2013
Harlequin (UK) Limited, Eton House, 18-24 Paradise Road,
Richmond, Surrey TW9 1SR

© Michelle Willingham 2013

ISBN: 978 0 263 23271 4

Harlequin (UK) policy is to use papers that are natural, renewable and recyclable products and made from wood grown in sustainable forests. The logging and manufacturing process conform to the legal environmental regulations of the country of origin.

Printed and bound in Great Britain
by CPI Antony Rowe, Chippenham, Wiltshire

Michelle Willingham grew up living in places all over the world, including Germany, England and Thailand. When her parents hauled her to antiques shows in manor houses and castles Michelle entertained herself by making up stories and pondering whether she could afford a broadsword with her allowance. She graduated *summa cum laude* from the University of Notre Dame, with a degree in English, and received her master's degree in Education from George Mason University. Currently she teaches American History and English. She lives in south-eastern Virginia with her husband and children. She still doesn't have her broadsword.

Visit her website at www.michellewillingham.com, or e-mail her at michelle@michellewillingham.com

Previous novels by this author:
HER IRISH WARRIOR*
THE WARRIOR'S TOUCH*
HER WARRIOR KING*
HER WARRIOR SLAVE†
THE ACCIDENTAL COUNTESS††
THE ACCIDENTAL PRINCESS††
TAMING HER IRISH WARRIOR*
SURRENDER TO AN IRISH WARRIOR*
CLAIMED BY THE HIGHLAND WARRIOR**
SEDUCED BY THE HIGHLAND WARRIOR**
TEMPTED BY THE HIGHLAND WARRIOR**
WARRIORS IN WINTER

Available in Mills & Boon® Historical *Undone!* eBooks:
THE VIKING'S FORBIDDEN LOVE-SLAVE
THE WARRIOR'S FORBIDDEN VIRGIN
AN ACCIDENTAL SEDUCTION††
INNOCENT IN THE HAREM
PLEASURED BY THE VIKING
CRAVING THE HIGHLANDER'S TOUCH

And in M&B:
LIONHEART'S BRIDE
  (part of *Royal Weddings Through the Ages*)

**The MacEgan Brothers*
†prequel to *The MacEgan Brothers* mini-series
***The MacKinloch Clan*
††linked by character

To Drew and James,
who will always be princes of their mother's heart.

Chapter One

The outer borders of Lohenberg—1855

Karl von Lohenberg had always been a bastard. For twenty-five years, he'd merely thought it was a personality disorder rather than a reflection of his birth.

He'd been raised to believe he was a prince, the *fürst,* who would one day be king of Lohenberg. And only a fortnight ago, one word had stripped away his future: *bastard.*

His father had ordered him out of the palace, granting him land and a manor house near the borders, as if to say: *hide him where he won't cause any trouble.*

Bitterness smouldered within him, at the way they'd turned their backs on him so quickly. Did they believe he was planning to kill or overthrow the true prince? Were the years of obedience and loyalty nothing to the king and queen? They treated him like a lighted fuse, leading to a keg of gunpowder.

Karl was stronger than that. He knew, well enough, that he'd never regain the throne of Lohenberg. It rightfully belonged to his half-brother Michael, and he wouldn't blacken the royal family or his country with scandal, fighting for something that wasn't his.

He'd given his life to his homeland, believing that one day he would be king, responsible for the lives of many. He *liked* being in command, and by God, he'd been good at it.

Fate might have picked him up by the collar and beaten him into a bloody mass, but he wasn't about to slink quietly into the shadows to lick his wounds. This was his life, and he intended to live it on his own terms.

For there was another way to restore his position. Cold-hearted and villainous, yes, but it *was* a solution.

He simply had to marry a princess.

Karl reached into his pocket and pulled out the letter he'd received a few days ago like the shred of hope it represented. His betrothed, Princess Serena of Badenstein, was leaving the palace on an impromptu holiday to her grandfather's hunting lodge in Hamburg. Alone. The letter from her sister Anna thanked him for his promise to accompany Serena as her protector.

At first, he hadn't understood the letter. He'd made no such promise, since he'd known nothing about Serena's plans. They hardly knew one another, for Karl had only met the princess twice in the six years they'd been betrothed. She was beautiful, with a heart-shaped face, dark blond hair, and green eyes that held years of unhappiness.

Not once had he seen her smile. When they'd first met, she'd eyed him with distrust and more than a little fear. He didn't know what falsehoods her family had told her, but he wasn't *that* bad. He wasn't a man who caused small children to flee into hiding. Usually.

Why would the princess make a journey where her sister felt she needed protection? Wouldn't she have her father's guards and a hundred servants to keep her safe?

His instincts warned him that something was wrong with this so-called holiday. It was doubtful that Serena had invited him at all. More likely, the princess had lied to her sister, to appease her.

But Anna had turned the tables, letting Karl know that his bride was up to something. He didn't doubt that Serena would carry out her plan of leaving the palace, but why was she planning to go alone? Was she running away? Or meeting someone else—a lover, perhaps?

Grimly, Karl folded the letter, his mind taking apart each possibility. It was too soon for anyone in Badenstein to know of his fallen status. At the time Anna had sent this letter, he'd still been the heir to the Lohenberg throne.

If he joined the Princess on her holiday, as Anna had suggested, his presence might grant her protection—but it would also compromise Serena's reputation beyond repair. She'd have no choice but to wed him, even if he never laid a hand upon her.

There would be hell to pay afterwards, but he could live with that. Once he became her prince consort, the scandal would eventually die down, and she could live her life as she wished.

Karl stared outside the window of the inn where he and his men were staying. The skies were growing dark, and he was within a few hours' ride of the palace. In the morning, he would put his plan into action. With any luck, he could claim the princess as his bride before anyone learned the truth about his lost kingdom.

Serena dragged out the small trunk she'd packed with a few days' worth of clothing. Today she would leave the palace, seizing the freedom she craved. She would depart Badenstein with a handful of servants and reclaim her life. Although the risk of discovery was terrible, it was worth it.

Beneath her tightly laced corset, her broken ribs had finally healed after so many weeks. Though it sometimes hurt to breathe or to lift her arms above her head, she'd grown accustomed to the pain. And after today, everything would be different.

Serena ran her hands over the brass-bound trunk and then ordered Katarina, one of her most trusted ladies, to ensure that the trunk was placed inside the coach she'd carefully prepared. Her heart was beating so fast, she pressed her hand to her chest as if she could steady it.

She had no doubt it would be only a few days before the messengers alerted the king that she was missing. Nothing escaped his notice, and Serena had to plan this carefully, so as to avoid getting anyone else in trouble.

For now, she would go to her grandfather's hunting lodge. Her father owned several estates in Badenstein and in Germany, but the lodge was rarely used any more since it had fallen into disrepair. Although they might search for her there, perhaps not until they'd investigated the other houses. It would grant her some time. She hoped to sell some jewels and purchase a small house or property somewhere no one would find her.

Her head spun with all the details, and she worried about being caught. If her father learned of this…she shuddered to imagine it. Princesses were not supposed to run away. And although she had enough loyal servants to help her, it might not be enough.

For now, she would concentrate on getting out of the palace. She couldn't think too far ahead, or the worries would consume her. One moment at a time, one hour at a time, she decided. And before she left, she needed to see her mother.

Serena chose a single rose from the arrangement in the crystal vase upon the end table. Queen Clara had always loved flowers. During the spring, she often sat in the garden where she could admire the blossoms.

Flanked by her ladies, Serena walked down the long corridor leading to the east wing. Before she reached it, two footmen blocked their way and bowed.

'Your Highness, His Majesty has commanded your presence.'

A layer of ice coated her stomach, but Serena lowered her head in acquiescence, following the footmen to her father's chambers. Each time the king summoned her, she knew what was coming—a punishment for some imagined misdeed. Every moment she spent in her father's presence was a mind-numbing game of trying to guess what sort of behaviour would help her to avoid his fists.

No one could protect her from His Majesty. Not the guards or her ladies, for they'd lose their positions. Not her younger sister or her mother, who was confined to a sickbed. She was defenceless against him.

Serena hated the pity in the eyes of the servants, for she didn't like appearing weak. But after the last beating had left her unable to move, she'd had enough. Six years of suffering was too much to ask of anyone. Nothing would stop her from escaping.

One of her ladies, Katarina, offered her a look of silent support. Serena squeezed the woman's hand, and then withdrew, needing the time to gather up her courage.

When the footman opened the door and announced her presence, Serena stepped forward. Her father, the king, stood with his back to them. He was a tall man, with greying hair and a physical form that rivalled his best guards. King Ruwald prided himself upon his strength, and he wore close-fitting clothing to show off his muscular arms and legs.

'Were you planning to go somewhere?' he asked softly, dismissing his men and her ladies with a hand. Serena curtsied and stared down at the Oriental carpet, her hand clenching her mother's rose.

Do not make him angry. Be demure and modest in your bearing. And perhaps he'll leave you alone.

The king moved closer, until he stood directly in front of her. 'Answer me.'

'N-no, Father. Of course not.'

'Don't lie to me!' He seized her by the arm, jerking her upright. The grip of his fingers was so tight, she gritted her teeth against the pain.

'My men informed me that you sent a trunk full of clothes to a waiting coach.' Softening his voice to a low murmur, he released her arm. 'Now why would you do that?'

'They're for Anna,' she lied, rubbing the bruised skin. 'The men were supposed to put the trunk with her belongings. That's all.' Tears spilled over her cheeks, as she stared down at the carpet.

'Do you think I don't see your defiance? I know everything you do. And you're going nowhere.'

His fist struck the back of her head, and stars exploded in her vision. The king knew exactly where to punish her so that it would not leave a visible mark. 'My men have their orders. You won't leave the palace.'

Why does he hate me so? she wondered. *What have I done?* Never had he laid a hand upon Anna, thank God. But for whatever reason, she infuriated her father. And she feared that if he lost control of his temper one day, she might not survive it.

Darkness swam in her vision, and she backed away, folding her body inwards as if to protect it.

As the king advanced toward her, Serena let out a broken supplication, 'Please, Father.'

But her words meant nothing to him as he curled his fingers and raised his fists.

Serena lay with her body pressed against the carpet. Though her father had left, she couldn't bring herself to move. Her hand touched the tender skin at her throat, the pulsing fear returning. She tasted blood in her mouth, and pain radiated throughout her body.

It only renewed her resolve to leave. *I won't stay here. I can't.* The door opened, and she saw the stricken faces of her ladies. Serena said nothing, but allowed Katarina to help her to her feet. The woman picked up the fallen rose with its crushed petals and held it to her.

Though not a word was spoken, she was certain they'd heard her father's tirade. Serena accepted the rose and leaned upon Katarina as she entered the hallway.

'Your Highness?' Katarina asked, her voice fearful. Her maid stopped walking and reached for a fallen lock of Serena's hair, pinning it back into place. In her lady-in-waiting's eyes, Serena saw the worry. But she could say nothing to reassure them.

'I am going to see my mother,' she insisted. *One last time, before I leave.* Her ladies surrounded her and led the way.

As she walked, Serena rested her hand against her bruised side, fighting to calm herself. Though not every servant was loyal to her, there were enough men and women to turn a blind eye to her escape. She believed she could get out of the palace with little trouble. The true problem was reaching the hunting lodge before the other guards caught up to her. They had no choice but to follow and bring her home again.

When they finally arrived at her mother's chambers and her presence was announced, Serena tried to smile.

Queen Clara was propped up with several pillows, her light brown hair streaked with grey. She wore a cap and a white nightgown, but the pale linen only accentuated her wan face.

'How are you feeling today, Mother?' Serena asked, handing her the rose.

Clara took it and smiled, before she waved her

hand, dismissing the ladies. 'Come and sit beside me.'

When the queen took her hand, her expression turned grim. Slowly, she reached out and touched Serena's reddened throat. 'What happened?' Her hand traced the marks, as if the caress could take away the pain.

A hard ball of fear rose up in her throat and Serena forced back the denial. Tears pricked at her eyes, but she could only lift her shoulders in a shrug. 'I've…tried to be better. More like the princess he wants me to be. But he seems to hate the very air I breathe.'

Clara closed her eyes, her hands gripping the coverlet. 'Your lady-in-waiting, Katarina, confessed this morning that your father has…taken your punishments too far at times. And she said you're planning to leave.'

Serena masked her frustration. It was her secret to keep—not theirs to tell.

'You should have told me about this,' her mother insisted, her face rigid. 'I thought he only…hit you once in a while. I thought it was discipline.' A tear slid down the queen's face. 'But Katarina said he broke your ribs.' Her mother's eyes stared hard at her, as if trying to determine if it was true. Serena dropped her gaze, unwilling to answer.

'*Why* would you hide this from me? I could have done something to help you.'

'And what would you have done?' Serena demanded. 'You're ill. If you tried to fight him, he would have taken his anger out on you. I'm strong,' she whispered. 'You're not.'

'I know it, but surely—'

'Don't try to stop me from leaving,' Serena warned. 'I…I need this time to decide what to do, Mother.'

The queen's shoulders lowered in defeat. 'You'll be married this summer,' she reminded her. 'And after that happens, your husband will keep you safe.'

Serena didn't believe it, though she nodded to her mother as if she did. Clara reached out and took her hand. She hid her dismay at how fragile her mother's knuckles were, how pale the skin.

'Take the next fortnight at our estate in Oberalstadt, if you need some time to recover. If your father returns and asks where you are, I'll tell him I sent you to visit my relatives.' Her mother tried to smile. 'And when you return, I'll do what

I can to protect you from his temper.' Her gaze shifted over to the wardrobe that contained her day dresses. 'Perhaps I'll be strong enough to speak to him myself.'

Serena doubted if her mother could do anything, but she demurred. 'I love you, *liebe Mutter.*'

The queen reached up and touched her cheek. 'I'm sorry for being so weak. If I had more strength…' Her voice trailed off with unspoken words.

Serena lowered her strength. 'You'll be fine.' *And so will I.* She kissed her mother's cheek and squeezed her hands, praying that she would see her again one day.

After she left, she passed the tall windows that lined the east wing. As a young girl, she'd sometimes raced her sister down the hall, while sunlight spilled through the large panes of glass. Now, she walked at a more dignified pace, as befitted a princess.

Raindrops spattered down the windows, but even the wretched weather couldn't destroy the bottled up hope inside of her. Freedom lay just within her grasp.

She returned to her chamber, waiting for her father and Anna to depart for Sardinia. Anna would be presented to the widowed king as a possible candidate for his new wife.

When Serena glanced in her looking glass, she saw the redness surrounding her throat. Without asking for permission, her lady-in-waiting Katarina brought out a lace fichu and drew it around Serena's neck to cover the skin. 'Does it hurt, Your Highness?'

'I'll be fine.' But when Serena stared at herself in the looking glass, her face was pale, her green eyes rimmed with red. Despite all of her careful plans, she couldn't repress her shiver. Her father might have killed her this afternoon.

She touched the back of her head, and the barest pressure sent a wave of pain within the skin. Katarina dampened a cloth from the washing basin and sponged at her hair to remove the traces of blood. Though her lady was gentle, Serena closed her eyes at the pain.

Soon you'll be gone from here. And he'll never hurt you again. She clung to the thought, taking comfort from it.

'The coach is waiting in the forest,' Katarina whispered beneath her breath. Before she could say another word, there was a knock at the door. When Serena nodded for Katarina to answer it, her lady-in-waiting announced, 'Your Highness, the Princess Anna is here to bid you farewell.'

Anna entered with three of her ladies trailing behind, and Serena went to embrace her. Her sister wore a rose taffeta travelling gown with seven flounces and a silk bonnet with a matching rose ribbon. A dark woollen cloak was tied around her shoulders. She held her gloved hands together, worry creasing her smile.

'I'll miss you,' Serena told Anna. It was true. Despite her desperate need to escape, she would think of her mother and sister often. Perhaps one day she could send for Anna, or make arrangements to come and visit her after her sister was married. But the tangled sadness in her heart wouldn't soften. She was afraid of never seeing them again, and it hurt to imagine the loneliness.

Anna appeared worried. 'I know that…a royal marriage is expected of me. But I would be lying if I said I wasn't afraid. What do I know of the king of Sardinia?'

'You'll be fine. And the weather will be much

warmer.' She braved a smile, but Anna didn't answer it.

'I still don't understand why you'd want to leave for a holiday alone.' A worried expression pulled at her sister's mouth. 'With only a few servants?' Anna pressed her hands together. 'How can you manage? You need at least seven ladies, simply to get dressed in the morning. Fifty would be a more appropriate number.'

Serena only smiled. 'I want a quiet holiday, not an army surrounding me.' Besides, she'd sent word for the caretaker to assemble a household of servants within the hunting lodge. It was far easier to make an escape with six servants, rather than fifty.

Anna would have none of it. In a whisper, she added, 'You shouldn't defy our father. What you're planning will only make him angrier.'

Her sister reached out and touched the fichu at Serena's throat. The knowing look in her eyes made her wonder if Anna suspected the punishments she'd endured. Had someone told her?

'The king will never know I'm gone.' Serena stepped back, adjusting the fichu to hide her reddened skin. 'I'll be fine.'

'You can't go off on your own,' Anna insisted. 'Someone might try to kidnap you or worse.'

'It's only meant to be a short holiday. By the time you return from Sardinia, I'll already be home. No one need ever know of it.' The falsehood rolled easily off her tongue, and she pretended as if it wouldn't matter at all. She could only pray they wouldn't find her.

'But why would you go to Hamburg?' Her sister looked as if she'd suggested living in a beggar's cottage. 'We haven't gone there in years. And there's nothing at all to do. Except…catch fish.' Anna wrinkled her nose with disgust.

Serena didn't answer, but merely hugged her sister again. 'I'll miss you.'

A tightness rose in her chest at the thought of leaving Anna, but when her sister squeezed back, she fought back the shadow of pain from her bruised ribs. A flash of fear came over her, remembering her father's beating.

You don't have a choice, she reminded herself. *You have to go.*

'I'll return in a few weeks,' Anna promised. 'And hopefully the king of Sardinia will choose someone else. You're fortunate that the *fürst* of

Lohenberg will be your husband. At least he's quite handsome.'

There was an enigmatic look in her sister's eyes, as if she wanted to say something else. Instead, Anna drew back and said a final farewell.

After her sister had gone, Serena ordered her ladies to help her change into a navy blue woollen travelling gown and a dark cloak. She raised the hood over her hair and covered her gown with the voluminous fabric.

'Shall I come with you to the lodge, Your Highness?' Katarina asked, her voice fearful.

Serena shook her head. 'You'd only be punished. If you stay here, you'll be safe.' She'd arranged for a coachman, footman and four guards to accompany her.

Katarina pressed her forehead to Serena's hand in a deep curtsy. 'As Your Highness wishes.'

'Go back to my father's library. The guards I hired are standing outside the doors. Bring them to me.'

But her lady-in-waiting hesitated a moment. One by one, her other ladies surrounded her, and Serena saw the worry in their eyes. Then Katarina spoke, 'Your Highness, you must know that…we would do anything to protect you. What you've endured from His Majesty—' Her lady bowed her head and flushed with embarrassment. 'It's so very wrong. And though there are servants loyal to him, rest assured, we will help you to leave, as best we can.'

Serena looked at the faces of her ladies. These women had been with her for years, and they were so much a part of her life, she hadn't thought of how lonely it would be without them. 'Thank you,' she whispered.

'There was a...problem with your coach,' Katarina said, biting her lip. 'The footman, Herr Henley, will explain, but—'

'We haven't much time,' one of the other ladies interrupted. 'I'll go and fetch the guards.' With a curtsy, the young woman departed.

Serena turned back to Katarina. 'What problem?'

Katarina shrugged. 'Just something unexpected. Your sister, Princess Anna, arranged it.' With that, Serena relaxed. Anna would do nothing to interfere with her plans.

A quarter of an hour later, the men arrived. Among them was Gerlach Feldmann, captain of her father's guards. He looked uneasy about the journey, but of all the guards, she trusted him the most. He'd assembled men to help her, at great risk to himself.

Serena bid her ladies farewell, and raised her hood to hide her hair. The guards led her through the scullery maids' quarters, to avoid notice.

Throughout each twisting corridor, her lungs tightened with fear. Although her ladies and many of the servants would not betray her, she doubted if every servant could say the same.

When they reached the grounds outside the palace, Serena ran through the rain, clutching her cloak around her. Her lungs burned with exertion as she fled into the wooded grounds just beyond the gates.

She never looked back. With a surge of energy, she raced as fast as she dared toward the coach that awaited her. It would take a full day to reach her grandfather's lodge, but that didn't matter. She would savour each mile that took her far away from the palace. No one would stop her now.

'Your Highness,' the footman, Herr Henley, interrupted. 'There is something you should know.'

Serena lifted her hand to dismiss him. 'Tell me once I'm inside the coach.'

The rain was pouring down, soaking through her hood and cloak. The waiting footman opened the door for her, and she let him assist her within. She sank down upon the cushioned seat, lowering her hood.

Then she stared in shock at the prince who was seated inside the coach, directly across from her.

Chapter Two

'You seem surprised to see me,' Karl said, knocking twice on the ceiling of the coach to signal the driver onwards.

His bride, in fact, looked as if she wanted to throw open the door of the coach and flee. Not quite the reaction he'd hoped for, but it came as no surprise.

'*What* are you doing here?'

His suspicions were now confirmed. Princess Serena had indeed lied to pacify her sister.

'Was I not invited?' Karl asked, keeping a neutral expression on his face. 'Your sister Anna sent a letter, thanking me for taking care of you.'

Beneath her breath, the princess muttered something about killing her younger sister. 'You are *not* coming with me to Hamburg. Or anywhere else.'

Even in her bedraggled state, she held herself

like a crown princess. Likely he was meant to apologise and cower beneath the regal order. Instead, Karl rested his hand upon the door of the coach to prevent her from trying to leave.

'She informed me that you intended to take a holiday with only a few servants.' He kept his tone neutral, but there was no doubt that his bride was growing more indignant by the second. 'She was concerned about your welfare. And your reputation.'

Confusion shadowed her eyes. 'Why would there be any harm done to my reputation by going alone?'

'Some might believe you were going to meet a lover. Without your father's knowledge.'

'Oh, for heaven's sakes.' Her green eyes sparked with indignation. 'How on earth could I have a secret lover, when I've been betrothed to you for the last six years. *When* would I have had time to meet someone?'

'One of the palace guards, perhaps…or your groom?'

'There is no one at all.'

'Good. Then I won't have to kill them.'

She stared at him as if she didn't know whether

or not he was serious. Before she could make another remark, he levelled a hard stare at her. 'What is your true reason for going?'

The princess eyed the rain outside and lifted her chin. 'My reasons are my own. Now get out of my coach.'

'No.'

'I have nothing to say to you. And if you don't leave now, the rest of my father's guards will catch up to us. I'll have you arrested for kidnapping me.'

'You might like being kidnapped by me,' he said softly. Leaning in closer, his knees touched hers. 'Think of it as getting better acquainted.'

Serena seemed to hold her breath when his hands came upon either side of her seat. Her green eyes were frozen with fear. 'You shouldn't be here,' she protested. 'It's not proper.'

'I don't care about what's proper or right, Princess.' He reached out and captured her gloved hand, despite her attempt to snatch it back. 'But I do care if my intended wife is trying to run away.' He caressed her palm with his thumb, and her lips parted with startled surprise. 'Or am I wrong?'

She cast a frightened look outside the window. 'This has nothing to do with you.'

Whether or not that was true, he strongly suspected she was fleeing from something. Or someone.

'You have no right to interfere with my plans,' she insisted, pulling her hand back.

'Don't I?' He changed tactics, for it was nearly time to put the second part of his plan into action. 'Did it not occur to you that every man who has helped you on this…journey…could face charges of assault or treason?'

'Not if I absolve them,' Serena pointed out. 'I won't be gone for…very long. When I return, I shall take full responsibility for my orders.'

She believed it; he could see it in her innocent green eyes. She really thought that her word was strong enough to vouch for the men.

'Every last one of these men will lose his post.' Karl leaned forward, resting his forearms upon his knees. Once again, she drew back. Whether it was an aversion to him or another fear, he didn't know.

'They will never work in the palace again, and every person who saw them leave will know of their involvement in this frivolous holiday of yours.'

Her face reddened with fury. 'It's not frivolous at all.'

'It is when it affects men's lives.' His gaze hardened upon her. 'Do you have any idea what these people endure for your sake? They would throw themselves in front of a bullet to save your life. And yet, a single word from you would destroy them.'

Her hands clenched in her lap. 'You don't understand—'

'No, it's you who doesn't understand.' The coach was slowing down, and Karl saw the open land shift into another wooded forest. The coachman had obeyed his orders, and slowly, the vehicle came to a stop. He opened the door, and outside the rain pounded so hard, it was difficult to see. 'I'm sending them back.'

'Do not presume to undermine my orders.'

'I'll presume whatever I wish. Your Highness,' he added with a dark smile. Before she could make a single move, Karl reached for the princess and captured her waist.

She let out a hiss, clutching her side. 'Don't touch me.'

It didn't surprise him. Princess Serena was a

woman accustomed to getting her own way, and she wasn't about to obey him meekly. Despite her gasp, Karl lifted her outside the window, into the freezing rain. 'I can't breathe,' Serena insisted, and he shifted his hold lower, still carrying her as he strode away from the coach. When he raised a hand to the coachman and her escorts, he signalled them to return to the palace.

But her guards didn't obey. Instead, they closed in with weapons drawn.

'Princess Serena?' Captain Feldmann queried, awaiting his order. He held a bayonet, the sharp point directed toward Karl.

He couldn't fault them for loyalty. He set her down, giving her a chance to make her choice. Rain poured down over them, dripping past the princess's hood and soaking her gown.

'Do you want anything to happen to them?' Karl demanded of her, beneath his breath.

His bride gripped her cloak, her face crestfallen. He was counting on her to consider the truth of his words.

'If you want to leave, I'll escort you myself with my own men.'

She stared at him, and he could see the words of

argument forming in her mind. 'It's your choice,' he continued. 'Go with me. Or return to the palace.'

Her hand went to rest against her throat, and it almost seemed that she was fighting back tears. He couldn't understand why, but at last she nodded.

'Return to the palace,' she ordered her men. '*Fürst* Karl will see me safely to my grandfather's lodge.'

The captain withdrew his bayonet and knelt before the princess, his knee sinking into the mud. 'Your Highness, my men will be forced to search for you.'

She offered him her palm, raising him up. 'Then don't let them find us. Take them to all the other estates before the lodge. I just…want a fortnight to myself.'

'You truly wish to go with the *fürst?*' Captain Feldmann questioned.

The princess sent him a glance, but to her credit, she nodded. 'He will not harm me. You'll be in less trouble if I go with him and his men.' Despite her calm tone, her face revealed her displeasure at the prospect.

One by one, her guards disappeared into the

woods. When they'd gone, Karl took her hand and gestured toward his own coach, which lay waiting down the road. 'My coachman Samuel will accompany us from here on out.'

The princess stood motionless, staring at her departing servants while the rain drenched them both. 'I cannot believe I'm even considering this.'

Karl wasn't about to let her change her mind. Instead, he led her to his own coach, where his footman opened the door. Lifting her inside, he settled her upon the soft cushions. Within moments, his coach changed directions, travelling northwest instead of south.

The rain had soaked through Serena's cloak and her dark blond hair hung in tangled waves beneath her hood, across her shoulders. She was trembling, and her eyes glittered with anger.

'Why are you really here?' she demanded. 'And don't tell me it's because my sister sent you. You didn't care enough to come and see me more than twice in the six years since we've been betrothed.'

'I think you know why I came, Princess,' he said smoothly. 'To make sure you weren't eloping with some other man instead of me.' He removed his hat and set it beside him. The cold rain had dampened his face, and his clothing was soaked from the bad weather.

Serena kept her hands folded primly in her lap. 'Your Highness, let us be honest with one another. We were only betrothed because my father wanted to secure the alliance with Lohenberg. After we are married, what we do with our lives won't matter. I don't believe for a moment that you have any interest in me.'

'You're wrong.' He reached out and lowered her hood, brushing his fingertips against her damp cheek. In her eyes, he saw the startled shock. 'I find you very interesting indeed, Princess.'

He could see from the look on her face that she wasn't at all looking forward to their union. Whether she disliked him or was afraid of him, he couldn't be certain. 'Our marriage can be more than political.'

She turned her face to the window, the melancholy sinking in. 'Sometimes I wish I could live like an ordinary woman, just for a few days. Free to make my own decisions.' Her voice held a note of misery, as though she believed herself a prisoner.

'Is it such a hardship, wearing diamonds and silks?'

'Sometimes,' she admitted.

When he saw her shivering, Karl reached beneath the seat for a blanket. He passed it to her, and she huddled within the wool, struggling to get warm. Outside, the rain continued, and he could see his breath within the interior of the coach.

She stared outside the window and said, 'This isn't the way to my grandfather's lodge.'

'We can't go there,' he admitted. 'If we do, they'll find you within a few hours.'

Her face paled. 'Then you really are abducting me.'

'Yes.' He made no apology for his actions. 'You'll still have your holiday away from the palace,' he reassured her. 'And I'll bring you back within a week.'

As my wife.

The panicked expression that flashed over her face was real, and Karl didn't understand it. It wasn't as if he meant any harm toward her. She was simply the means to an end. After they married, he'd let her do as she pleased.

'Where are you taking me?'

'To the island of Vertraumen, off the coast of Lohenberg. We'll take a boat there tonight.'

Her eyes narrowed upon him, as if she expected him to take advantage of her. 'I am not sharing a room with you. Or a bed.'

'Not now,' he agreed.

'Or later.' She pulled the blanket around her, as if it could shield every last inch of skin from his view. 'Just because I've decided to continue this journey doesn't mean that I want anything from you.' She nodded to him as if he were a servant. 'You can do as you please, and I'll stay out of your presence.'

Time was slipping through his fingertips, and Karl was well aware that once his fallen status was revealed, the princess could easily cast him off. What he needed was to elope with her, to coerce her into this marriage before he brought her home again.

But she didn't even like him. And that was a problem. He needed to find a common ground with her, to somehow bridge the distance of the past six years.

'No, Princess.' He leaned forward, and she responded by inching as far away from him as she could. 'I don't intend to stay away from you at all.'

Outside, the rain pounded a rhythm against the roof of their coach while the horses quickened their pace. When he crossed to sit beside her, she cowered against the back of the coach, curling up her body tight. The fear in her eyes was completely different from the woman who had argued with him not five minutes earlier. Her hands were clenched in front of her, as if she were trying to shield herself.

Her response was entirely too violent. Something was wrong.

'Princess,' he said quietly. 'What are you running away from?'

Her face had gone so pale, he thought she might faint. Slowly, she lowered her hands, but her breathing was unsteady. She didn't meet his eyes, but stared down at her gloved hands. 'Nothing that concerns you.'

She was lying. But whatever the reason, her decision to leave was more complicated than he'd supposed.

'You have nothing to fear from me,' he insisted. 'Not now. And not when we are married.'

Her green eyes held nothing but suspicion. Droplets of water clung to her cheeks, one sliding down her slim neck. He noticed the reddened skin beneath the fichu, but the clouded daylight made it difficult to see clearly what had caused it. When his gaze fixed upon her lips, he wondered what it would be like to kiss her. Would she be cold and heartless? Or was there another woman hiding behind her hauteur?

'Will you please return to your own seat?' she pleaded.

Karl released her hand and moved to the opposite side of the coach. And when she turned to look outside the window again, he realized that this courtship would be far more difficult than he'd thought.

After travelling all afternoon and most of the night, they arrived upon the island of Vertraumen at midnight. Serena was so exhausted she could hardly walk, but she wasn't about to accept help from Karl.

It made her feel vulnerable without her ladies surrounding her. *This was what you wanted,* her mind retorted. *A chance to be alone.*

But the man who had brought her here was not at all predictable. She'd mistakenly believed that Karl was a quiet, passive man. Instead, he'd taken charge of her kidnapping, changed her destination, and brought her to a place where it would be more difficult for her father's men to find her.

Worse, he'd brought only two servants with him. Though perhaps it was to make them less noticeable, his lack of men struck her as unusual. Every royal household travelled with dozens of servants—especially guardsmen, to protect them from highwaymen or bandits.

Did he think he was invincible from danger? She knew better than to believe she was safe. Though Captain Feldmann might lead the others astray, unless she travelled a great distance from here, eventually they *would* find her. The thought of facing her father's punishment terrified her.

But you haven't been caught yet, she reminded herself. There was still hope.

Her hands were shaking as the coach stopped in front of a set of iron gates. Karl opened the door and led her outside toward a two-storey brick manor house with two turrets on either side. Ivy grew across the side of the house, and a curved gravel driveway nestled near the front steps. The rain continued to pour down on them, but Serena hardly felt it. Inside, she was sick about what she'd just done. And now, she was about to spend the night with a man who was not her husband.

Even if he slept in the farthest bedchamber from her, no one would believe that she hadn't been compromised. Her reputation was now in ruins. If she ever returned home, the gossipmongers would believe the worst.

She was beginning to understand her sister's reasoning. Though she loathed the idea of sharing a home with the prince, all would be forgiven if she married him.

She stared at the man who had orchestrated her abduction. For that was what it was, surely. He'd brought her here, and she didn't understand his reasons for it. He was the *fürst* of Lohenberg. Surely his responsibilities were far too important for this.

He was hiding something from her…but what?

When they reached the gates of the estate, they were locked tight. There were no lights visible within the house, and a sinking feeling took hold in Serena's stomach.

The *fürst* turned to his men. 'This house belongs to my father. Where is the staff?'

The footman and coachman could only exchange blank looks.

'Do you mean to tell me that there is no one prepared for our arrival?' Serena predicted. 'And we're locked out?'

He sent her a dark look. 'We're not locked out.' Turning around, he led them to the back of the walled manor, down to another padlocked gate. He ran his hands along the stone wall, counting stones right and then down, until he loosened a brick.

After several minutes of pulling at the stone, he withdrew an iron key. It fit into the padlock, and Karl opened the door. When he met her incredulous stare, he said, 'I spent many summers here as a boy.' To his footman and coachman he instructed, 'Go inside and see if there's anyone here.'

'Did something happen?' Serena asked. 'Could the staff be sick or in trouble?' Never had she journeyed to an estate where there was not a staff waiting. Even if they didn't expect their arrival, most were ready to welcome them at a moment's notice.

'We'll find out in the morning,' he assured her. 'It won't be like this for long.' But the look on his face held tension, as if he, too, suspected that all was not right.

Serena followed Karl through the garden. It was overgrown with weeds, as though no one had tended it in weeks. She saw a small henhouse, and a hole in the back of the garden wall, where one of the hens struggled to squeeze through.

A few moments later, Samuel and Bernard managed to force open the back door. When they walked inside, the kitchen looked abandoned, with no food anywhere, or signs that it had been used recently. It appeared ghostly, with the interior of the manor house cold and dark.

Serena huddled within her cloak, feeling more lost than ever. By now, she should have been comfortably ensconced in her grandfather's home, dreaming of her future plans. Instead, she'd been taken to this place with a man she hardly knew.

The prince gave orders for Samuel and Bernard to light the fireplaces within the dining room and to prepare two chambers. While they departed, he turned to face her. 'It was never my intention to bring you to a place so unprepared for our arrival.'

'Then what was your intent?' Her voice came out with a tremble that revealed her fear. It wasn't so much the poor conditions of the house, but more, that she didn't know this stranger standing before her. Her betrothed husband was staring with a look that reached deep inside, as if he were taking her measure.

'I've already given you that answer.'

To become better acquainted. But what did he mean? Was he intending to seduce her? It felt as if she'd run from one set of problems, only to encounter something worse.

'Stay away from me, *Fürst* Karl,' she warned. She wanted to run far away from him, to hide herself. But she knew she couldn't escape. The fear inside mingled with another unfamiliar sensation. The blood rushed to her face, while her body grew colder from the chill of her damp clothing.

'You're afraid of me.' His voice resonated in the stillness, his breath clouded in the air. He reached for her gloved hand, but when she tried to pull it back, he held it captive.

'I don't know you.' Her voice came out in a slight whisper, revealing every bit of her fear.

In response, his grasp upon her hand softened. His thumb slipped beneath one of her glove buttons, stroking her skin. She jerked her hand away, shocked that he would take such a liberty.

'You will,' he said quietly, releasing her hand.

What if I don't want to? she thought. Everything about the prince made her uncomfortable, from his demanding presence to his rigid expression. She couldn't deny her sister's admission, that Karl was indeed handsome. His dark hair framed a strong, lean face. When she looked into his hazel eyes, flecks of green and brown mingled with hints of gold. And his firm mouth hadn't smiled at all.

He reminded her of a highwayman, who had stolen her away to his private residence. Beneath her cloak, she gripped her arms, terrified of what would happen to her now.

Inside the house, the prince guided her through a series of sitting rooms until at last they reached the dining room. He pulled a chair beside the fire his footman had built. 'Sit down and warm yourself.'

Serena sank gratefully into the chair, waiting for the tiny blaze to grow larger. The *fürst* left her side for a moment to give the footman another order for food and hot tea. Though she ought to be hungry, her stomach twisted at the thought of food. Right now, she wanted to be away from the prince, alone in a room where she could collect her thoughts. So much had changed so fast, she couldn't quite grasp what to do.

'I'm too tired to eat,' she protested when the *fürst* returned. 'Really, once I get warm, I'll just go to my room and sleep.' If she rested her head against the back of the Chippendale chair for even a moment, she thought she might fade into a dreamless exhaustion.

She closed her eyes for a brief moment, but there was no satisfaction at having made her escape. Instead, she envisioned countless guards, searching every pathway, every road.

Her heart pulsed within her chest, though she tried to blot out the fear. She tried to comfort herself by imagining a steaming hot bath, a clean nightgown and a soft bed. There would be time to make plans in the morning after a good night's rest.

A horrifying thought occurred to her. Without

a staff here, she had no one to help her undress. Even worse…had Karl brought her trunk from the other coach? Did she have anything at all to wear?

'I will need a ladies' maid to attend me,' she informed him. 'Please send Bernard to find someone.'

'It's after midnight. I'll send him to the village, first thing in the morning.'

'No, not in the morning,' she corrected. 'Now.'

He sent her an annoyed look. 'I'm certain you'll survive one night without a lady-in-waiting to tuck you in or brush your hair for you.'

She sent him a look of disbelief. The prince didn't understand what she was saying. There was no possible way for her to sleep unless someone helped her out of her corset and petticoats. But her alternative was to ask *him* for help. And that was most definitely not going to happen.

'What about my trunk of clothing?' she asked. 'Did your footman bring it?'

His face showed no reaction at all. All he would say was, 'There may be clothes that were left here by the governor's wife.'

Then she truly had nothing at all to wear. Serena didn't know whether to laugh or cry. Nothing at all had gone right with her escape from the palace. The only thing that would make it worse would be if the guards caught up to her this night and forced her to return to the palace.

The sound of a man clearing his throat interrupted them. When Serena looked up, the footman Bernard looked embarrassed. He held a wooden tray containing a teapot, two cups, a covered plate and a jar of preserves. 'Your Royal Highnesses, I must apologise. There was very little food in the house. I found some eggs in the hen house and prepared what I could.' He bowed and set the tray upon the dining-room table, apologising as he left.

Serena lifted the cover and winced at the sight of the overcooked scrambled eggs. They were badly burned on one side, while the rest was runny. 'I suppose he did try to cook for us.'

'You wanted to know how ordinary people lived,' the *fürst* pointed out.

She didn't want to eat, but it would be rude to ignore the footman's valiant effort. When she ventured a taste of the overcooked eggs, it surprised her to realise how starved she was. When she offered the plate to Karl, he shook his head. 'I'm waiting to see if you survive.'

There was a hint of roguery in his voice, and she raised an eyebrow. 'Did you want me to be poisoned?'

'Not at all. I've no wish to be a widower before I'm a bridegroom.' He poured her a cup of tea. Serena took it from him, but the drink was weak and tea leaves floated on the surface.

She stared down at the watery brew and wondered if she ought to tell him that she was ending their betrothal. 'How long are you planning to keep me here?'

'How long were you planning to spend your holiday?' he countered.

She could feel his gaze upon her, though she didn't meet his eyes. 'I was going to stay three days at my grandfather's lodge.' After that, she'd intended to leave again, perhaps taking a train somewhere far from Germany or Badenstein.

He ate his own eggs, but all the while, his eyes were studying the room. 'Your father's men will come after you.'

'I know it.' A cold chill spread over her skin, and she pushed her plate aside, walking to stand by the fire. 'They'll try to force me to return.'

'The king will be angry with you for taking such a risk.'

She said nothing, though her hands had begun to tremble. It was easy to hide her fear behind the guise of cold.

The prince left his own plate and came to stand before her. 'Marry me here, on the island,' he commanded. 'And when we return, I'll shoulder any trouble that arises.'

She shook her head slowly. Not only did she have no intention of marrying him or anyone else, but she wasn't going to return.

'You'd prefer to wait until the summer?' he mused. 'After being here with me, I don't know if the king would allow it.' He took her hands and drew her to stand. 'We'll wed tomorrow.' Within his voice, she heard the commanding air, the expectation that she would do his bidding.

She was not a household maid, bound to obey. But neither would she have this argument now, not when she was too tired to think clearly. 'We'll discuss it later. Where do you think the servants went?'

'I don't know. But if Bernard can't find them, I'll hire a new staff.' His posture stiffened, his bearing almost that of a soldier. This was a man accustomed to issuing orders and being obeyed.

He reached to her hood and lowered it to her shoulders. 'A lot could happen in the week we spend together, Princess.'

She stepped back. 'Or nothing at all.' Her mind was made up. In the morning, she would decide where to go and how to get there. Although it terrified her, she had to make her own decisions and decide what she wanted to do with her life.

An awful thought occurred to her. If she refused to wed the *fürst,* would he reveal her whereabouts to the king? She stared at Karl, not knowing what sort of man he was.

'I'm tired,' she said at last. After all the travelling, the need to rest was overpowering. And though she could not change out of her gown, perhaps she could find a way to sleep in her clothes. 'Do you think my room is prepared?'

'All should be in order.' The *fürst* led her toward the main staircase. While he escorted her up the stairs, Serena glanced behind them. There was no footman, no one else but the two of them. It felt awkward without her ladies, and she suddenly realized that she could be in danger if the *fürst* wanted to press his attentions upon her.

When they reached the door to her chamber, she ordered, 'You may leave me now.'

He raised an eyebrow at her tone, but she ignored it and fumbled with the doorknob, trying to escape him as quickly as possible.

'I am not your servant,' he said quietly, resting his hand against the door frame.

'Neither were you invited.' She tried to push her way past him, but he refused to move.

The suffocating fear rose up, and Serena crossed her arms over her chest, turning away from him. If she could have melted into the wall, she'd have done so. The harsh memory of her father's fists discoloured all else, and she squeezed her eyes shut, terrified that Karl would touch her.

Don't hurt me. The plea echoed in her mind, and she swallowed hard, her heart racing.

But he didn't lay a hand upon her. Silence fell between them, and when she at last dared to open her eyes, Karl had gone. A shattered breath of relief filled up her lungs, and her hands were shaking as she forced the door open and retreated into the tiny chamber.

When she found a key, she locked the door and leaned back against the wood. Only then did she let the tears fall. It had been a gruelling day, and she felt so lost, so uncertain of what to do.

The interior was freezing, though the footman had lit a fire. Serena drew close to the coals, feeling as though she'd never get warm. Her cloak and gown were still damp, and the heavy wool itched her skin. The tiny chamber had only a single bed, a table with a washbasin and pitcher, a desk and chair and a window with rose curtains. Serena walked over to the window, resting her fingers upon the cold surface of the glass.

It's going to be all right, she tried to convince herself. But she'd been unprepared for *Fürst* Karl von Lohenberg. Everything about this man confused her. She didn't know how she was meant to behave or what to do about his insistence on eloping.

It doesn't matter. She would find a way to keep him at a distance, and surely he would leave her alone once he understood that she wasn't going to wed him.

She dragged the chair across the room, huddling in front of the fire. What she wouldn't give for a ladies maid right now. Her corset was cutting into her skin, and she couldn't sleep at all, not wearing so many heavy layers.

Why did the *fürst* have to interrupt her plans? She would have been fine on her own. And at least she'd be asleep right now in a comfortable bed, perhaps with a warm brick wrapped in flannel at her feet. A tear dripped down her cheek, and she returned to her chair beside the fire, feeling foolish and angry. Crying wouldn't help.

It was as if her fairy tale had gone all wrong. The handsome prince was supposed to rescue her, not kidnap her. He wasn't supposed to put her in a dusty manor house with no servants and terrible food, keeping her imprisoned in a wet gown.

And he thought she would want to marry him after all that?

A hysterical laugh trapped in her throat. No. Not even if he offered himself on a golden platter with a ribbon tied around his neck.

In the quiet of the night, her nerves sharpened. She found herself staring at shadows, wondering if she was truly safe here. Karl had made no further move to touch her, but she didn't trust him. He was here for a reason, and though she didn't know what it was, her instincts warned that it wasn't good.

In the coach, she'd been shocked by the way he'd closed in the space between them, sitting beside her. She'd barely heard a word he said. All of her attention was drawn to the fierce eyes staring at her as if she were a confection he wanted to feast upon.

If she'd been an ordinary woman, she might have welcomed the idea of a handsome prince wanting to court her. But the constant emotional and physical battering by her father had weakened her, until now, she couldn't bear to have anyone close. Much less the prince.

A light knock sounded upon the door, interrupting her thoughts. 'Who is it?'

'It's Karl.'

Why had he returned? She didn't want to see him now, not when she was so tired. 'What is it?'

'Will you let me come in?'

No. Stay far away from me.

But she stood and crossed the room, resting her cheek against the door. 'Why?'

'You asked me for a ladies' maid.'

Had he found someone? The thought of getting

rid of these clothes, of being able to sleep, was so intoxicating, Serena pulled the door open.

But there was no maid standing there. She was about to shut the door again, when Karl stepped inside her chamber. 'I misunderstood what you meant earlier, when you asked for a ladies' maid. You can't sleep, can you? Because there's no one to help you undress.'

No. Not a chance. If he believed she would let him anywhere near her, he was sorely mistaken.

'It's only a few more hours until dawn. I'll wait until we've found someone.' She took a step backwards, which was a mistake. The *fürst* advanced toward her, and she searched for a way around him.

His hazel eyes were unreadable, his emotions masked. 'What do you need help with?'

'Go back to your own room. I don't want you anywhere near me.' The very thought of the prince unbuttoning her, of unlacing her corset, was an invitation to trouble. She'd rather go without sleep than risk him touching her.

'So instead you'll remain in discomfort for the next few hours because of your pride?' He took her shoulders and softly guided her to stand by the fire. When she felt his hands moving down the buttons of her gown, she jerked away.

'I said *don't!*' She covered herself with her arms, backing toward the door. 'I don't need your help now. I don't want you here.'

His supercilious belief that he could take the liberty of undressing her was too much. Why would he think she would want that?

'Get out,' she whispered, not bothering to hide her tears.

The prince lifted his hands and backed away. When the door closed behind him, Serena lowered her head to her hands and wept.

Chapter Three

A few doors away, Karl sat down upon the bed and removed his boots, trying to push back the fury that darkened his mood. He'd gone to her chamber, meaning only to help her with the buttons and laces, but she'd behaved as if he were about to ravish her. Good God, he'd only meant to help her.

A suspicion was starting to take root. She'd left the palace, supposedly for a brief holiday. And yet, she hadn't taken a large enough retinue with her, nor had she received the king's permission.

Whatever she was fleeing from meant more than her reputation. She'd agreed to leave behind her servants, her family and her home, ruining herself as a consequence.

Why? Her answer, that she'd wanted to live like an ordinary woman for a few days, seemed disproportionate to her actions. No, her behaviour spoke of a woman who had been hurt by someone.

Every time he'd come too close, Serena had tried to shield her body…like a woman who had experienced physical violence. But who on earth would dare to harm a woman of royal blood? Any guard would tear the man apart.

Likely, whoever had threatened the princess was still at the palace…someone who had utterly destroyed his bride's confidence. He could barely touch her hand without her cowering. And he remembered the reddened skin around her throat, as if someone had tried to strangle her.

Fury blackened his mood at the thought of someone harming a woman. He stood and strode across the room, staring outside at the midnight sky. Nothing had gone at all as he'd expected. His bride-to-be had fled the palace because someone was hurting her. And though she was safe now, it would take a great deal of time to gain her trust. Time he didn't have.

Karl pushed open the door and strode down the narrow corridor. The wooden floor was cold beneath his stocking feet, but he wanted to explore more of the house while he rearranged his plans.

Logic and reason had governed his actions in the past. He believed in ordered solutions to solve problems. And yet, he'd never met a woman who adhered to logic. They were changeable creatures whose moods altered as frequently as their gowns.

He spent the next hour going through the different rooms in the house, inspecting each of them, while he turned over the problem of Serena in his mind. Perhaps it was best to pretend as if they were on a holiday of sorts. If he provided her with a relaxing environment, one where she felt safe, she might soften toward the idea of marriage.

He wandered down a set of stairs and through the hallway until he stood in front of Serena's door once again. Although he listened, there was only silence.

Karl wanted to say something to her, to somehow make her understand that he hadn't intended to offend her. 'Serena,' he said quietly.

She didn't answer.

He felt like an idiot talking to a closed door, but perhaps she was listening.

'I apologise for my earlier actions,' he said. 'I meant only to help you.'

He waited to see if she would answer him, yet once again, there came no reply. Finally, he admitted, 'I promise, I'll find you a maid within a few hours.'

Still nothing. He turned around and walked back toward his own room. When he opened the door, he risked a glance back at hers.

Her door opened slightly, and he saw her watching him from behind it. She met his gaze for a brief moment, long enough to let him know that she'd heard him.

And when she closed the door again, he wondered what he could do to earn her trust.

Serena couldn't remember a night worse than last night. Her neck and back were sore, and though her gown had eventually dried by the fire, she was ready to fall asleep standing up. But the *fürst* had promised her a maid this morning. If all went well, she might be in clean clothes within a few hours.

Clothes. Her eyes flew open and she let out a groan. She'd forgotten to look for a spare gown last night. It seemed doubtful that any would have been left behind.

And yet, what did that matter? It was ridiculous to fret over clothing when the larger question of her future loomed over her. She had to make decisions that would take her away from Vertraumen, away from the prince.

A knot of uneasiness clenched inside of her. *Fürst* Karl didn't seem like the sort of man who had any intention of letting her go. He'd come all the way from Lohenberg to join her, and although he'd permitted her to leave the palace, it had been on his terms.

Would she now have to escape him, in addition to her father? Worries assaulted her mind as she fumbled with the buttons that the *fürst* had unfastened last night. Her hands struggled with the tiny holes, until at last she was forced to admit defeat.

A choked laugh caught in her throat. She couldn't even dress herself. How did she ever expect to abdicate her throne and live apart from her family?

Serena walked over to the window, opening the rose curtains. It was early morning, and she stared out at the clouded island. The sea wasn't visible from the house, but a low fog clung to the hills, obscuring everything.

Would the guards keep their word, searching the

other estates first? Or would they follow Karl's path, bringing her back immediately? Troubled thoughts of soldiers dragging her from the house, facing endless miles of travelling, plagued her mind. She questioned her decision, wondering if it was better to face her father's punishments than to venture forth on her own. In the end, hunger drove her away from her worries and out of the privacy of her chamber.

Serena walked down the staircase, winding her way through the house toward the dining room. Before she reached it, her attention was caught by an open door. Inside, she found the library, filled with books.

She couldn't resist going inside, and she ran her hands over the leather-bound volumes. There were books on philosophy, poetry and science, as well as a few tattered books on household management. In the corner of the room, she saw a large wingback chair facing the window. She imagined curling up within it, enjoying hours of quiet reading. A smile came over her face.

It faded a moment later when the *fürst* entered the room. His posture was as straight as Damascus steel, his face devoid of any emotion. If she hadn't noticed the shadows under his eyes, she'd have believed he'd slept all night.

'There are eggs, if you're hungry,' he said. 'I've already given orders for Samuel to go and fetch more food from the village.'

He escorted her into the dining room, saying, 'By tonight, you should have all the comforts you're accustomed to. Including a maid.'

She nodded in thanks and then questioned, 'Was there any sign of the king's men following us?'

'It's doubtful that they'd find us here. Vertraumen is fairly isolated, with only a few ships that travel to the mainland.' Serena recalled that his men had awakened a fisherman last night and paid him double his fare to take them across to the island.

'At this time of day, most of the boats are out fishing,' the prince continued. 'And even if your father's guards do come, I won't let them take you against your will.'

She sent him a doubtful look. If her father's men arrived to take her home again, there was nothing he could do to stop them.

As she seated herself at the table, the prince joined her on the opposite side. Serena lifted the covered plate and saw that the eggs were slightly better than last night. While she ate, she sensed the *fürst* watching her. Though she tried to ignore his gaze, it intimidated her. She saw the intensity within them, as if he wanted *her* instead of the food. She imagined his mouth seizing a kiss, and she recalled the heat of his hand upon her palm.

He was both dangerous and unpredictable. A man who wouldn't hesitate to go after what he wanted. And he seemed to want *her*.

Tentatively, she met his stare, not knowing if she'd imagined it. The prince's dark hair was short, his face bristled, from not shaving in the past day or so. He reminded her of an outlaw with his devil-may-care attitude. There came a flicker of a smile at his lips, as if he'd guessed what she was thinking.

Serena forced herself to look away, finishing her food though it tasted like sawdust.

'I thought we'd go into the city today,' the prince offered. 'You could buy a new gown.'

Thank goodness. Nothing was more appealing than getting rid of the soiled navy blue travelling gown. Though at first she was grateful, the idea worried her. She'd never been allowed to leave the palace without a dozen escorts, much less venture among the citizens of Badenstein.

'Won't it be dangerous? Wouldn't they recognise their crown prince?'

'Even if I walked among them, most wouldn't know me. Vertraumen is separate from the mainland, and they keep to themselves. My father's face is on their currency, not mine.' He folded his napkin and stood. 'And, it's easier to learn the needs of your country when you spend time amongst the people. You should try it.'

'Do you disguise yourself?'

'I wear plainer clothing, but most people aren't that observant. So long as you don't behave like a princess, I doubt anyone will notice.'

'What if it isn't safe?' She was less worried about the citizens and more afraid of being recognised. Someone might send word to her father.

The prince's mouth tilted in a silent challenge. 'It will be fine. And we'll find out what happened to the household staff while we're there. We'll learn more if we blend in among them.'

'I don't know,' she hedged, uneasy about the prospect. 'I've never gone out without my guards or my ladies. Who will protect us, if they discover who we are?'

'You don't look very much like a princess right now,' he pointed out. 'And I am quite capable of protecting us.'

'How would you do that?'

The *fürst* departed for a moment and returned with his great coat. Inside, he showed her a revolver. 'In the past five years, there have been at least ten assassination attempts on my life.' His gaze centred upon her. 'I'm certain you've experienced the same.'

She nodded. It was a part of being a princess, an unfortunate reality that terrified her. One of her ladies had become deeply ill when some food had turned out to be poisoned.

'There were two attempts this year.' A shudder gripped her at the memory. God willing, if she escaped the palace, there would be no more threats.

'You'll be safe enough,' the prince said, discreetly hiding the revolver again.

Her stomach twisted with nervousness. She'd never ventured out in disguise before, and she frankly preferred to stay at the manor house where she could make her plans. 'Perhaps you should go without me,' she urged. 'You could send the seam-stress here with the patterns and material.'

The *fürst* rested his hands upon the table. Softly, he asked, 'What are you afraid of?'

She studied the china plate, knowing that she sounded like the worst sort of coward. When she glanced into the other room, she saw the sunlight spilling onto a *chaise longue*. Outside was the freedom she'd wanted so desperately. And already she was allowing the shadow of her father to dictate her decisions.

'I've hardly ever been outside the palace,' she admitted to the prince. She didn't know if she dared to try it. What would it be like to wander among the other people, like a commoner? To be viewed as a woman instead of a princess…she'd once dreamed of such a thing.

Serena lifted her gaze to his, expecting to see frustration upon his face. Instead, the prince was merely waiting for her answer. 'It will be safe,' he repeated.

She didn't truly believe him, but what choice did she have? If she didn't learn how ordinary people lived, how would she ever survive apart from her family? Assuming she avoided her father's guards, that is.

'All right,' she conceded at last. 'But promise me, if we're discovered—'

'We won't be.' He brought her cloak over and handed it to her. 'Remove your jewels before you go.'

Serena took off her earrings and set them upon the table, reaching behind for the clasp of her pearl necklace. It had an intricate fastener, and she had no idea how to get it off.

'Will you let me help you?' the *fürst* asked.

She wanted to refuse, even though she knew it was foolish. Instead, she conceded, 'You may.'

When his hands rested upon her shoulders, her skin prickled with an unfamiliar sensation. He reached for the pearls, and the strand rolled across her neck like a caress as he worked with the clasp.

His fingers moved over the pearls, and the heat of his hands permeated her throat while she breathed in the scent of his skin. Serena tensed as he freed the clasp, but all he did was set the necklace down upon the table. If he saw the bruises around her neck, he made no comment.

'There are three buttons unfastened,' he murmured against her ear. Heated tremors raced through her at the feeling of his warm breath upon her skin. 'Would you like me to fix them or leave them alone?'

She kept her gaze staring straight ahead. Taking a deep breath, she nodded. 'Please help me with them.'

Once again, his hands touched her nape, adjusting each button slowly. Before the prince pulled his hands away, he lifted a fallen lock of hair and twisted it, pinning it away from her face. The intimate gesture made her cheeks flood with colour.

'Th-thank you,' she stammered, rising up from the table. She reached for the earrings and necklace, searching for a place to hide them.

Karl nodded toward the sideboard, and she stored the jewels in a drawer. Then he handed her the cloak she'd worn yesterday. 'Are you ready?'

Not at all.

But Serena donned the cloak and raised her hood. If she ever wanted a glimpse of the outside world, now was her chance.

Karl led the princess outside the manor house, though he made no move to touch her hand. She reminded him of a skittish bird, ready to take flight at the least provocation.

'Are you certain we should walk?' she asked. 'Isn't there a curricle or a carriage here?'

'There is, but it would take time to ready the horses. Bernard has gone to hire staff from the village,' he reminded her. 'And if we are to remain unnoticed, it's better this way.'

'What about an escort, or someone to guard us?' She looked around as if she weren't at all certain he was capable of protecting them.

'Samuel will follow in a few moments.' Karl started to walk and after a sigh, the princess squared her shoulders and continued beside him. In her bearing, he could see her exhaustion. Her face was pale, her eyes weary from lack of sleep.

Although he told himself that it was only temporary, it made him aware that he'd done a poor job of taking care of her. She needed servants of her own and new clothing. Of the women he'd known in the past, most had been enamoured of baubles and beautiful gowns. Money and wealth were all that mattered to them, and his mistresses had given themselves freely, so long as he was generous.

Princess Serena was different. She seemed more eager to escape the palace than to surround herself with luxury. And if he wanted to wed her within days, he had to learn what she wanted most and fulfil that desire.

The path from the manor house led downhill to a small village. Out upon the sea, several fishing boats had gone out for the day's catch.

'When we reach the village, I'm going to hold your hand,' Karl warned. He didn't want her to overreact when he touched her. 'We'll pretend to be a married couple.'

She stopped walking and studied him. 'Why would I need to hold your hand?'

'Because it will let the others know that you're under my protection.'

The closer they walked to the capital city, the more nervous Serena became. Her face was pale, her hands clenched together. He was beginning to wonder precisely how sheltered she'd been. Was she so afraid of visiting the city, or did he frighten her that much?

When he took her palm at last, she looked petrified. 'Breathe, Princess.'

'I am breathing!' But her steps slowed when they reached the main cobbled street. There were rows of houses higher upon the hillside, while several shops lined the streets. The air held a stale, salty aroma, and he saw only a few people walking, most of them elderly.

'It's too quiet,' she offered, keeping her voice in a low whisper. 'I don't like this.'

'It's practically abandoned.' In the past, he remembered market stalls with fresh fruits and vegetables, meats, cheeses, fish and bread. Even flowers in the springtime. When they passed a baker's shop, there were only a few loaves of bread for sale.

Something wasn't right about this place. It was as if most of the people had deserted the island. But why?

Karl led Serena deeper into the town, drawing her to one side as a cart rolled past. The princess gripped his hand, and when a few villagers walked past, eyeing them with curiosity, she leaned closer.

He caught the scent of her hair, and the unexpected warmth of her body as it brushed against his. A flare of interest caught him, and he resisted the urge to pull her closer, knowing it would frighten her. The princess was so cautious, it was like coaxing a butterfly to land on his palm.

'Don't be afraid,' he murmured. 'They don't know who you are.'

She stopped walking and turned to him, her expression filled with worry. 'It's not easy for me. I keep thinking someone will come down the street and attack us.'

'If any man tries, I'll shoot him,' Karl promised. He took her hand and brought it to his coat where the revolver rested. She studied him as if she didn't quite believe he knew how to handle the weapon.

'Shall I demonstrate?'

Her eyes widened a moment, before she realised he was teasing. Her shoulders lowered, though she didn't quite relax. 'That won't be necessary.'

'You're under my protection, Princess. No man will harm you.'

She eyed him with suspicion. 'You might.' Her troubled gaze lacked any faith in him, as if she expected him to invade her bedchamber late at night.

'If that were my intent, I could have done so last night.' He studied her, not letting go of her hand. 'And why would I want to harm the woman I'm going to marry?'

She sobered, her gaze lowering to the ground. Karl tilted her chin up to face him. Worry filled up her green eyes, but he held her steady gaze. 'You're safe with me.'

'I hope so,' she whispered. She stood with perfect posture, in spite of her tangled hair and the exhaustion lining her face. Though she'd tried to cover her throat with a fichu, the reddened skin had darkened into bruises. It reminded him that some men were worse bastards than himself.

With her hand in his, Karl led her farther down the street, where a small stone church stood with a single steeple. It looked a hundred years old, and in his mind, he could almost envision a bride with flowers in her hair, smiling up at her bridegroom on their wedding day.

He doubted if Serena would smile at him, not after the way he'd abducted her. And while he couldn't give her the wedding day of her dreams, he hoped she could accept a marriage between them, despite his lost birthright. Though it was an inauspicious beginning, she would eventually have everything she wanted—he'd make sure of it.

When they reached the end of the cobbled street, Serena turned to him. 'Why are we here?'

Karl started to answer, but the words caught in his mouth. Her demeanour was hesitant, and he suspected that bringing up the wedding again would only add to her fears. 'No reason,' he lied, bringing her back up the other side of the street.

He searched the row of shops until at last he saw a linen draper's. When she frowned a moment, he ordered, 'Go inside. I'll buy you more clothes.'

The confusion on her face was replaced by gratitude. Serena's lips nearly curved in a smile, and she took a tentative step forward, staring at the interior of the shop. It smelled pleasant, like freshly brewed tea. Upon a table lay rows of handkerchiefs and shawls, as well as a third row of aprons. She stared at the merchandise as if she'd never seen such articles before.

The female shopkeeper sent Serena a guarded smile. In Lohenisch, she greeted her, asking, 'May I help you, madam?'

Before the princess could answer, Karl interrupted. 'My wife's belongings were lost overboard when we made the crossing to the island. She'll need a new wardrobe. If you can find seamstresses who can work quickly and deliver the first gown tonight, I will double your price.'

The woman gaped at him, 'Forgive me, my lord, but it's clear to me that this is your first time upon our island. There are few of us left on Vertraumen. I am the only seamstress here.'

Karl exchanged a look with Serena. Correcting the woman, he said, 'No, I visited the island years ago. It wasn't always like this.'

'We're losing more of the islanders each day,' the matron admitted. 'Soon, there won't be anyone left.'

'Why would they go?' He couldn't understand how the island province would suffer in such a way.

The woman's face turned solemn. 'The crops have failed us over the past few years. We've no grain for bread or to feed our livestock. We rely upon the fishermen to sell their catch on the mainland. Most have gone to Germany or Prussia to find work and homes for their families.'

'What caused the crop failures?' Karl asked. In the past, he remembered fields of barley and even a few vineyards lining the hills. Although this island wasn't as large as some, it had been self-reliant.

'Flooding, mostly. We've had terrible rains these past two years.'

'Have you appealed to the king of Lohenberg for help?' he asked. Though he'd served on his father's council, never had any problems been reported from the island. He wondered if the governor was to blame.

'Our island isn't the king's concern, so it seems,' she responded. 'He did nothing.'

Karl remained silent at the woman's assertion. If he were responsible for the island, he'd order relief supplies and grain. He'd try to bring in new equipment to mechanise their farming and—

You're not their prince any more. Your only hope for a kingdom lies with Serena.

His jaw tightened at the thought. He didn't like the idea of relying on anyone else's whims to make his future.

With her hair pinned up in a messy arrangement, Serena looked vulnerable. Tentatively, she examined yards of fabric and trim, and Karl nodded to the shopkeeper. 'Let her purchase whatever she wishes. And one of the dresses must be ready by this evening.'

The woman eyed him for a moment, her face

furrowed as if she didn't believe she could accomplish the task. 'I have pieces of a gown partially sewn, but I must ask that you pay a portion of the cost beforehand. And I'll need to take her measurements to adjust the fit.'

From her embarrassed expression, it seemed that others must have cheated her in the past. Karl withdrew a stack of gold coins and set them in the woman's palm. 'This should cover the cost of two gowns. One for tonight, and another within the week.' Then he turned back to Serena. 'Do you want me to stay while she measures you?'

The princess's face reddened. 'No, I'll be all right on my own. But please…wait outside.' She looked uneasy about being alone, and he wondered if he ought to stay, regardless of her wishes.

In the end, he decided that his presence would only worsen the awkwardness between them. 'Send the dress to the governor's manor tonight,' Karl ordered. 'And I need you to acquire a suitable ladies' maid for my wife. Perhaps if you've a daughter or an acquaintance…?'

The woman's face paled. 'My lord, the governor's house is locked up. Are you certain you're speaking of the right place?'

Karl gave a single nod. 'I am.' He offered nothing further, letting her draw whatever conclusions she would.

Over the next hour, Serena inspected the fabric pieces that the dressmaker had begun stitching. It was a cream-coloured taffeta gown, trimmed with a cranberry ribbon. Although it would need to be taken in at the waist, Frau Bauherzen believed she could make it fit. There was also a matching cloak in the same shade of deep red.

It was strange, ordering a gown without jewels or lace, one that would never be worn to greet ambassadors. The simple design had a vee waist and box pleats that fell to the floor. A lady might wear this gown to pay calls, but it was entirely too plain for a princess.

Serena rather liked it.

'Do...all the island women purchase clothing this way?' she asked, feeling foolish at the question. Everything she'd ever worn had been created only for her. She'd never been inside a shop before, and she had to resist the urge to touch everything.

Frau Bauherzen sent her a curious look. 'I'm sorry, madam, but I don't understand.'

'Nothing.' She shook her hand, realising that she would only give away her identity if she asked more questions.

'May I take your measurements now?' Frau Bauherzen enquired.

Serena followed her behind a curtain, and the woman offered to help her remove her outer gown. 'I'd rather remain dressed,' she murmured, afraid that the dressmaker would discover her bruises, 'if you don't mind.'

Though the matron respected her wishes, Serena had to fight against her embarrassment at being touched. Her ladies in the palace already knew her measurements, and whenever she needed a new gown, it was simply delivered the day before the event. She had multiple wardrobes filled with day dresses, riding habits, ceremonial ballgowns, hats, gloves and stockings.

'Your husband is a generous man,' the woman offered, measuring the distance from Serena's waist to the floor.

Serena didn't know how to answer. Generous with coins, certainly. But how would he react when she informed him that she would not be marrying him? Already Karl had proved to be strong-willed and dominant. She suspected he wouldn't accept her refusal well at all.

'Forgive me,' Frau Bauherzen apologised, 'but I did wonder how you managed to go inside the governor's house. It's been locked up for several weeks now.'

Though the woman's tone was unassuming, Serena wasn't about to reveal their identities. She gave the only truth she could. 'My husband has connections with the Royal House of Lohenberg. But we were surprised to learn that the staff had gone.'

'They fled a few months after the famine,' the matron admitted. Her face coloured, and she added, 'Were I you, I'd go back to Lohenberg. There's nothing here any more.' She folded her hands, busying herself with writing more measurements.

'What about the rest of the islanders?' Serena asked. 'How are they surviving?'

Frau Bauherzen set down her pencil and shrugged. 'The rest of us have no choice but to stay. We can't afford to leave.' She lifted the taffeta gown and began pinning the waistline. 'I don't know what brought you here, but Vertraumen has no future any more. Not for any of us.'

Serena didn't like hearing the resignation in the woman's voice. 'I'll ask my husband to speak with the king of Lohenberg. It may be that he can get help for you.'

'I wish it could be so,' Frau Bauherzen responded, 'but it's been two years now. And... nothing.'

Though she knew it was none of her business, Serena couldn't stand back idle when people were suffering. Surely they could bring in more food and workers to help restore the island. 'We'll see what can be done,' she offered.

'About what?' came the voice of the *fürst*. He entered the shop, taking Serena's gloved hand in his.

The matron cleared her throat, her face bright with embarrassment. 'I was only explaining to your wife about the troubles that have been going on in Vertraumen.'

'So I've heard.' The *fürst* guided Serena to stand behind him. 'I will send word to the king on your behalf.'

The woman sent him a sudden look, as if she were wondering who he was. A moment later, she seemed to dismiss it. 'Thank you, my lord. In the meantime, I should…get started on the gown. I will bring it to the manor house as soon as it's finished.'

Before Serena could say another word, the *fürst* guided her outside, leading her away from the village. 'Bernard and Samuel have purchased supplies, and they will bring them to the house. We're going back now.'

'But I thought you wanted to explore the village?' She was confused at his sudden decision. 'Has something happened?'

He nodded. 'I'll tell you more when we reach the manor.'

'I want her found.' *Freiherr* Albert von Meinhardt swept his fist across the desk, sending a brass candlestick flying. It struck the ground, but Captain Gerlach Feldmann didn't flinch. He'd been prepared for the *freiherr*'s outrage. As the king's closest advisor and a distant cousin, Albert had secretly held a fascination with the princess. Had she not outranked him, Gerlach suspected the man might have offered himself as a potential bridegroom.

'Why did you let her leave?'

'She was travelling with the *fürst* of Lohenberg and went willingly.'

'Against her father's orders!' the *freiherr* shot back. 'You defied the king by letting her go.'

'And was I supposed to offend the prince?' Gerlach held up his hands, feigning ignorance.

'Your loyalty is to His Majesty. Not to the *fürst* of Lohenberg.'

'She's only been gone one day,' Gerlach said. 'She must have gone to one of her father's estates.'

'Send two dozen men to each of the estates,' the *freiherr* ordered. 'Betrothed or not, if word of this reaches the people, the princess will be ruined. I don't have to remind you what will happen when the king learns of this.'

'Or what will happen to Princess Serena,' Gerlach said beneath his breath. He'd seen the effects of the brutal beatings first hand, and it sickened him to see her bruises.

'What His Majesty chooses to do with his disobedient daughter is his own affair.'

Gerlach didn't answer, for he knew the *freiherr* would do nothing to offend the king. The man was blind to the princess's suffering, and he was glad

Serena was far away from the palace. Thankfully, by obeying the *freiherr* and sending men to each of the estates, it would grant the princess more time, for Gerlach knew she wasn't there. Though he feared her escape could only be temporary, he hoped she would succeed.

'As my lord commands,' Gerlach said, lowering his head to acknowledge his orders.

'Captain Feldmann,' von Meinhardt continued. 'If she isn't found, the king will hold someone to blame. It won't be me.'

The implication wasn't missed on Gerlach, and he bowed. He'd known the risk in aiding the princess, but he'd wanted to do what was right.

'I've ordered the arrest of your wife,' the *freiherr* informed him. 'She will be held prisoner in your place, while you find the princess.'

The ground seemed to disappear from beneath his feet. Was that man that heartless to arrest an innocent woman?

'My wife has done nothing wrong,' Gerlach protested. 'You've no right—'

'No, *you* had no right to ignore the king's orders. And perhaps this will motivate you to find her sooner.'

Gerlach gritted his teeth to hold back words he was going to regret. The *freiherr* was a dangerous man, especially when angered. And he didn't know if the baron was aware that they had a son. If he mentioned the boy, he sensed that von Meinhardt would imprison him, as well. He couldn't hide the fury and resentment on his face, his hands clenching into fists.

'You're dismissed, Captain,' the *freiherr* said. 'The sooner you find the princess, the sooner we'll release your wife. And take you in her place.'

Chapter Four

The *fürst* quickened his pace, keeping his hand around her waist. Serena knew it was merely to ensure that she kept up with his stride, yet the warmth of his hand felt too familiar. She tried to move away from him, but his hand only curled around her in a protective grasp.

'Please,' she said softly, 'don't touch me.'

She expected him to ignore her request; instead, his hand dropped away, his face sobering. He waited for her to say more, but Serena felt her cheeks redden. What could she say? That any kind of touch bothered her, reminding her of the beatings she'd endured? His penetrating gaze pushed down her defences, leaving her to feel desperately uncomfortable.

The prince took the edges of her fichu and parted

them, revealing her bruised throat. 'This was why you left the palace. Wasn't it?'

He knew.

Serena couldn't find the right words to answer so she remained silent.

'Who did this to you and why?' he demanded.

She flinched at his harsh tone. Without answering, she took the edges of her fichu, and used the lace scarf to cover her neck.

There was a flash of anger in the prince's eyes before he returned his gaze back to the house. Though he hadn't pressured her for the answers, she sensed that he was only biding his time.

The prince led her to the back entrance of the house, locking it tightly behind them. As they continued through the maze of rooms, the silence continued. At last, they reached the drawing room.

The *fürst's* posture was rigid as he walked over to a carved wooden clock that hung upon the wall. After checking the time on his pocket watch, he adjusted the hands of the clock and swung the pendulum.

'While you were with the dressmaker, I spoke with one of the other islanders. He said that they have been without a governor for weeks. With hardly any provisions left, some have resorted to stealing.'

'Frau Bauherzen told me about the hardships. I think you should send word to your father and appeal on their behalf.'

The prince reached for the clock key and inserted it, winding it up. But even after he swung the pendulum a second time, there was no sound of ticking from within the clock. 'I agree. I'll have the king send troops to restore order and help with supplies.' He folded his arms and stared at her. 'It would be best if we married today or tomorrow, before we leave. I can arrange it this afternoon, if that would suit.'

It took an effort to keep her mouth from dropping open. He spoke of marriage as if it were having afternoon tea. 'I'm not going to marry you.'

'I promised I would keep you safe,' he said quietly. 'Marrying you is my means of doing so. Surely you understand that it will silence any gossip about us. We've no choice in the matter.'

Serena had no intention of surrendering her freedom to his whims. Although he was right that her virtue was already destroyed by being with him, she had no desire to wed any man. It didn't matter what people believed, for she intended to disappear and live where no one would find her.

She straightened and walked over to him. 'You will return to Lohenberg. And I'll go to my grandfather's hunting lodge, as I'd planned.' It wasn't the truth, for she hadn't decided where to go, but it was all she could think to say.

'You can't go there. Your father's men would bring you back to the palace within hours.' He closed the clock door and turned to face her. 'Unless that's what you want.'

Most definitely not. If they found her, she would bear the full brunt of her father's temper. Serena closed her eyes at the thought.

'Who were you running away from?' he asked. His gaze fixed upon her throat, and the anger in his expression unnerved her.

She ignored the question. Even if he believed the truth, there was nothing he could do about it. 'Why did you kidnap me?' she countered.

The *fürst* moved so close, she could feel the warmth of his breath against her mouth. Though he didn't touch her at all, it took all of her courage to hold her ground. 'Why do you think, Princess?'

Her body seemed drawn to his words, the heavy

woollen gown feeling restrictive. She thought of his hands upon her nape, unfastening the buttons last night.

He believed he was still going to be her husband, that he had the right to touch her in this way. When she dared to look at him again, the heat in his eyes held her transfixed.

'You're trying to ruin me,' she whispered.

'You're already ruined,' he responded, reaching out to cup her face. His hands were gentle upon her skin, but embarrassment blazed upon her cheeks. 'I'm trying to tempt you.'

A sudden chill swept over her, and Serena took a step backwards. He let her go, and the darkness in his eyes took on a shadowed look. This was a man accustomed to getting what he wanted. And he wanted her.

Her mouth went dry at the thought of sharing his bed. Karl von Lohenberg looked as if he knew exactly how to seduce a woman, how to lure her into wickedness.

But she couldn't allow herself to be caught up in him. Though he'd helped her to escape Badenstein, she would find another way to repay him.

A way that didn't involve marriage or sharing his bed.

'Anna should never have written to you,' she said to him. 'I would have been fine on my own.'

'There are many men who would take advantage of a woman travelling alone.'

'I wouldn't have been alone. I had guards.'

'What you did wasn't safe. Half-a-dozen bullets would have ended their lives, and you could have been kidnapped.'

'I *was* kidnapped,' she reminded him, 'by you.'

'For your own good.' He folded his arms across his chest. 'Can't you imagine what would have happened to you, if another man had stolen you away?'

She sent him a pointed look. 'And your intentions are more honourable?'

'I offered to marry you.' He took another step forward, pressing her back against a *chaise longue.* 'You'll admit, I've not once forced my attentions on you.'

'Yes, you have,' she countered. 'Last night. And—and—you've been entirely too forward.' With him standing so close, she wished she hadn't spoken. It sounded like a challenge, instead of a criticism.

'I've never hurt you, Princess. And I promise, when I touch you, it will only bring you pleasure.'

She couldn't breathe when he was looking at her in this way. Her fingers dug into the *chaise longue,* and he backed away, shielding his thoughts.

'I know a priest who can perform the ceremony, and in the next few days, we should explore the island. Then, I can provide a detailed accounting of the conditions here. Once I've sent word to the king, we'll return to Badenstein.'

She said nothing, refusing to belabour the issue, when he wasn't listening to her. Her head ached, and she was so tired, her vision blurred.

The prince lifted the clock from the wall and took it with him as he crossed into the dining room. Now what did he want that for? Serena followed him, not understanding his intent when he rang for the footman.

When Bernard arrived, the *fürst* ordered him to fetch a set of tools. The footman seemed not at all surprised at the request and hurried to obey.

'What do you need the tools for?' Serena asked.

'I'm going to fix the clock.' He took off his coat

and rested it on the back of a chair. She stared at him, shocked to see a man of his rank performing such a menial task.

'Why?'

'Because I can.' He pulled a chair out from the dining room and sat. 'You're free to do as you please. Bernard will bring us luncheon, soon enough. I hope he acquired a cook as well as the food, or we might end up eating eggs again.'

Serena took a few steps toward the library, feeling somewhat uncertain of what to do. The prince's dismissal was unexpected, and she leaned against the door frame, distracted with thoughts of her own plans. For so long, she'd obeyed her father's orders, never allowed to think for herself.

Not any more. She walked amid the books, tracing her finger along the spines. Possibly she could find an atlas and make a list of possible locations to live.

There were many Greek islands, and she envisioned living somewhere warm, with olive groves lining the hills and soft sand beneath her shoes.

'You're smiling,' came the voice of the prince. 'What are you thinking of?'

Serena blinked and snatched a book from the

shelves. 'Nothing.' She risked a glance at the prince.

From his vantage point at the table, she could see him watching her. Beside him lay the clock face. He turned back to his work and began loosening various parts of the apparatus, working as though he'd manufactured clocks all his life. Her gaze fell upon his hands, his long fingers that moved with expertise. He was completely focused upon his work, though she sensed that his mind was not at all on the mechanical parts. It was a distraction, nothing more.

Serena couldn't fathom his reasons for wanting to take it apart, but it intrigued her. He tilted the clock toward the sunlight so he could see better, and she glimpsed a structure of gears. His dark hair was cut short, but across his cheeks, she saw the darkening shadow of stubble. Though it should have made him appear rough and unkempt, instead it made him look dangerous.

'You may as well come closer,' he said, nodding toward her. 'You can't see very well from over there.'

She didn't move. 'Perhaps I don't want to.'

He set down a small wooden mallet, a slight

smile playing upon his mouth. 'Or you could pretend to read that *Treatise on Hydraulic Engineering* that you're holding. I suppose you'd find it fascinating.'

Serena glanced at the book she was holding. She hadn't even looked at the title, and it struck her that his vision must be quite good to have viewed the title from so far away. 'It might be interesting.'

'Not likely.' The *fürst* beckoned to her. 'Come and stand beside me. You can help.'

It sounded more like an order than a request, and she remained where she was. 'I've never taken a clock apart before.'

'I could use someone with smaller hands.'

Reaching inside a clock didn't bother her at all; it was the idea of sitting so close to him. 'I might break it.'

'The gears are made of metal. You can't break them.' He gestured toward the chair beside him with a pair of tweezers.

Just being near this man made her unsettled and afraid. She didn't know what on earth possessed her to obey, but then, he was fixing a clock, nothing more. And she *was* curious. She stood beside him, and the prince ordered, 'Take your gloves off.'

'I'll just watch.'

'Off.' His expression turned provocative and measured. 'Unless you'd rather I removed them for you. I'm good at that.'

He reached for the fingertip but she pulled her hand away, unrolling the kid glove from her hand. 'You needn't threaten me.'

'It was an invitation, Princess.' His voice grew deeper, as if he were physically touching her.

Her skin flushed at his words, and she removed the other glove, setting it aside. Inside the clock, she saw gears and a large spiral-shaped coil of metal. He brought her hand to touch the part. 'That's the mainspring,' he informed her.

The prince leaned over her shoulder as he pointed out the other parts of the clock. He could have been speaking Greek, for all that she remembered of the names. Instead, she was conscious of his physical form, and the way her body nestled against him, almost in an embrace. When she breathed, she could smell the male scent of his skin.

It felt strange to be this close to a man, particularly one who believed that they would one day be intimate. Her hands trembled as he guided her hand to one of the clock parts.

'Do you see this gear?' He pointed to a smaller grooved circle. 'It slipped out of alignment. I want you to see if you can move it back into place.'

She fumbled with the tiny piece, and the prince was saying something about where it was supposed to go. Instead, she found herself studying his hands and the way his fingers moved over the pieces.

'That's it,' he praised, when she locked it into position. 'Now, if you'll hold it there, I'll tighten it.'

She held the gear in place, and his fingers brushed against hers as he made the adjustments. The gentle pressure of his hands both frightened and fascinated her. Never before had any man been so close to her, not without the intent to harm.

When the prince had finished fixing the clock, he didn't move away. Instead, his hazel eyes regarded her, as if he wanted far more than she could give. This was madness. Just being near him made her breathless, and she didn't like feeling this way.

'You're trembling,' he murmured. 'What are you afraid of?' He caught her hand in his, and the warmth of his palm against hers did nothing to abate her nerves.

'I'm afraid of you,' she admitted. And the way he made her feel inside.

When she pulled her hand back, he made no move to stop her. His mouth tightened, as if he didn't like what she'd said. Even if it was the truth.

He fitted the remaining pieces back together and wound up the clock. When he tilted it up and swung the pendulum, she heard the rhythmic ticking.

'It works.' She hadn't truly expected it to. But there was a sense of satisfaction in having fixed something that was broken. She reached for one of her gloves, but the *fürst* took it from her.

'Of course it works. I can fix anything.'

She sent him a doubtful look. 'Not anything.'

He picked up her fallen glove and stroked the exterior, as if he were caressing her skin. 'With the proper instructions, yes. Anything.'

One by one, he fitted her fingers within the glove, and slowly eased it over her palm. The sensation of her fingers sliding against the soft leather caused an echoing ripple over her body. She didn't know why he was intent on touching her, but even the slightest gesture sent her senses on edge.

'I started taking things apart when I was a child,' he told her, reaching for the second glove. 'Anything I could find. I wanted to see how it worked.'

'Why?'

'Because it was more interesting than reading about it. And some would say I'm good with my hands.' The wicked look in his eyes suggested that he was no longer speaking of taking things apart.

Serena couldn't stop her mind from envisioning his hands moving over her bare skin, awakening her to the pleasures of the marriage bed. The nearness of him, the way he tantalised her with the barest touches, made her all too aware of how bold he was. Already she had almost no ability to control her responses.

Distance was what she needed. She pulled her hand from his and went to stand by the fire. 'Who taught you to fix mechanical things?'

'The gardener, Herr Pflicht. After I tried to build a steam engine out of a tea kettle.'

A smile tugged at her mouth, despite her efforts to stop it. She could almost envision a young boy, experimenting with a tea kettle. 'Did it work?'

'It sank to the bottom of a rain barrel. Cook was furious.'

Her smile softened. She could imagine the mischief he must have caused.

The prince came over to stand before her. 'Did you ever get into trouble as a girl?' he asked.

'I wasn't allowed to do anything improper.' Her days were spent with lessons or learning how to behave like a princess. Any slight misbehaviour had earned her time spent locked up in the library. She'd consoled herself with books to fill the hours. Her father hadn't believed her capable of learning anything except embroidery and etiquette, and if he'd known how much she'd adored learning, he'd have found another place to punish her.

In reading, she'd found her escape. She'd read about exotic places around the world, dreaming of a house of her own overlooking the sea. She'd wanted a home where she could be herself, where no one would judge her.

The prince's gaze centred upon her throat, and before Serena could move away, his hand hovered above the lightly bruised skin. 'Why did this happen to you? How could anyone lay a hand upon a royal princess?'

'I'm not as protected as you might believe.'

For no one could protect her from the king. Serena started to move away, but the prince's hand suddenly reached around to her nape. He stroked the back of her neck, threading his fingers into her hair. She froze in place when his fingers moved over the fragile skin of her throat, his thumb caressing the bruises.

'Don't,' she whispered, trying to pull away.

He returned his hand to the back of her head, leaning in. 'Who hurt you?'

Serena's blood pulsed, her skin prickling with fear. When his forehead touched hers, the heat of his skin entranced her. His hands moved down to her shoulders, and she sank deeper under his spell. 'I want you to stop,' she confessed. 'Please. I can't—I don't—' She closed her eyes, so terribly confused when she was near him.

'Don't what?' His mouth rested just above hers, and Serena wondered if he was going to kiss her.

Karl saw the way Serena was fighting against herself. Fear penetrated her expression, and her hands were clenched. She looked as if she wanted to be far away from him, as if she dreaded his touch.

He wanted to ignore propriety and taste the soft lips that lay so close. Her green eyes held worry, her cheeks flushed with uncertainty. After seeing the bruised skin of her throat, he understood that he couldn't push her. Someone had hurt her badly, though he couldn't understand why.

It would be reckless to damage what little trust she had in him, by forcing a kiss. Karl released her and returned to the clock on the table. He lifted it and brought it back into the other room. While he distracted himself with mounting it on the wall, he wondered what he was supposed to do now.

He stared at the blurred reflection of his face in the glass clock cover. He'd mistakenly believed that Serena would welcome a marriage, if only to preserve her reputation. But she was running away from someone who had tried to hurt her.

Frustration unfurled inside him, for she would say nothing about it, and he couldn't understand why. He'd been patient with her, thus far, but it was wearing thin.

Karl turned around and closed the distance between them. 'Are you still afraid of me?' In the silence between them, all that could be heard was the clock ticking.

She nodded slowly. But then, she lifted her gaze up to meet his. Karl reached for a fallen, tangled lock of hair and tucked it behind her nape. 'Go and eat your luncheon without me. I'll join you in a moment.'

She nodded, clutching her arms at the casual touch. It infuriated him that she was so mistrustful, as if she believed him to be a monster. When she didn't move, he couldn't tell if it was frozen fear or something else.

'I'll…wait for you.' Her arms crossed over her chest, and he sensed that she was trying to overcome her nerves. The softness of her skin, the shadowed look of her eyes, spoke of a woman who had been hurt. A woman who no longer trusted anyone.

'That wouldn't be a good idea.'

'Why?' she whispered.

'Because if you stay, I'm going to kiss you.' He wanted to taste her mouth, to coax her into wanting more. To see if she might…desire him.

Her innocent eyes widened, and Serena looked behind her, as if to see whether anyone was watching. But there was no one near, no eyes watching them. With his fingers, Karl traced a path down the back of her neck, feeling the gooseflesh rise beneath his touch.

'And if I don't want you to?' she whispered.

'Then go into the dining room right now. I won't stop you.'

Her face paled, and she crossed her arms over her chest, as if to shield herself. For a moment, she considered it, lifting her face to his. Karl drew his hands to the back of her head, sliding his fingers into her hair.

The moment his hands touched her hair, she winced and pulled away. Then, as if she couldn't bear his presence any more, she fled.

After she'd gone, Karl stared at the face of the clock. *What did you expect? That she would want a man like you?*

The brittle anger at himself threatened to break free, so he took a few moments to suppress it, along with the physical frustration Serena had conjured. She wanted nothing at all to do with him, and it was doubtful that would change.

When they reached the dining room, his footman was standing next to a covered tray of food.

'I must apologise, Your Highnesses,' Bernard said, bowing after he set down the tray. 'I fear that a cook won't arrive until tomorrow. I…did the best I could, but I'm not much good in the kitchen.'

'I'm certain that whatever you've prepared will be better than anything the *fürst* or I could manage.' Serena gave the footman a polite smile, and he pulled out a chair for her before Karl dismissed him.

When Bernard had gone, Serena's expression changed into wariness. 'For an island experiencing a famine, I wonder what he managed to find.'

Karl lifted the covering and revealed two plates containing grey slabs of meat and limp vegetables. Eyeing the princess, he said, 'We could starve by the time a real cook arrives.'

'What sort of meat do you suppose it is?' She poked at it with a fork.

'Overcooked.' He attempted to cut it, but the meat wouldn't give way. 'I don't know if we should eat it.'

'It would hurt his feelings if we didn't try.'

The princess doggedly began sawing at the meat. Karl tried some of the vegetables, which were hardly more than mush. At last, he gave up and pushed the plate away. 'This is a disaster.'

Serena was trying to chew the unpalatable bit of meat with no success. Karl tossed his napkin upon the table. 'Come on. We'll go somewhere else to find better food.'

'But where, if there's a famine…?' She cast a glance outside, uncertain of what he meant.

'I have a friend who lives upon an isolated part of the island, one that few people know about. We'll share a meal with him and I can learn more about what's been happening here over the past two years.' He stood beside her chair. 'Unless you're too afraid to leave.'

The dare was meant to provoke her, for he needed her to come with him. He didn't know if the old priest still dwelled among the abbey ruins, but it was possible.

'I don't know,' Serena said, lowering her gaze. 'It doesn't seem safe.'

'Our alternative is to suffer through two more meals here before we can leave,' Karl said. 'If you're willing to risk it.'

Chapter Five

Serena's instinct was to say no. The poor food was only a temporary inconvenience, whereas she needed to make her plans for the next few weeks before her father's soldiers could track her here. 'I'm not certain it would be a good idea.'

'If you'd rather not eat, that's your decision.' He shrugged and rang for Bernard.

While he gave orders for a horse to be readied, Serena touched her fingers to her mouth. It seemed surreal to imagine that only moments ago, the prince had wanted to kiss her. She'd thought about it, wondering what a kiss would be like. But the moment his hands had touched the tender bruises on the back of her head, all she could remember was her father's fists. She couldn't bear the thought of physical closeness. Never before had she experienced an affectionate touch from a man, and the look in Karl's eyes had made her panic.

I don't understand him, she thought to herself. *Why would he want to kiss me?*

She stared down at the grey meat, wondering what she was going to do about the prince. He'd had no qualms about abducting her from the palace, and although he kept insisting on marrying her, he'd never forced himself upon her. It wasn't at all the behaviour of a man intent on ruining her reputation.

Serena moved into the drawing room to stare out the window. In the hall, Bernard helped the prince don his great coat and gloves. Not once did *Fürst* Karl take his gaze from her. He studied her, as if he sensed the maelstrom of thoughts tangled inside her. Then he crossed the room to stand before her.

'I'll admit, I'm not a patient man. I like doing things my way.' His hazel eyes bored into her. His gloved hand moved over to tip her chin. 'But you needn't be afraid of me. I don't hurt women. Ever.'

There was iron resolution in his tone, like he was offended by her fear.

His hand moved over her cheek, tracing a path to the bruises at her throat. With the gentlest touch, he sent waves of gooseflesh over her skin. She wanted so badly to move away, but her feet remained locked in place.

'Why do you persist in touching me?' she whispered. 'You don't behave like a prince at all.' More like a man bent upon seduction.

'Perhaps I'm not a prince any more,' he responded. 'Perhaps I really am a villain.'

'I don't know what you are.'

'I'm the man who's going to marry you,' he said, drawing his hand down to hers.

She steadied her thoughts, and eyed him. 'No. I'm not going to wed you.' Even if she never returned to Badenstein, marrying Karl would forever trap her into the life of royalty, having to rule over Lohenberg one day. She wouldn't let that happen.

Before he could voice an argument, she removed the fichu and bared the darkened bruises. 'I've been told what to do, all my life. And this was my reward for obedience.' She let him see the marks upon her skin, taking a deep breath as she did. 'I won't endure it any longer.'

He didn't release her from his grasp. 'Do you think your father's men will let you go, Princess?'

His grip tightened around her waist, pulling her against him. 'They'll search until they find you.'

'I—I know they'll search. But they won't find me.' She took his hands and gently extricated herself.

His expression hardened. 'You're the heir to the throne. Running away isn't feasible. Especially alone.'

'I could hire servants to protect me. If I travelled far enough—'

'No.' His tone was brusque, unyielding. 'It won't work. Your only option is to wed me. Trust that I'll keep you safe.' He reached out his hands to her, waiting for her to take them.

'Trust a villain?' she mused. 'I thought I wasn't supposed to do that.'

'You're not.' He led her outside to where Samuel had prepared horses. 'But I'm not giving you a choice.' Before she could stop him, the *fürst* lifted her onto his horse and swung up behind her.

'What are you doing?' she demanded, feeling more than a little uneasy about the powerful thighs pressed against her. When he reached around her for the reins, it was like being within his embrace.

'Abducting you again,' the prince responded

as he signalled the horse forward. He drew the edges of his coat around her, offering warmth. He spurred the horse, and as they rode together, Serena could smell the faint exotic spice that clung to his coat. With the prince's arms around her, she felt even more apprehensive. Sharing a horse with him was intimate, and it frightened her to be this close.

She suspected that, the more time she spent with *Fürst* Karl, the greater the chance of succumbing to temptation. Inwardly, she admitted that she'd wanted him to kiss her. She'd wondered what it would be like to feel his mouth upon hers, coaxing feelings of yearning. To be touched with affection instead of the intent to harm.

The sunlight glowed in the sky above with puffy white clouds. Green hills gleamed like emeralds, and for a moment, Serena absorbed the beauty. An island such as this made a wonderful place to escape the world. She imagined a small house nestled in the hills, overlooking the water.

He guided them toward a more isolated part of the island. There were no cottages or shops anywhere, but only miles of grassy, damp meadows. In the distance beyond the sand, the brown-grey water of the North Sea was rough, with high waves sloshing against the rocks.

'Have you ever seen the sea before?' he asked against her ear.

His breath sent a rush of warmth through her. 'I have. But not this close.'

The prince pulled back on the reins, tightening his grasp around her. Serena tried to glance back to see if Samuel or Bernard had followed, but there was no sign of them. Karl caught her gaze, and asked, 'Still afraid?'

'A little.' She stared at the violent water, and the wind drew a light, salty mist against her skin. Gazing out at the churning sea, she felt the contrast of the cold air and the warmth of his body.

'There's nothing calm about the sea, is there?' he said.

'It's beautiful.'

'When I was a boy, I wanted to swim in it,' the prince admitted. 'Nearly froze my...'

'Toes?' she guessed.

He flashed her a wicked look on his face, and she realized he hadn't been referring to his feet at all. 'Not quite. But I lost my desire to swim.'

He directed the horse back to the grassy field.

Ahead, she spied stone ruins nestled at the top of another hill, with a dark forest obscuring the road. Serena craned her neck and asked, 'What is that place?'

'It's where we're going.'

She frowned, not understanding. Behind them came the sound of horses. Bernard and Samuel emerged to watch over them. Karl waited until they were close enough and ordered, 'Give us a few moments, and then join us at the abbey.'

An abbey? She couldn't understand why he would take her to such a place, especially when he'd claimed it was for food.

Karl urged their horse forward, up the winding pathway. When they entered the forest, the shadows grew darker. It was now late afternoon, and the sunlight filtered through the treetops, casting soft rays of gold upon the deep green ferns and moss.

'It feels almost enchanted,' she whispered. 'Almost from another time.'

'The shadows can be frightening at night,' he said, slowing the pace so she could look around.

'I can't believe you'd be afraid of anything,' she remarked. With his unyielding demeanour, she'd never supposed the prince would imagine anything beyond what he could see.

'I used to be afraid of the dark,' he admitted. 'When I was a boy, I had nightmares about being locked away in a cupboard.'

She glanced back at him and saw a tension on his face, as though it bothered him still. 'My mother used to come and comfort me, if I ever cried from a nightmare.' An aching tightened her throat, for she missed Clara's calm presence. Her mother's illness was taking her away, and it hurt to think of the time when she would be gone.

'My mother hated me,' Karl said. 'She wanted nothing at all to do with me, much less when I was having nightmares.'

His confession startled her. 'What about your father?'

Karl shrugged. 'The king had better things to do than coddle a young boy. I learned to get over my fears on my own.'

'But they loved you,' she insisted. 'You were their son.'

'No. They had an obligation to me, but love was never part of it.'

She couldn't think of anything to say, for his

even tone suggested that he'd spoken the truth, nothing more. When she craned her neck to look into his eyes, she saw the echoes of her own loneliness. Her father hated her for reasons she couldn't understand.

And the prince knew what that was like. For a brief moment, she'd glimpsed the man behind his cold shield. There was a similarity between them that she'd never guessed.

'I'm sorry,' she whispered, turning away.

They continued riding uphill until he stopped the horse near a small stream and tethered it. 'We'll walk the rest of the way.' The path grew steeper, and he offered his hand to help keep her balance.

'Who are we going to see?' she asked.

'An old priest who served my father, years ago.' His face grew solemn, as if he didn't like mentioning the king of Lohenberg.

'A priest?' She stopped walking, folding her arms across her chest. 'Why are we visiting a priest?' Her suspicions prickled, for she knew the *fürst* was still insisting upon marrying her.

'Because I want to hear more about what's been happening on the island, and Father Durin will know the needs of his parishioners. He's also fond of food and can provide us with a meal.'

Her suspicions sharpened, for it couldn't be a coincidence that he'd brought her to visit a priest. *He can't force you into marriage,* she reminded herself.

The prince reached to the ground and picked up a long wooden staff, handing it to her. 'Use this walking stick, in case you start to lose your balance.'

Though she accepted the staff, leaning upon it, she eyed the *fürst,* questioning his motives. He behaved as if nothing at all were amiss.

When they emerged from the forest, Serena saw the ruins of the abbey. Truthfully, it seemed to be built upon the remains of a castle structure. The main section was intact, but several towers were crumbling. A small moat encircled the structure, and water flowed beneath the drawbridge and down the hillside.

The *fürst* took the staff from her and ordered, 'Stay behind me.'

'Why? Isn't it safe?'

'I don't know if Father Durin is still living here,' he murmured. 'And if he's gone…'

She understood what he meant. Following his

orders, she moved behind him. The *fürst* led her across the drawbridge and up the wooden staircase that led to a large set of double doors. He lifted the iron knocker and rapped sharply upon it. Serena took another step back, uncertain of what to expect.

When a hand touched her shoulder, she let out a yelp. Behind her stood a middle-aged man with a long sword in his hand.

The prince's reaction was instantaneous. He moved in front of her, shoving her back toward the top of the stairs while he held the walking stick like a quarter staff.

The older man's mouth slid into a smile. In Lohenisch, he said, 'So. The fallen prince has returned.'

Serena pressed her back against the door, not knowing what he meant. Fallen? Before she could ponder it further, the old man laughed and sheathed his sword.

'We came to share a meal with you, Father Durin,' Karl said. A moment later, he switched into an unfamiliar dialect, and the only thing Serena recognised was the question behind it.

The older man withdrew an iron key from a

pouch at his waist and pushed his way past the prince. 'Come inside, and we'll talk.' He didn't cast Serena a single glance, nor did he ask why she was here.

The interior of the ruins was dark, and Father Durin brought them into a gathering space. A large chandelier hung in the centre of the room, filled with lighted candles. Although Serena could see bits of the sky through the roof, with the fire-place lit, the chamber wasn't too cold.

'And who is this?' the priest asked. 'Looks a bit fine, to me.'

'She's my betrothed wife,' Karl answered. He sent the older man a piercing stare, and the priest responded with a nod. Serena sensed that something was unspoken between them, and whatever it was made her spine prickle with unease.

'Why did you come to Vertraumen? Were you banished by the king?' Father Durin asked Karl.

The prince rubbed his chin and sent the man a dark look. 'Food first. Then we'll discuss the rest.'

The old man gave a shrug and disappeared down a narrow corridor. Serena studied the tall ceilings and walked the perimeter of the room. The long, narrow space might have been used for worship, she now guessed. Tall Gothic windows stood out on either side. Some were covered up with stone, while others had bits of cracked glass remaining. Outside, she saw that Samuel and Bernard had arrived with the horses and were tending them in the courtyard.

'What did the priest mean when he called you fallen?' she asked Karl.

His mouth drew into a line. He hesitated before answering, as if choosing his words carefully. 'He was mocking me. As I told you earlier, my father and I don't get along well.'

Though she supposed it could be true, she wondered if there was more to it than that. The *fürst* had travelled with only two servants, instead of a household of at least fifty or more men. What could have happened?

'How do you know the priest?' she asked him.

The *fürst* turned to face her. 'I spent a few summers here, after I turned ten. I had tutors for lessons, and Durin trained me in weaponry. I learned how to shoot and how to defend myself.'

'A priest trained you?' The idea seemed implausible, but then, how many priests greeted their guests with a sword?

He nodded. 'He wasn't always a priest, but a member of my father's guard until he grew old. My father sent me here in secret when the queen didn't want me at the palace.' His eyes grew shadowed, and he would say no more.

In her mind, she imagined a young boy, not yet a man, ignored by his family. It wasn't unusual, for many royal families in Lohenberg and Badenstein sent their sons and daughters away to be educated. Like her younger sister, Serena had attended boarding school for many years, before she'd finished her schooling with private governesses. 'Were you lonely?'

'I learned the skills that were necessary. And that was my father's intent.' He stared at the walls, and then added, 'I also brought you here for another reason.'

'To talk me into marrying you?' she guessed, crossing her arms.

'Yes.' He glanced outside. 'I have a marriage licence from Lohenberg, and Samuel and Bernard can be our witnesses.'

Narrowing her gaze, she said, 'I've already told you that I don't intend to wed you, or any man.'

'So you've said. But you might enjoy marriage

to me.' The sudden flare in his eyes made her take a step back. He was staring at her the way he had in the drawing room. Like he wanted to kiss her.

Serena felt goose bumps rise over her skin, and she couldn't tear her eyes away from him. Inside, her body grew warmer, and she wondered what it would be like to be touched by this man. Her heart seized up, and her hand moved to her throat. The skin was still tender from her father's grip, and she closed her eyes at the memory.

You can't escape the king, an inner voice warned. *No matter where you go, he'll find you. Unless he believes you're dead.*

She straightened and informed the prince, 'I'm sorry, but no.'

'You fled the palace because you were afraid. And yet, you won't let me protect you now.'

He took slow steps toward her, and she retreated until she backed up against a long wooden table. 'I'm going away, and I don't intend to return. What happened in the past doesn't matter.'

'It matters to me,' he said. He continued walking slowly, and Serena didn't move. When he reached the table, his arms moved on either side of her, trapping her in a silent embrace. A shiver of warmth spiraled through her.

'If I wed you,' she said quietly, 'I would become a Princess of Lohenberg.' The thought of being imprisoned within yet another palace, forced to surrender her freedom, made her tense. For so long, she'd been ordered around, criticised for her actions and her manners, until the idea of ruling over a country seemed impossible. 'It's not the sort of life I want any more.'

'Why not?' The look in his eyes made her falter. He believed she was his promised bride, a woman meant to belong to him.

'Our betrothal was made when I was fifteen years old,' she reminded him. 'When neither of us had a choice.'

Serena turned away from him, trying to free herself from his embrace. He confused her with the strange feelings he'd conjured. 'Let me go,' she breathed, pushing at his arm.

Karl's hazel eyes glittered as he stared back at her. But he did lift his hands away, granting her space. Wordlessly, she retreated to the other side of the hall, needing space.

At that moment, Father Durin returned. 'My

cook is preparing a meal for us to share. Come, have some wine and we will talk awhile.'

'I thank you for your hospitality, Father Durin,' Serena answered. 'I hope the food shortage has not made our visit a hardship.'

The priest shook his head. 'There is plenty of food upon Vertraumen, if you know where to look. I have a garden of my own, and I hunt for the meat I desire.'

'Are you the only priest living here?'

He nodded. 'The others who came before me preferred to live in the village. I wanted my privacy, which is why I chose the ruins as my home. I have everything I need here. The forest provides me with meat, the sea with fish and the earth gives the fruit of my labour.' He sent a look toward Karl. 'Now, what has brought you here?'

'I understand the islanders are leaving because of the famines. Tell me how the king should intervene and help them.'

The priest seemed to relax at this and began revealing information about the island and its difficulties.

Over the next hour, they ate a feast of roasted venison, fish and spring greens. Serena was so hungry, it took all the years of royal training to keep from devouring the food down to the last crumb. The longer the men spoke, the more her mind drifted away from their conversation about drainage and farming.

When Karl asked about the former governor, the priest confirmed that the man had fled. 'There were riots from the lack of food. The governor locked up the house and fled in the night with his family.' Father Durin added, 'Although the people are doing the best they can to survive, we're losing islanders every day.'

'Your father the king should know of this,' Serena insisted. 'Send word to him, and he can re-establish the leaders. It's a province of Lohenberg, after all.'

Karl's gaze grew distant, and he met the priest's discerning stare. A silent message seemed to pass between them.

'But it's not your concern any more,' the priest said. 'Is it?'

Karl sent the man a dark look. 'Lohenberg will always be my concern, regardless of what's happened.' He tossed a few coins on the table. 'Thank you for the meal. We'll go now.'

Regardless of what's happened? Now what did he mean by that?

As he took her hand and led her from the ruined castle, Serena wondered exactly what had caused such a rift between the prince and his father.

Chapter Six

He never should have brought her to Durin's home. The old man had voiced too many suspicious comments, and Karl knew Serena had formed her own doubts.

When they reached the forest, he dismissed Samuel and Bernard, who had walked up to the abbey ruins. He commanded them to take the supplies Father Durin had offered back to the manor house.

'What are you going to do about the island?' Serena asked when Karl walked alongside her through the forest.

'I'll visit the different towns and find out what's been causing the famine. Then I'll send recommendations to my father.' In his mind, he'd already begun a list, but he needed further information.

'Why didn't the governor alert the king?'

'Likely he feared he'd be blamed for the problems.' When they reached the steep slope, Karl offered his arm. He walked through the woods by memory, knowing the path well. He heard the sounds of a raven cawing and the light crunching of leaves as an animal scurried through the brush.

'I can see why you were afraid of these woods, as a boy. I can almost imagine something coming out of the shadows.' Serena moved closer to his side, and his arm came around her waist.

He stopped walking a moment, fixing his gaze upon her. 'Nothing will happen to you when I'm here.'

'You can't protect me from everything.' In the shadows, he couldn't see the expression on her face, but he heard the regret.

'Because you won't allow it.' He slowed their pace when the path grew steeper. Using the trees for balance, he kept his arm around her.

'I'm afraid that they'll find me again,' she confessed.

Within her tone, he heard the unsettled worry, as if she expected soldiers to drag her away to a dungeon. 'Would it be so terrible to go home?'

'I've been imprisoned in a place where I cannot

make my own decisions. I'm ordered around and beaten when I disobey.'

His temper darkened at her confession. Deep inside, his anger brewed—not at her, but at the one responsible. Someone had undermined the princess's confidence, making her believe that she had no choice but to flee. The more he looked at her, the more he saw the broken pieces of her spirit. Someone had bruised not only her body, but her confidence.

With great effort, he calmed his temper and kept his voice soft. 'It wouldn't have to be that way,' he said. 'Do you think I'd let anyone lay a hand upon my wife?'

She closed her eyes, as if to hold back tears. 'No. But you should choose another princess. I would never be the right wife for you.'

He said nothing, for she was the only wife he could have. Without a title of his own, without a kingdom, he would be reduced to nothing. His only hope of becoming a prince was to wed her.

And she no longer wished to be a princess.

Once again, fate was mocking him. It wasn't possible to find another bride, and Serena would learn of his lost title, soon enough.

It was growing dark outside, the trees casting shadows over the path. Serena wouldn't look at him, and she'd clutched both hands against her chest. In the fading light, her dark blond hair held tints of gold. She looked fragile, and in that moment, he wished he weren't such a bastard. An honourable man would do what he could to help her, to let her go.

You haven't a shred of honour. You tried to use her, and this is what you deserve.

'You despise me, don't you?' he said quietly.

Her face turned back to his, confusion in her green eyes. 'No. You might be overbearing and stubborn, but you aren't that terrible.'

He didn't believe her. 'I stole you from the palace and brought you to the most forsaken place on earth.'

Serena's mouth faltered as if she didn't quite know what to say. In the end, she offered, 'It hasn't been easy, that's true. But it's not so bad on the island.'

'And your reasons for not wedding me…is it only because you don't want to be a princess?'

She walked alongside him to the water's edge, her shoes pressing footprints into the damp sand.

'If you were an ordinary man and I, an ordinary woman, you'd want nothing to do with me.'

'You underestimate yourself.' He reached out to her, his hand grazing hers. 'Though I already know you want nothing to do with me.'

Her eyes were studied him with nervousness and interest. 'You are an overbearing tyrant.'

'I don't like it when I don't get my way,' he said, stopping in front of the water's edge. The air had turned cooler, the afternoon shifting into evening. The setting sun slid behind a cloud, the golden rim haloing Serena's hair.

'I'm not marrying you,' she whispered again, her gloved hands touching his.

'I know.' He drew her hands around his waist. 'You'd never want a man like me.'

'What kind of man are you?'

'Demanding.' He moved in, touching his nose to hers. He could feel her tremble, the fear he'd conjured by his nearness. 'You're right to stay away.'

'What are you doing?' she whispered.

'I've already ruined you,' he said against her cheek. 'It seems unfair that I should be blamed for your undoing...and I've never even kissed you.'

'That's unnecessary,' she said. But though he'd released her waist, she didn't try to escape him.

'I disagree. I think you should at least be forced to kiss a tyrant. Before you decide that I'm not what you want.'

Her eyes were wide, and she started to glance over her shoulder when he leaned to brush his lips upon hers. He'd already butchered any attempts at courtship or good manners. He had nothing else to lose.

Serena stood like a stone pillar, too afraid to move. He lifted her hands to his shoulders, guiding her into the embrace. He framed her face with his hands, sliding his fingers into her hair. She didn't know how to kiss, and her innocence pleased him. There was a sweetness to her, an awkwardness that made him want to teach her what he wanted.

Her mouth softened, and he took her deeper, winding her arms around his neck, bringing her body against his. The softness of her feminine shape against him was like a rich liquor, intoxicating and sweet. He kissed her fully, capturing her mouth and giving her no chance to pull away. She was entirely at his mercy, and he could taste the shock against her lips.

He didn't care. If he was to be incriminated and refused as a bridegroom, he wanted it to be about him, not his non-existent throne.

For a long moment, she did nothing except stand motionless, accepting his mouth upon hers. But as the kiss went on, she suddenly caught the rhythm. When her lips moved against his, kissing him back, he was caught by the tantalising warmth of her mouth.

He wanted to show her that there could be more between them if she'd allow it. With his palms, he caressed her spine, drawing her close, until her chest was against his. She was starting to soften beneath his onslaught, and when her mouth opened wider, he slid his tongue inside.

A soft moan of surprise came from her, but he didn't stop. He invaded her mouth, not allowing her to catch her breath. When she dared to slide her own tongue against his, instinctive needs pulled at him, to bare her skin and feel her softness against his hard length.

Serena broke away from him at last, her hands pressing against his chest. Her shoulders were tense, and he felt the slight tremor in her body. 'I shouldn't have let you kiss me, *Fürst* Karl.'

'Karl,' he corrected. 'Just Karl.'

'I cannot call you by your first name. It isn't proper.'

No, but he wasn't a prince any more. The title felt like a mockery of his former status. 'When we're alone, it doesn't matter what you call me.'

Her fingers reached up to her swollen lips, and she looked fearful of what she'd done. He said nothing more, for he'd pushed her farther than she was ready. Even if she had kissed him back.

When they rode along the edge of the water, Serena sensed that they were being watched. Though the prince had allowed her to ride the horse the footman had brought for her, she kept close to his side. Bernard and Samuel took the lead, with the supplies tied to their horses and torches to light their path.

The moonlight cast a shimmering band of silver upon the quiet waves. The prince drew closer to her, keeping his voice low. 'We have visitors, Princess. And I don't think they've come to pay a call.'

She clenched the reins of her horse and followed

the direction of his gaze. Along the edge of the hill, she spied the flare of torches.

'What do you want me to do?'

Karl withdrew the revolver from his coat and cocked it. 'You're going to stay with me. Bernard and Samuel will keep them occupied while we ride to the manor. It's not too far.'

'What about them? What if—?'

'They'll be all right,' Karl assured her. 'Both of them are armed, and they are trained to protect us.'

Inside, she struggled to remain calm while Bernard and Samuel came to ride alongside them.

'How many?' Karl asked. From the sombre look of the men, Serena suspected they were outnumbered.

'It's too dark to tell,' Bernard answered. 'But we'll hold them off as long as we can.'

The prince absorbed this knowledge and pointed his revolver skywards, firing a single shot.

'What was that for?' Serena asked.

'Reinforcements,' was all he would say.

Serena huddled against the horse, wishing she understood what threat they were facing. Her answer came a moment later, when four men emerged from the shadows, carrying their own torches. All were armed.

Karl brought his horse close to her, and murmured, 'When I give the command, ride toward the hills as fast as you can. Don't look back, and don't stop. I'll follow you.' She nodded, knowing that her life might depend upon blind obedience in this instance.

The leader of the men came forward, and his body was painfully thin, the bones of his cheeks showing. He held a gun in his hands and his men moved to flank them. 'Give us your supplies,' the man ordered.

'Put away your weapons,' Karl countered. 'Come to the manor house in the morning, and you can have a share in our food then.'

'You're the new governor, aren't you?' the man said. 'Sent by the king to keep us starving.'

Karl said nothing, but repeated, 'Put down your gun.' Serena saw the ruthless air upon the prince's face, just as he levelled his own revolver at the leader. When a gunshot sounded from behind her, Serena jerked in startled response. Karl roared, 'Go!' He slapped her horse's side and fired the gun toward the men.

She bent low against the horse's mane and urged her mount forward, terrified at what was happening behind her. Just as ordered, she didn't look back, though she heard the sound of someone pursuing her. Whether it was the prince protecting her or someone else, she kept up the horse's pace.

In the darkness, her navy gown was an asset, keeping her hidden from the assailants. Her heartbeat pounded to the rhythm of the horse's hooves, and she prayed for the safety of Karl and the men. If anything happened to them, she would be utterly alone.

Serena closed her eyes, willing away the thought.

When she reached the manor and dismounted, she struggled to remember how to get into the back garden gate. Her hands were shaking so badly, she couldn't pry any of the stones loose.

The sound of another horse approaching made her huddle into the shadows, praying it wasn't one of the thieves. She eyed the stone wall, wishing she'd paid more attention to where the key was hidden.

When the rider drew closer, she held her breath.

Then her horse whinnied from behind, giving away their presence.

'Princess?' came a voice, and she recognised the *fürst*. Thank heaven. She emerged from her hiding place, and he withdrew another key from his waistcoat, unlocking the gate.

'What about Bernard and Samuel?' she breathed.

'Father Durin is with them.' The prince's voice held a note of strain, and he added, 'I suspect they will join us shortly. Most of the thieves fled after the priest arrived with his weapons.'

Karl brought her inside the house, and Serena felt the welcoming warmth of the interior. She went to the fireplace, her body trembling more from fear than the cold.

His face tightened, and he suggested, 'You should try to get some sleep. I'll wait for the men to return. I doubt if the thieves will trouble us again.'

In his voice, she heard a slight edge of…something wrong. Serena turned to look at him. She studied the prince, her eyes passing over his hardened face, past his tight jaw and mouth, down to the great coat he wore.

There.

She moved forward, parting the edges of his coat before he could stop her. The prince's upper arm was stained with blood. 'You were shot,' she breathed with horror. 'How bad is it?'

'The bullet grazed me, nothing more. It's just a little blood.'

Just a little? His shirt sleeve was turning red. Without waiting for him to argue, Serena gripped his hand and guided him upstairs into his bed-chamber. Her heart was staggering in her chest, but she forced herself to behave in a calm manner.

'Sit down,' she commanded, 'and let me look at it.'

He started to protest, but she ignored him and forced him to sit on the bed. She poured water from the pitcher upon his dressing table into a basin, locating a handkerchief to tend the wound.

Karl sat down, his posture as rigid as stone. His eyes held pain, but he didn't voice a single complaint. Serena helped him to remove the coat, and she reached for the buttons of his waistcoat. Her fingers were shaking, and she fumbled with the small buttonholes.

'I'm sorry,' she apologised. 'I'm trying to hurry with these.'

'I don't suppose you've had much experience unfastening buttons.'

She sent him an embarrassed look. 'You're right. But I'll manage.' When she'd freed the last button, she loosened his shirt, and bade him to lift his arms. Though his face turned pained at the effort, Karl obeyed.

The sight of the raw, angry flesh sobered her. Though she'd never tended a bullet wound before, Serena had watched Katarina treat Serena's injuries in the past. Cold water had soothed her own pain, and so she touched a wet handkerchief to Karl's skin. He flinched, but didn't make a sound while she tended him. To her relief, the linen absorbed the blood, revealing only a shallow abrasion.

'I don't think it's too bad,' she murmured as she wiped the blood. A strange sense of peace descended over her mind, pushing away the feelings of helplessness. The prince would heal, and she wasn't going to be left alone.

Serena tore a strip from the bed sheets and held the damp handkerchief in place while she tightened the length around him. As she worked, she couldn't help but notice his muscular chest. A light dusting of hair covered his pectorals, and between his ribs, his abdomen was firm.

A dryness caught in her throat, and her face warmed with modesty. Though she knew he needed help in wrapping the wound, it felt strange to touch a man's bare skin. It was warmer than she'd expected, like heated stone.

She wondered what it would be like to see the rest of him. Though she'd seen statues and paintings before, she blushed to think of a fully naked man.

If she'd eloped with him this afternoon, would this have been their wedding night? Her skin tightened against her clothing, her mind imagining lying in bed with a man like Karl.

Though he was often cool, his demeanour overbearing, she couldn't forget the way he'd kissed her. It was almost as if he couldn't get enough of her, as if he craved her touch.

He stared at her now with interest. She remained in place after she'd tied off the bandage, wondering what to do now. Her breathing quickened, and his hands came to rest upon her waist. He looked tired and in pain, but in spite of his discomfort, there was no denying the need in his eyes.

'Is there anything I can get you for the pain? I could try to find some laudanum.' The close proximity made her feel threatened, and Serena took a step away. Not because she thought he would hurt her, but because she was afraid of her response. With each moment she spent in his company, he was taking down her defences. Right now, she couldn't trust herself to be around him.

'I can bear the pain,' he said quietly. 'Thank you for tending the wound.' He studied her, adding, 'You were quite resourceful.'

She nodded, feeling suddenly shy by the compliment. The truth was, she'd surprised herself. Tending a wounded man was something she'd never done before, but she'd managed to hold back her fears.

Warmth brushed at her cheeks, and she offered, 'Do you want me to help you put your shirt back on?' Though it was bloodstained, at least it would keep him somewhat warmer.

He nodded, and Serena lifted it over his head, guiding his arms back within the sleeves. She held out his waistcoat, but he only took it from her, not bothering to put it on. Hazel eyes stared into hers with an unfathomable expression.

'Since you helped me, it seems only fair that I return the favour.'

Serena didn't understand his meaning and sent him a questioning look.

'You haven't slept in two days,' the prince said. 'I can see the weariness in your eyes.'

She started to protest, but he reached out to take her hand. 'Do you trust me, even a little?'

She wanted to say no, that two days wasn't long enough to trust anyone. But he had done what he could to keep her safe. 'A little, I suppose. But not very much.'

'I want to help you get some sleep tonight. Since you have no ladies' maid to assist you.'

It was then that she understood exactly what he intended. He wanted to help unbutton her gown, loosening her corset. Words of protest flew to her lips, but she couldn't seem to gather up her thoughts.

'You're about to fall asleep standing up,' he predicted. 'And rest assured, I've no intention of taking advantage of you. Especially not with a gunshot wound.'

'I don't know if it would be a good idea,' she admitted. Yet, she'd gone so long without sleep, her vision was starting to blur. Just the thought of a warm bed and being able to sleep made her crave it even more.

'It's a courtesy, nothing more. I think I can unfasten a few buttons without bothering you too much.'

Her sensibilities were screaming at her, and Serena had no idea why she was even considering it. Never in her life had she done anything improper. And yet, within the past two days, she'd broken so many rules of propriety, her reputation was beyond repair.

She'd spent time alone with the prince, even allowing him to kiss her. Now, they were standing together in her bedchamber, and he was wanting to undress her.

'I should go,' she whispered, closing her eyes.

The prince came to stand behind her. He stood so close, she could almost feel the heat radiating from his skin. 'But you won't. Not yet.'

His hands moved to rest upon her shoulders. When his fingers flicked open the first button, something stirred within her. One by one, his hands moved down her spine, until she felt the cool air against her back. She gripped her arms across her chest, and with each touch of his fingers, her breasts grew heavy and tight.

She shouldn't be standing here, allowing him to undress her. Inside, her conscience was screaming at her for the wanton behaviour. But she'd been without sleep for so long, the desperate needs were drowning her brain's common sense.

Serena felt a pressure against her nipples, almost as if he'd touched them instead of the last button. His hands moved down to the tight laces of her corset, and she couldn't quite catch her breath.

Her skin was burning, and the unexpected response confused her. He loosened the knot, and as he adjusted the laces, she felt the heavy corset growing less constricted. When she believed she could raise it over her head without any trouble, she held the front of her gown tightly and turned to face him. Her shoulders were bared to him, and the look on his face was of a man starving for her.

'Go back to your room,' he ordered. 'Now.' His hazel eyes held a fierce expression, and she fled without question.

When she reached her bedchamber, Serena turned the key in the lock, before allowing the dress to fall to the floor. The corset was more difficult to remove, but she arched her back, lifting it over her head. She kept her chemise and a single petticoat on, for she had no nightdress.

And when she slid beneath the covers, her aching body resonated with the memory of his touch. Her mind played over the image of his hands on her skin.

She rubbed at her bruised ribs, staring into the darkness. Karl could have been killed this night, leaving her with no one. And although she had no wish to wed him, neither did she want anything to happen to the prince.

Her mind drifted back to the kiss he'd taken. She rested her face in her hands, remembering the firm command of his mouth. Why had he done it? She hadn't been thinking clearly, but it was as if he'd shattered an invisible pane of glass. His mouth had been so warm, and she'd felt the stirrings of an intangible need.

And she simply didn't know what to do about it now.

Chapter Seven

Karl was haunted by the vision of Serena's bare skin. He'd mistakenly believed that he could help her unfasten her gown and corset without responding. He couldn't have been more wrong.

As he'd loosened every button, baring more of her skin, her womanly scent had aroused him to the point of physical pain. He'd wanted to kiss her bare back, to cup her full breasts and strip away every layer between them.

But then he'd seen the bruises that ran from her back around to her ribs. The yellowed skin revealed the healing, and it made him aware of just how abused she'd been. From the extent of the damage, he guessed that her ribs had been broken.

Seeing her healing injuries had changed everything. Though he couldn't understand how this could have happened to a royal princess, he wasn't going to let it happen again. He wasn't going to let her leave on her own, with no one but strangers to take care of her. She was too innocent to fully understand the danger.

He stared into the firelight, wondering what the hell he was doing. Somehow, he had to convince her that marrying him was her best option and that he would never harm her.

Karl lay back on his bed, a fiery ache plaguing his side. He remembered Serena's smooth hands passing over his skin and the way she'd touched him with such gentleness. She'd been so tense when he'd unlaced her, as if she believed his control would snap and he'd force himself upon her.

She didn't know just how close to the edge he'd been.

Though he'd brought her to the island with the intent of seducing her, forcing her to marry him... he couldn't do it any more. The sensible solution would be to bring her back to Badenstein and let her go. But there was no way in heaven or earth he could allow her to be threatened again. If she returned, she'd only become a victim, and it would be his fault.

Damn it all, nothing had turned out as he'd

planned. Karl rose from the bed, wincing at the bullet wound. He stood by the cold fireplace, wondering what he should do now. If his princess preferred to be a commoner...

A startling idea occurred to him. He'd simply have to convince her that being an ordinary lady wasn't everything she believed it was.

In the morning, a soft knock resounded at the door. Serena buried her face under the coverlet, hoping the person would go away and let her sleep for a few days more. The warm cocoon of her bed wouldn't allow her to emerge.

The knock grew louder, and the door opened quietly.

'My lady?' came a woman's voice. 'I've brought your new dress, and your husband bid me to awaken you.'

Serena peeked over the covers and saw Frau Bauherzen standing at the door. In her arms, she held a package wrapped in brown paper. The woman apologised, saying, 'I came last night, but no one was here. It was getting late, so I had to return home.'

'May I see the dress?' Serena asked, reluctantly

rising from the bed. Frau Bauherzen unwrapped the package, revealing the cream gown trimmed with cranberry ribbons and a matching red cloak.

'Shall I help you?' the matron asked.

Serena sent the woman a grateful look. After she used the pitcher and basin to wash, she gripped the bedpost while Frau Bauherzen assisted her with her corset and petticoats. Then she raised her arms while the woman lifted the gown over her. It was still a little large, but Serena was so grateful to be in clean clothing again, it didn't matter.

'Thank you so much.' she smiled.

The woman bobbed a curtsy, but worry lined her face as she reached out to point toward Serena's upper arms. 'I see you have some bruises, my lady. Are you all right?'

Serena's smile faded. 'I suffered a fall down the stairs, several days ago,' she lied. 'I'll be fine.' Frau Bauherzen murmured her sympathies, but Serena could tell she was still uneasy about them.

'Shall I tend your hair?' the matron asked.

Serena sat at the dressing table, thrilled beyond words to have assistance. Though she was self-conscious of the bruises, she hoped they weren't too noticeable. She could wear the cloak outdoors to cover her arms, or perhaps find a shawl.

Frau Bauherzen helped her untangle her hair, brushing it to a smooth sheen before coiling it and pinning it into a soft chignon.

When at last she was ready, Serena offered, 'Whatever your family needs, I shall ensure that you receive it.' She started to instruct the matron to speak to Bernard, but then realised she didn't know what had happened last night. 'Come with me downstairs, and I'll make the arrangements,' she finished.

She reached the dining room and saw Bernard standing near the door. He appeared weary, and when she asked after his welfare, he admitted that he'd suffered no injuries.

'I am very glad to hear it.' She smiled and told him to provide Frau Bauherzen with a share of the supplies they'd received last night. 'What happened after I left?'

'I relived my past days as a palace guard,' came the voice of Father Durin from the dining room. Serena hurried forward and saw the priest seated across from the *fürst*.

'I hope you weren't hurt?'

'Not at all,' the priest assured her. 'And I recognised a few of the men from my parish. When they saw me, they realised their wrongdoing. I'm convinced that they'll make amends.'

Serena breathed a little easier, but when she caught the prince staring at her, she felt self-conscious. His eyes drifted over her new gown, settling around her figure. The heat in his gaze made her feel exposed with the short sleeves. And then, when he studied her bare arms, he stood from the table.

'We need to talk,' he said.

'What you need is a chaperon,' the priest grumbled from behind them. At the pointed look on his face, Serena flushed.

Before she could voice a reply, the prince guided her into the library and closed the door. His knuckles curled across the door frame, gripping the wood. 'Those bruises didn't happen last night, did they?'

'No.' Serena covered up her arms with her hands. 'I told you I was beaten at the palace.'

Karl crossed the room to stand in front of her. He removed a glove and reached out to trace the bruise on her upper arm. As soon as he touched her, Serena drew back. 'Running away from the problem won't solve it. This man should be punished for what he did to you.' His voice held the razor edge of his temper. 'Have you even told the king?'

She let out a breath, afraid that trusting him with the truth would only entangle him further.

'Serena,' Karl said quietly, 'let me protect you.' Though he didn't touch her, gooseflesh rose up over her skin in the cool air.

His words conjured up last night, when he'd nearly taken a bullet for her. He'd kept his word, bringing her away from the danger and keeping her safe. She wasn't used to that. But neither could she wed him and bring him up against the wrath of a king.

'I know there are thousands of little girls who wish they could be a princess,' she said quietly. 'But I hate everything about it.'

'Why?'

'Because it's a prison.' She regarded him. 'Don't tell me you haven't wished for a single day, all to yourself. With no one telling you what to wear, what banquets you'll attend, what you can and cannot say. If you could give up being a prince, you would.'

'I would never turn my back on my country.'

She heard the stiffness in his voice, the disbelief that she would so willingly leave her birthright to someone else.

'You have a responsibility to your people,' he insisted. 'You've never had to worry about survival, like so many others.'

She narrowed her gaze at him. Raising her arms to him, she revealed the bruises again. 'Haven't I?'

'You're giving up too easily, Princess.'

'Why does it matter to you?' she whispered. 'Find another princess to wed. Let me live my own life.'

He reached for her gloved hand, and within his palm, her fingers felt small. Heat permeated the glove, reminding her of the way his hands had moved over her buttons. She couldn't stop thinking of his bare fingers touching her spine and the intimacy of him unlacing her corset last night.

Her body softened, and she couldn't draw her attention away from the man who was watching her with such unveiled desire. She half expected him to pull her to her feet, dragging her into a breathless kiss. It startled her to realise that she wouldn't mind that at all.

'You couldn't give up your crown if you wanted to,' he said.

'I could,' she countered, 'and not hold a single regret.'

His expression turned into a challenge. 'Would you care to make a wager on that?'

What did he mean? At her curious gaze, he continued, 'Three days, Princess. We'll live together in the abbey as ordinary people. No servants. No luxuries.' He removed her glove, turning her palm over. With his fingertips, he stroked the soft skin. 'I don't believe you could survive it. These palms have never known what it is to work.'

She frowned at his prediction. 'Are you suggesting I'm not capable of living the life of a commoner?'

His mouth curved in a slight smile. 'If, after three days, you still want to give up your throne, I'll help you. I'll take you to a country of your choice and help you purchase property of your own. Even hire a few servants, if that's your wish.'

Serena stared at him. He'd offered to grant her deepest desire, to have absolute freedom to live her life as she chose. 'There's more, isn't there?' she ventured. 'You're not expecting me to…give myself to you?'

'No.' He released her hand, his eyes filled with daring. 'But regardless of whether you agree, people will believe you've shared my bed. Your reputation is already compromised.'

She crossed her arms, suddenly feeling the chill in the morning air. 'Then what are you suggesting?'

'If, after three days, you've decided you'd rather live the life of a princess, you'll wed me. Immediately.'

'I won't,' she whispered.

He took a step forward, standing so close, their lower bodies touched. His mouth moved against her ear, whispering, 'By the end of the three days, you'll want to be my wife.'

She put her hands against his chest, bringing distance between them. 'You're going to lose this wager, *Fürst* Karl.'

He took her hand in his. 'Are we in agreement, then? You'll go where I take you to live and become a commoner?' Lifting her fingers to his lips, he added, 'You'll cook for us…and keep our home clean?'

There was doubt in his voice, as if he didn't believe her capable of completing such tasks. Just because she'd never cooked a meal in her life or ever swept a broom didn't mean she wasn't able to do so. There were books to show her how.

'Will you keep your promise, if I win?' She knew that it would be nearly impossible to purchase property and a house, as a woman. But if Karl made all the arrangements, she could remain far away from her father. Safe and free to make her own life as she chose.

He gave a single nod. 'As long as you wed me, if I win.'

She shook his palm, sealing the agreement between them. It would be difficult, but she was determined to prove him wrong. She was no hothouse lily who would wilt if there was no one to serve her. The *fürst* didn't know or understand her at all. She was looking forward to the challenge.

In three days, she could survive anything at all.

Badenstein—two days later

There was no sign of the princess. Not at any of the estates. *Freiherr* Albert von Meinhardt cursed to himself, his anger flaring. He'd sent separate groups of men to every estate in Badenstein, Germany and Prussia. And…nothing. It was as if she'd disappeared.

The king's Captain, Gerlach Feldmann, hadn't seemed surprised. For a man responsible for letting the princess run away, he didn't appear eager to get her back.

The man's defiance to the king was clear, even if Feldmann's actions had the guise of obedience. Clearly, his loyalty to Her Royal Highness needed to be broken.

Captain Feldmann had a son—a young boy of nine, who had been living with the boy's grandmother, after his mother was imprisoned. Now, it was time to use that influence. Although others might view it as heartless, Albert merely saw it as a means to an end. Feldmann would have no choice but to find the princess, if his son were threatened.

Albert sat back in his chair, reaching for a pen and paper. As he began writing to the king, he filled the letter with false reassurances that they had found the princess and were bringing her home. King Ruwald would be livid, but Albert intended to redirect his rage toward the bastard prince of Lohenberg.

For it was his fault, wasn't it? The princess would never have fled without the man's help. Finding out that the prince was illegitimate had been a stroke of fortune, for it meant that the princess could no longer marry him.

The thought pleased him greatly. The princess's impulsive escape had destroyed her virtuous reputation, and it meant that she had to wed quickly. But no longer could she become the bride of a prince—not after this.

The king's anger would know no bounds. But there was a solution Albert could offer. Though his blood was not royal, he was of noble birth. He was a baron with lands of his own. Perhaps the king would bestow a greater rank upon him, if he agreed to Albert's proposition. He could marry Serena himself and restore her honour.

It didn't matter that the princess despised him. She would learn to yield to his authority, for she was young enough to be trained to his bidding.

Albert glanced over at the velvet-draped bed. In his mind, he envisioned her naked body waiting for him. He shifted in his seat as the physical lust swelled inside him. He had to inform the king of his daughter's disobedience and of the necessity to end her betrothal to the bastard prince of Lohenberg.

The words flowed from his pen as he offered himself up to the king as a means of saving the princess. He wanted her with every breath in his lungs, needing to possess her beauty.

And when he called a servant, giving the order to seize Feldmann's son, he knew that he would get what he wanted. No matter what the cost.

'Take this to my father,' Karl commanded Bernard. The sealed letter contained his instructions for revitalizing the island. He'd requested troops to bring order to the towns and to provide relief supplies. After talking with Father Durin last night, he'd sketched ideas for drainage ditches that could assist with the flooding.

The distraction had kept him from thinking of Serena. Three days alone with her. Three final days to win her as his wife. He'd posed the wager as a last, desperate means of gaining her hand in marriage. And he needed to win.

He'd arranged for them to stay in the ruined

fortress while Father Durin remained within the manor house. Though the priest had voiced his disapproval, Karl had promised that at the end of the three days, he could perform the ceremony. In the meantime, Father Durin and Samuel would take turns guarding the forest surrounding the fortress while Bernard travelled back to Lohenberg.

'I will obey, Your Highness.' The footman bowed. 'But I fear it isn't safe—especially after last night. These islanders cannot be trusted.'

'Which is why you will return to Lohenberg and bring back soldiers and supplies. The king must know what is happening within the province.'

'What about the princess?'

'We will remain in hiding at the abbey,' Karl said. 'So long as no one knows we are there, it should be safe enough.' He lowered his voice and walked outside, waiting for the footman to follow. 'I will protect her, no matter what happens.'

On the night when they'd been attacked, Karl had nearly taken the bullet aimed for her. He didn't regret it at all. It was strange to think of, but after everything she'd suffered, he wanted nothing else to happen to her.

And even though it would hurt her to learn the

truth, he wanted to believe that Serena would forgive him. In these three days, he had to show her that he wasn't a monster or a man unworthy of being her husband.

'And what of you, Your Highness?' Bernard cleared his throat.

Karl lowered his voice. 'I am no longer the Prince of Lohenberg. What happens to me doesn't matter, does it?'

'To us, you will always be our prince,' Bernard protested. 'Your Highness, we know what Lohenberg means to you.'

'It's no longer mine to rule,' he replied. 'My brother holds that honour now.'

'If something should happen to you—'

'No one would care,' Karl answered honestly. 'My best hope is to win the princess's hand in marriage. Now go to the king, as I've commanded.'

Bernard bowed low. 'You have our loyalty, Your Highness. And I will return as soon as possible.'

'I'm going to win this wager,' Serena informed the prince as she rode with him toward Durin's fortress. The *fürst* sent her a pointed look that said he didn't believe her, but Serena only smiled.

Though she was uneasy about being alone with the prince, he'd offered her an agreement she couldn't turn down. She needed his help in buying property, and once he'd settled her someplace safe, she'd have everything she needed.

All she had to do was live alone with him for three days in a ruined abbey.

Her mother and sister would fall into hysterics if they learned of how far she'd fallen. Virtuous ladies never spent time with men unchaperoned. They also didn't run away from home with the intent of living the life of a spinster.

But it wasn't the less-than-desirable circumstances that bothered her most. She could live with a leaking roof or terrible food—it was the prince himself who made her worry.

Already he'd kissed her once, and she'd relived the memory of his mouth each night when she'd fallen asleep. His firm lips, the unquenchable needs he'd evoked, haunted her still. Though she didn't believe he would take her against her will...she feared that he would use seduction as a weapon. He might use those stolen moments to weaken her resolve and make her want more than she was willing to give.

But I can still refuse to marry him. That was within her power, no matter how he tempted her. No matter how difficult the three days were.

Serena lifted her face to the salt spray, eager to arrive at the priest's ruined abbey. Karl rode alongside her, his face shielded of any emotion. 'You're so certain you're going to win?'

'Of course I am.'

His gaze passed over her cloaked attire, and he frowned. 'And you were able to get dressed on your own?'

She nodded, revealing none of the tactics she'd had to resort to. Although Frau Bauherzen had not come this morning to help her, Serena had worn her new gown backwards, leaving the corset behind. Though the fabric was extremely tight, she'd managed to button it up by herself, a feat she was quite proud of.

Even so, she felt uneasy without the whalebone garment holding her curves back. The creamy taffeta strained against her breasts, leaving a few gaps in the buttons.

Three days, she reminded herself. There would be no one except the prince to witness her fashion faux pas. And with the red cloak pulled tightly around her, the gown wasn't visible.

When they reached the path that led through the forest toward the ruins, Father Durin was waiting for them.

'It's safe,' he pronounced, 'and all is prepared for the two of you.' With a stern look toward Serena, he added, 'I expect to preside over your wedding at the end of the three days.'

Serena said nothing, letting the priest believe what he wanted. Karl dismounted and helped her down. He then lifted the bundle of supplies from the horse and set them on the ground.

The priest mounted Karl's horse and took the reins of Serena's mare. As he started to depart with the animals, she grew suspicious. 'Why is Father Durin taking the horses?'

'Because commoners walk, Princess.' His tone held a nonchalant air that needled her.

'Not all of them.' With the disappearing horses, Serena now realised that the food supplies she'd packed would have to be carried by hand. Uphill.

She adjusted the ties of her bonnet and stared at the higher ground. He'd done this on purpose. *Fürst* Karl wasn't about to play fair with this wager and intended to cheat every step of the way. Already he was leaving her to carry the supplies alone.

'Aren't you going to help me?' she demanded.

He rested a hand on one of the trees and sent her a slow smile. 'No.' Crossing his arms, he leaned back against the trunk. 'But if you want to admit that you do need servants to help, we can end the wager this moment.'

Serena glared at him, unwilling to give up so soon. Bending over, she grasped one of the bundles with both hands. It was quite heavy, due to the books and food supplies she'd packed. She struggled to lift it as she made her way up the hill. Karl was going to make this an impossible task, without question. But two could play that game.

She had to stop and rest several times, and the exertion made perspiration dampen her face. When at last she reached the top of the hill, she set the bundle down in front of the stone wall. The prince had retreated inside the fortress, and he returned with a bow and arrows.

'What are those for?' she questioned.

'I'm going to hunt for our meat tonight.' He

nodded back down the hill. 'Don't forget the other bundle of supplies.'

'I haven't.' She stood up and untied her cloak, folding it and setting it down near the entrance. The sudden look of shock on the prince's face made it worthwhile.

'*What* in God's name are you wearing?'

'My new dress.'

She started to walk down the hill, but he caught her arm. 'If you haven't noticed, it's on backwards.'

Serena shrugged. 'I'm well aware of that. But, as you pointed out, we're going to live as commoners. And since there was no one to help me dress myself this morning, I did it as best I could.'

His expression was incredulous. 'You're not wearing a corset. And what you are wearing is indecent.'

'My cloak covers most of it. And how was I expected to put on a corset with no one to help?' she demanded. 'Many of the poor women don't wear them.'

She kept her tone even, not letting him see how embarrassed she was. He was right; the gown fitted too tightly, and if she forgot about her posture and kept her shoulders back, it revealed bits of her chemise.

'Put the cloak back on,' he ordered. 'You cannot walk around in such a state of undress.' His iron gaze was arrogant and unyielding, but she saw the interest in his eyes.

'In a moment. The sun is warm and—'

Karl picked up her fallen cloak and strode forward. Without another word, he tied it around her neck, arranging it so it covered every inch of her gown.

'I'll return in a few hours. In the meantime, you should get better acquainted with the abbey and prepare our chambers. Unless you want to leave sooner than the three days.'

'Or unless you do,' she reminded him. Though he behaved as if it didn't bother him to live this way, she was convinced it was a facade. He was a man accustomed to issuing orders and living like a prince. She brightened, wondering if he would give up by the end of this night.

The prince ignored her remark. 'Father Durin left the fortress in quite a state. I'll expect it to be clean upon my return.'

From the look in his eyes, she fully expected that

the priest had sabotaged the interior. But she was made of stronger stuff than anyone could imagine.

'I'll see you later,' she said. 'Happy hunting.' And when she continued down the pathway, she untied her red cloak again, letting it fall to the ground behind her.

Karl hadn't managed to get a deer or rabbit, despite hunting for hours. His shirt was filthy from crawling around in the underbrush, and eventually he'd conceded defeat and bought fish from a local fisherman. It was better than returning empty-handed.

Outside, it was growing dark, and he wondered how he would find the princess when he returned. A heaviness hung in the air, like an impending rain. And he knew for a fact that Durin's roof leaked, which would make the night uncomfortable.

He wasn't going to feel any guilt over it. Serena would change her mind after three days, and when Karl made it clear that she would never again suffer from her father's abuse, she would wed him, and he could return to the life he'd known.

He would claim the role of prince consort, helping Serena to govern Badenstein. Though her father would want to interfere, once he'd wed her, there was little the king could do about it.

Karl brought the fish around to the back of the fortress. The kitchen was enclosed in a smaller stone building, farther away from the main hall. The ruins had once been an abbey, made up of smaller enclosures and the large space. To his surprise, he smelled something…sweet?

He set the fish down upon a stone table and washed his hands, using a dipper of water.

'Princess?' he called out. He searched inside the fortress but couldn't find her in the large hall or even upstairs. Eventually, he found her within the priests' quarters. She was seated near a bright fire, reading a book, and upon the hearth, he saw small biscuits baking.

The fire cast a soft glow over her features, and her long blond hair was pinned away from her face beneath her bonnet. She'd discarded the red cloak again, and he was drawn to the curves revealed by the tight taffeta. She was slender, but her breasts strained against the fabric, tempting him with the hidden flesh.

'I brought a book of cooking receipts with me,'

she said, holding up the bound volume. 'And I made these from flour, sugar and a little butter that I found.' Wincing at his appearance, she remarked, 'My, but your shirt looks as if you rolled in the dirt.'

Karl unbuttoned it and lifted it over his head, handing it to her. 'Then you'll have to wash it, won't you?'

Her face grew pink at the prospect, but she pointed toward the table, gesturing for him to set it down. 'How does one wash a shirt?'

He shrugged. 'Doesn't your book tell you?'

Serena pursed her lips together. 'Not quite. It has wonderful instructions on how to cook—everything from the herbs to use and how long to prepare the food. But I don't think there's anything about washing clothes.' She lifted her shoulders in a shrug. 'I suppose I'll just put it in a pot of boiling water and try to find some soap.'

She picked up one of the warm biscuits and offered it to him. At the sight of his bare chest, she blushed again and stared at the ground. Karl took the biscuit, and the smooth buttery taste crumbled into his mouth. They weren't terribly sweet, but the fact that she'd made a successful attempt at cooking was unexpected.

'You see? It's not so bad living like this.' Serena ate another biscuit, and waited for his reply. Karl could only nod, feeling more and more like the bastard he was. She'd been beaten and abused by her father, and what had he done in return? Forced her into three days of living like a servant.

It was no way to treat a woman, particularly one he intended to marry. Karl stared at her, wondering what he was supposed to say now. In the end, he offered, 'You don't really have to wash my shirt.'

She stepped in front of him. 'Oh, no. I won't have you claiming that I reneged on our wager by refusing to launder your shirt.' With a pointed look, she added, 'You can borrow clothing from Father Durin. Perhaps a hair shirt might teach you humility.'

'I doubt it.' He took another biscuit and crooked his finger in a silent gesture to follow him. 'I have fish for our supper.'

Serena picked up her book of cooking receipts and his shirt, following him back to the kitchen where he'd left them. 'I'll cook them, once you've cleaned them.'

'Our agreement was—'

'No.' She stopped him, taking his hand. 'You're not leaving me with this.' Before he could say another word, Serena brought him to stand beside her. 'You're very much mistaken if you believe that ordinary women stand by and do all of the work while their husbands watch. I've already made biscuits. If you want the fish, then you clean them.' Before he could protest, she pointed a finger at him. 'Unless you wish to give up?'

Chapter Eight

'I'm not giving up our wager. But there are other tasks to be done. I have to cut wood, if you want to stay warm tonight.' The prince came up beside her but she would have none of his excuses.

'And you have to fill that large pot with water.' She pointed to an iron cauldron hanging above one of the hearths. 'If I'm to wash your shirt.'

'That won't work with me, princess. Our agreement was that you'd complete the tasks of an ordinary woman for three days. Not that you would coax me into doing them for you.'

She rested a hand on the door frame, studying him. 'I never agreed to be your slave for three days. I agreed to work at your side.' His expression was emotionless, his eyes holding no promises. 'Why would I want to wed a man who thinks I'm incapable of doing anything right?'

'That isn't what I think.'

She cast a glance toward the fish. 'Then at least show some fairness in this wager.'

His hazel eyes hardened, but he picked up a knife. Serena opened her book of cooking receipts and skimmed the pages for a way to cook the fish. Then she searched for information on how to launder a man's shirt but came up with nothing. There was a cake of lye soap, so she decided to slice it up and add it to the cauldron. Once the prince got the water boiling, it would melt the soap and make the water better for washing.

After the better part of an hour, she found Karl with a pile of fish parts and two tiny fillets, barely larger than her palm.

She covered her mouth with a hand, and he glared at her. 'Don't you dare laugh.'

'They're rather…small, aren't they?'

He stood up. 'The size doesn't matter, Princess.' He dipped his hands into a basin of water and washed them, keeping his eyes locked upon her. 'I think you'll find that there's not a single bone in them.'

'I might still be hungry afterwards,' she ventured.

His smile turned wicked. 'Then there are other ways I could satisfy you.' He leaned a hand upon the table. Before she could move, he cupped the back of her neck and pulled her in for a kiss. His mouth was warm, taking hers in a softly demanding conquest.

It shook her down to her knees, though Serena tried to keep her balance against the table.

'I'll take care of your needs, Princess.' He stepped away and added, 'I'll start a fire in the hearth and fill the pot with water. Then I'll prepare fires to warm up the abbey interior. Bring the fish inside when it's ready.'

When he'd gone, she steadied her breathing, understanding that the kiss was only another weapon in his arsenal. He'd made it clear that he intended to try and seduce her into marriage.

Serena distracted herself with the book while he made good on his promises. It would take a long time to boil the water for Karl's shirt, but she put it into the pot of water. Her gaze fell upon her own clothing, and she picked up her muddied cloak, adding it to the laundry.

As she studied the instructions for fish, using the book to guide her, Serena heard the sound of falling rain. Oh, no. She moved closer to the fire, praying it would stop before she had to venture out with the food.

But the weather only worsened. Serena looked down at her hands, and wrinkled her nose at the fish smell. On impulse, she held them out in the rain to cleanse them. It had grown warmer, thankfully, and the water felt good against her fingertips.

The fish needed a few more minutes before it was done, and as she stared out at the falling rain, a strange impulse came over her. As if she were under a spell, Serena took one step, then another, until she stood in the rain, letting the water spill over her.

It was something she'd never been allowed to do. And though she'd regret it later, right now, she wanted to feel the immense freedom of doing something foolish.

The rain soaked through her gown and bonnet, wetting her hair against her neck. She closed her eyes, lifting her head back, and smiling to herself.

'Have you gone mad?' a voice demanded.

Serena opened her eyes. At first instinct, she nearly darted back into the outdoor kitchen. But then, what could the prince do to her?

'I believe I have.' She walked forward, along the cobbled path, until she saw an enormous puddle. With her foot, she stomped within it, sending a splash of water upwards.

'I always wanted to do that,' she laughed aloud, wondering what had come over her. 'Even as a child I couldn't step in puddles.'

'You've ruined your gown,' he said.

'I don't care.' She held out her hands, as if she could embrace the rain. The feeling of breaking the rules, of doing something inappropriate, left her feeling wild. 'It's wonderful, isn't it?'

'It's wet.' He stepped beneath the shelter of the kitchen, his own hair dripping from the rain. 'And you should come inside.'

Rebellion swelled inside her, and she tossed her bonnet at him, letting the rain soak through her tangled hair. 'I don't want to.'

For a few more moments, she revelled in the storm, well aware that he was watching her. And that he didn't approve.

She stopped and watched him, never minding

the water pooling over her skin. 'Haven't you ever wanted to do anything foolish in your life?'

He shook his head. 'It's not the sort of man I am.'

With that, he retreated back into the abbey ruins.

After their meal, Serena stood by the fire in the great hall, drying her hair. Although rain fell through sections of the broken roof, the area by the hearth remained dry.

Karl pushed his plate aside, unable to take his eyes off her. He'd expected her to cry or complain about having to do everything alone; instead she'd revelled in the freedom.

He'd expected her cooking to be disastrous, but once again she'd proved him wrong. The fish had been perfectly seasoned and cooked tender, after she'd diligently followed the instructions in the cook book. His princess, it seemed, was more resourceful than he'd expected. It worried him, for he'd counted on her surrender.

Against the firelight, the wet gown outlined every inch of her corset-less form. He could see the rise of her nipples, and the slender dip of her waist. She had closed her eyes, as if she could absorb the heat from the fire into herself.

'Are you regretting your dance in the rain?' he mused, standing from the table and dodging water that poured from the leaking roof, forming puddles on the floor.

'No.' She stretched and let out a sigh. 'I may be wet and cold now, but I enjoyed every moment of it. I suppose I should go and check the laundry pot. Your shirt and my cloak will be clean by now, if I haven't cooked them.'

He crossed the hall, noticing the weariness on her face. Not a single complaint had she voiced, but the evidence of the gruelling day lay within her green eyes. When she left, he sat back and stared at the stone walls. She had succeeded living amid the hardships better than he'd ever imagined.

A quarter of an hour passed, and when she entered the hall at last, her face looked worried. 'There was…a problem with your shirt.'

'Did it shrink?'

'No.' She bit her lip, as if she didn't know how to tell him what had happened. With a dismissive shake of her head, she explained, 'It's very wet, and I couldn't wring it out well. I hung it to dry in the kitchen. I hope you don't mind.' She glanced down, as if expecting him to get angry. He thought of the bruises on her throat and the way she was shielding herself now.

'I won't need it while I'm sleeping,' he said. 'In the morning will be fine.'

She seemed relieved to hear it. 'You could find one of the priest's shirts, if you're cold.'

'I never get cold.' He crossed his arms over his bare chest, and noted how her gaze was fixed upon him. 'But I imagine you are, in that wet gown.'

Her face softened into a smile. 'I enjoyed myself.'

'It was foolish.'

'Do you not know how to have any fun?' she countered. 'Or were you always this serious?'

'I had fun as a boy, but there's no place for it as a prince. Duty matters most.'

'You believe that, don't you?' Her face turned sympathetic. 'Being foolish isn't such a bad thing.'

'You said your father never allowed you to do anything, either.'

'He didn't. But I learned how to entertain myself in all circumstances.' She sat down next to the hearth, tracing her finger across the cool ashes that lay just beyond it. 'Sometimes, I would draw pictures of houses by the sea. I dreamed of places I wanted to visit and imagined a quiet holiday from the palace with just me, my sister, and my mother.' She drew lines within the ash, and then ventured, 'What about you?'

He sat beside her. 'I spent all of my time learning to rule the kingdom.' He hadn't played, for he had no friends or siblings. His father had forbidden him any contact with other boys when he was growing up. And as for Queen Astri…after years of her madness, they had locked her away. Nothing he'd achieved had ever pleased them.

The memory of the lonely boy he'd been gave rise to a cold frustration. What reason was there to seek their approval, when they'd disinherited him and turned their backs? He owed them nothing. The stony emptiness inside hardened into resolve. He would gain his own kingdom to rule, and prove his worth as a ruler.

He didn't need them. Or anyone else.

Karl glanced over at Serena, and in her eyes, he saw sympathy. It wasn't right for her to pity him. He was using her for her kingdom, and he didn't deserve anything at all. 'It's growing late. You should get some sleep.'

She came closer, her hair in wet strands against her shoulders. The gown clung to her, the water droplets glistening upon her skin. 'Not yet.' With a sigh, she moved beside the fire, turning to dry herself.

'Going out in the rain wasn't a wise idea,' he pointed out. 'It won't be easy for you to sleep.'

Her gaze softened. 'No, but it felt good to do something I wasn't supposed to do.'

The hint of rebellion in her voice sent a flare of interest through him. He moved to stand beside her. With a hand, he reached out to touch her damp hair. The wet strands slid through his fingers as he saw her expression transform into apprehension.

'Why do you want to marry me?' she whispered. 'It would be far easier to find another princess.'

He stared at her, drinking in her soft features. The buttons gaped across her breasts, and he longed to cross the room and unfasten them, one by one. He wanted to peel away the fabric, revealing her bare skin. 'I have my reasons.'

Leaning in, he took her mouth in a kiss. Her soft lips were damp, and he tasted the rain upon them. Against her mouth, he ordered, 'Kiss me back, Princess.'

'This wasn't part of our agreement,' she breathed, resting her hands against his chest.

He moved his mouth to her temple, feeling her body shudder at his attention. When he took her earlobe into his mouth, she gasped, her hands grasping the back of his head. She wasn't fighting his advances, but instead held him to her. He tasted the skin of her throat, pulling her flush against him.

She aroused him, and he palmed her hips, letting her feel his desire. 'If we were married, I'd take you upstairs,' he murmured. 'I'd remove this gown and touch you everywhere.'

She emitted a shaky breath, still holding on to him. In her eyes, he saw the haze of her own forbidden desires.

'I'd take your breast into my mouth, using my tongue to make you ready.' His hand moved to the curve beneath her breast, his thumb close to her nipple, but not touching it. Her face flushed, and against the damp dress, he could see the taut buds.

He claimed her mouth again, kissing her hard until she returned the kiss. Her mouth moved against him, her hands touching his shoulders as she lost herself in the abandonment. With his knee, he parted her legs, his mouth hovering against hers. 'You'd feel wet for me here,' he said. 'And I'd fill you, moving inside you, until you cried out with release.'

Serena's mouth was swollen, her eyes filled with needs she didn't understand. But when he drew his hands down her bruised arm, she inhaled sharply.

'It still hurts a little,' she admitted, closing her eyes.

The physical reminder of her abuse made him stop. Though he wanted her badly, she wasn't ready for this.

'I'll show you to your room.'

Serena followed him as he led the way up the stairs. Karl brought her into the smallest bedchamber, and she grimaced at the sight of the straw mattress upon the floor.

'Must I sleep upon that?'

'Like an ordinary woman, remember?' Karl moved forward to stoke the fire he'd lit in the hearth earlier. It was still cold within the room, and she shivered.

'Get some sleep.'

Before the door could close behind him, she interrupted, '*Fürst* Karl?'

'What is it?' He turned back and saw her standing by the fire. In the dim light, her skin glowed, the droplets of water making him want to lean down to taste them.

'Today wasn't as bad as I thought it would be. It was rather nice, actually.'

Karl closed the distance between them and pulled her back into his arms. He could feel the quickening of her breath, the soft chills that ran over her skin. 'There are two days left.'

'And nights,' she added in a tremulous voice.

'You don't have to spend them alone,' he murmured. He moved his hands down her spine, drawing her closer.

Against his cheek, he felt Serena's face grow warm with embarrassment. His body was tight with need, but he wasn't about to let her go to bed without throwing down his own gauntlet.

He brought his mouth to hers, resting just above it in the hint of a kiss. 'Tell me to go away, Princess.'

'What have you done to my son?' Gerlach threw open the door to the *freiherr*'s study. He didn't care about proper etiquette or waiting to be announced. The man had taken Wilhelm, imprisoning him in the dark. 'He's only nine years old! What could he possibly do to you?'

'You've been remiss in your search, Captain Feldmann,' the baron responded. With a signal, a servant stepped closer. Although the man was smaller and Gerlach could easily overpower him, he kept his temper under rein. Wilhelm's well-being depended on him remaining calm.

'The coach stopped near the coast of Lohenberg,' Gerlach answered. 'The *fürst* paid passage to the island of Vertraumen. They are still there, so the fisherman said.'

'Now that wasn't so difficult, was it?' The baron's voice dripped with sarcasm. 'Go with your men and bring the princess back to the palace.' The thin smile upon the man's face made Gerlach long to break the man's jaw. 'I'll notify the king.'

'I want to see my wife and son,' he demanded. The thought of Marta and Wilhelm enduring imprisonment pushed him closer to the edge of murder.

The *freiherr* motioned for a servant to escort him. 'Take him below,' he ordered. Then he added, 'They won't be released until you bring back the princess. And you'll face charges for defying the king's orders.'

Gerlach shielded his fury and fear for his family. Though Marta was young and strong, no woman should have to endure what she had on his behalf. And as for Wilhelm…it infuriated him that the Baron held the power to harm a child. He followed the servant down the winding stairs that led to the prison cells, his heart growing colder with every step.

When he arrived below, the air was frigid. The prison guard led him to a wooden door with only a small slot that would fit a plate. When he unlocked the door, Gerlach strode inside and saw his wife sitting upon a bench, staring at the wall. Her blond hair was greasy, her face pale. When she saw him, she started crying.

He gripped her in an embrace, stroking her hair and murmuring words of comfort. Her tears dampened his shirt, and when he asked his wife if she was all right, she shook her head.

'No. They've taken Wilhelm into this place, and I've heard him crying at night.' She took his hands in hers, and gripped them hard. 'Get him out. I don't care what you have to do. He can't live like this.'

The cool fury tightened into a shield of ice over his heart. 'I swear I will.' Inwardly he wanted to damn *Freiherr* Albert to hell. The man cared nothing about right and wrong. He could only view the world through the king's commands.

'I'll get both of you out,' Gerlach promised. 'I swear it.'

And as he held her close, he wondered if he'd pay the price of their freedom with his life.

Serena found it impossible to sleep upon the rough pallet. She guessed it was near midnight, but she'd tossed and turned for hours, thinking of Karl. She'd ordered him to leave, and he had. Without a word or an argument.

It hadn't brought her the relief she'd expected. Instead, she'd felt dissatisfied and troubled. It was right to send him away, but her stomach twisted with the unsettled feelings. Perhaps food would satisfy her anxiety.

Her gown was still a bit damp, but considerably drier than it had been, so Serena pulled it over her head and buttoned it up the front. She didn't bother with stockings, but slipped her bare feet into her shoes. Inside the abbey, it was quiet, and she supposed the prince must be asleep in his own room.

She crossed through the hall and toward the spiral stone staircase. Holding on to the wall, she made her way down to the main hall. To her surprise, she found *Fürst* Karl sitting by the fire, staring into the flames.

'What is it?' he asked, when he saw her coming closer.

'I couldn't sleep. I was hungry, so I thought I'd see if there was food in the storage cellar.'

'The biscuits were good,' he told her. 'I suppose we could cook more, if you're willing.'

'No.' The idea of preparing another meal didn't appeal to her at all. 'I'll see what else I can find.'

'What were you hoping for?'

'I won't know until I see it.'

Karl stood from his chair and brought out a lamp, shadowing her as she moved to the back of the abbey, where another staircase led below ground.

'Will Father Durin mind if we take some of his food?' she asked him.

'No.'

The air grew cooler as she moved down the stairs. The lamp flared in the darkness, and it took a moment for her eyes to adjust. Then she spied different baskets and wooden containers. She opened one, then another, finding frozen slabs of meat, dried fruits and vegetables, and finally, a store of nuts.

'Hazelnuts,' she beamed, holding up the small wooden bowl. With a smile, she told him, 'At Christmas, I used to drink cups of chocolate while nibbling on these.'

'Then take them.'

'Was there something you enjoyed as a boy?' she asked. 'Anything that you loved?'

His eyes grew distant for a moment. 'When I was ten years old, we had an assortment of ice creams. Our cook made a raspberry ice cream once,' he admitted. Serena tried to imagine Karl as a young boy, gorging on raspberry ice cream. Somehow, the image didn't fit. He was always so serious, so rigid in his demeanour, she couldn't envision him as a child.

He returned to the staircase, raising the lamp while she followed with the hazelnuts. She hadn't found a nutcracker in the storage chamber, and it was raining harder now. There had to be something else they could use.

The interior of the abbey was cold, and several pots rested beneath the leaks in the roof. Serena moved to sit by the fire, and Karl joined her. 'These aren't shelled,' she explained. 'We'll have to find a way to crack them.' Eyeing their surroundings, she wasn't quite certain what to use. 'Do you know what we can use?'

'Wait here.' The *fürst* disappeared for a few moments while Serena warmed herself by the fire. She placed a few of the hazelnuts within the coals, to roast them while she waited. In the dark silence, it felt almost intimate to be sitting here, alone with the prince.

When he returned at last, he held two large stones. She hid her smile. 'So, we're to bash them apart with rocks?'

'Have you a better idea?'

'It wasn't a criticism,' she said, reaching out for one of the stones. It was larger than her hand and was heavier than she'd expected it to be. She knelt down beside the fire and laid out a handful of nuts. With a resounding whack, she struck the shells repeatedly, until they cracked open.

'I'm not certain I should be near you when you're attacking them like that,' he ventured. 'You look rather dangerous.'

'Not at all,' she corrected. 'I find it invigorating.' Gesturing toward him, she suggested, 'Why don't you try it?'

The prince picked up a single hazelnut, and with one crushing blow, he obliterated the nut. Serena stared at him with a raised eyebrow. 'Remind me not to make you angry. You've pulverised it.'

His mouth twitched. 'Perhaps a bit too much force.' He set the stone down. 'What if I allow you to crack the shells, and I'll remove the meat?'

'All right.'

They spent the next half hour cracking nuts, dividing their spoils between them. Serena nibbled at the hazelnuts and remarked to the prince, 'You know, you're not so bad to be around when you're not giving orders.'

'Is that a compliment or an insult?' he asked, handing her a nut.

She hadn't quite meant it that way. 'A compliment, I suppose.'

Karl picked up another nut and reached toward

her mouth. Serena tried to take it from him, but then realised he intended to feed it to her.

'Aren't you afraid I might bite?' she murmured, opening her mouth to receive it. When she bit down on the savory nut, his fingers grazed her lips.

He placed another nut in her fingertips, but guided this one to his own mouth. 'Are you afraid I'll bite?'

She shook her head, only to be proven wrong when he took her fingers into the warmth of his mouth, nibbling them gently. She pulled them back, staring at him. Something had shifted, and what had begun as a simple pastime was now becoming more sensual.

'I don't think you should—'

'—try to seduce you?' he finished. 'Are you still going to pretend that there's nothing between us?'

Karl pulled her up to stand in front of him. Her shoulders pressed against his chest while his hands spanned her waist. 'You asked me to leave you alone earlier. And yet, here you are.'

He reached to the pins that barely held locks of her hair in place, releasing them. Her hair dropped around her shoulders, and his hands moved the length of it aside. His mouth moved to her ear. 'You wanted me to stay, didn't you?'

She did, heaven help her. 'You frighten me.'

'You're afraid of the way I make you feel,' he murmured, nipping at her jaw. 'You know I'll bring you pleasure when you take me inside of you.'

The words were arousing, making her lean back against him. She didn't deny that he made her feel things she didn't understand. And if she didn't return to her room this very moment, she was going to regret it.

With all of her willpower, she stepped out of his arms and turned to face him. 'I don't doubt that you'll make another princess happy in your marriage bed. But it won't be me.'

And as she swept aside, returning to her chamber, she couldn't forget the shielded look on his face…of a man who didn't seem to care. Was it a mask? Or was it the truth?

Chapter Nine

Gerlach stood upon the shores of Vertraumen. It had rained all night, and his clothing was soaked. He stared at the green island, while the waves sloshed against the sand. In all his years of service, he'd never imagined he'd have to betray the princess like this

But there was no choice. His wife and son were at the mercy of the Baron, and once the king learned of his role in the princess's escape, all of them could pay the price.

He had to bring her back or risk harm to those he loved.

Along the edge of the sand, he walked for hours. Past the houses belonging to the middle class and a few of the wealthy. He searched for poverty, for only there would he find the sort of men he needed—desperate folk who wouldn't hesitate to bring him his hostage. And he needed men who could scour the island until the princess was found.

When he reached the outskirts of the town, he found shelters held together with wood and rusted nails. A child stood watching him from the door, a young boy perhaps three years of age. His face was dirty, and he looked hungry.

Gerlach's throat burned, but he walked toward the house. A father would do anything for his child's welfare. Even betray an angel.

He voiced a prayer of forgiveness, for what he had to do now.

The pounding sound wouldn't stop. Serena groaned and buried her head deeper under the coverlet. She was shivering, and the idea of removing her body from the bed was akin to freezing to death.

Only when the door flew open, did she shriek and open her eyes.

'What did you do to my shirt?' the prince demanded, tossing the garment at her.

'I...washed it?' She stared at Karl with groggy eyes, wondering why he was in her chamber. When she sat up from the wretched mattress, she saw her gown drying near the fireplace. Which meant she was naked beneath the coverlet and the prince was getting an eyeful of her bare shoulders and side.

'It's pink, for God's sakes! What did you put in the water?'

She closed her eyes and lay back down on the pallet. 'My red cloak. I thought I could wash both of them together.'

'Obviously not.' The words came out in a growl, and his ill temper was too much to endure at this early hour.

'How was I supposed to know this would happen?' He ought to be grateful that she'd washed it at all. Hadn't she spent most of yesterday cooking for him, straightening up the abbey and laundering their clothes?

'I thought you had a book.'

'It said nothing about washing a red cloak and a white shirt. Or washing clothes at all, for that matter.' Rolling over, she pulled the blanket tighter and offered, 'You might look fetching in pink.'

'Princess,' he growled. In his voice, she heard the threatening anger. And yet, she wasn't at all intimidated by him. Even with all his bluster, the prince had never dared to lay a hand on her. All he'd done was kiss her.

And that, admittedly, had been rather pleasant.

'Go away,' she ordered. 'I need to get dressed.'

'So do I,' he reminded her. 'And I'm not wearing that.'

'Fine. Go and look through the priest's clothes. I'm certain you'll find something black to match your mood.'

When the door closed, Serena kept the coverlet firmly wrapped around her body, in case he decided to invade her chamber again.

It took half an hour to get dressed, since she couldn't quite get her chemise and petticoats fastened the way she wanted to. The gown felt awkward buttoned up the front, but she reminded herself there were only two more days.

After that, she could have a lady's maid once more. She smiled to herself as she finger-combed her hair and prepared to face the second day.

When she wandered down the stairs, the hall was cold and dark. The morning weather had shifted into sunlight while the hearth had died down to coals. *Fürst* Karl was trying to stoke it and she saw him wearing an oversized shirt that bunched at his waist.

All right, so she did feel guilty about dying his shirt pink. But it truly had been an accident.

When the prince couldn't get the wood to light, he cursed beneath his breath.

'The logs are wet, aren't they?' she predicted. All around the hearth, she spied puddles from where the roof had leaked.

Karl nodded. 'It will be cold inside today.'

'But at least the rain has stopped.' She pointed up at the large glass windows. 'I thought I'd explore the area around the abbey today. From the top of the hillside, I imagine we could see all around the island.'

'There's too much to do,' he argued. 'We need more food and a fire.'

'I want to see if Durin has a garden, and I'll try to find some herbs and vegetables.' She walked to the doorway, adding, 'The book of cooking receipts that I brought with me has excellent drawings. I'm certain I can identify what I need.'

She reached for her cloak and held out her hand. 'Won't you come with me?'

He looked annoyed, as if he'd rather remain

within the leaking walls. But at last he relented. 'For an hour.'

It would be far longer than an hour, but she didn't tell him that. Serena handed him his great coat, saying, 'I'll go and fetch a basket and my book.' She intended to pack a picnic luncheon, as well. It would be her atonement for ruining his shirt.

Karl crossed the room and brought ammunition and his revolver. 'I'll bring the weapons.'

Because every picnic needed guns. Serena resisted the urge to roll her eyes.

Outside, the ground was damp, and Serena studied the book, recognising turnips in Father Durin's garden. It was too early for any other vegetables, but there were a few potatoes and carrots she'd seen in the priest's cellar last night. She might be able to prepare a vegetable stew.

From the herb garden, she selected cuttings of rosemary and sage, which she added to her basket. Karl looked impatient, as though he'd rather be anywhere else but here. His hand remained inside his coat, taking comfort from the revolver.

After she'd collected her plants, she continued climbing up the pathway leading to the top of the hill. Karl followed behind, but he looked disgruntled at the walk. The dark forest surrounded them, the sun skimming the edges of the trees, casting shadows over the lichen and moss.

Serena climbed higher on the pathway, holding on to the narrow trees to help keep her balance. The walk was more difficult than she'd realised, and perspiration dampened the back of her neck. She stopped a moment to rest, and when Karl caught up, he asked, 'Do you want to go back?'

'Not when I've come this far. It's only a little farther.' She caught her breath and continued ahead, until at last she reached the hill summit. The ground flattened into a small, grassy clearing with a stone altar in the centre, adorned with a carved limestone cross. It was old, overgrown with moss, but she imagined the monks climbing the hill and saying their prayers here.

She set down her basket and chose a spot in front of the altar. The air was cool, and she adjusted her cloak around her shoulders. Leaning back against the stone, she drew her knees up beneath her gown and stared at the glittering sea. The grey waters had calmed somewhat, though the waves were still choppy. In the distance, she spied a few lone fishermen with their boats.

Karl stood beside her, his eyes narrowed as he took in the view. He seemed unable to relax at all, for he studied the landscape with the eye of a man who saw only the problems and none of the beauty.

'Will you sit with me?' she asked.

'No, I'd rather stand. And we'll be going back soon enough.' He shielded his eyes against the sun and turned back toward the path.

'Not yet. I thought we could eat our luncheon here.' She opened the basket and revealed the food she'd packed: a flask of wine, some of the sugar biscuits, and a jar of strawberry preserves. Though it wasn't the most elegant selection of foods, she thought she'd done well enough.

Karl stared at the food, not speaking a word. It seemed that she'd confounded him once again.

'You really believed I would give up, didn't you?' she said softly. 'Even though I told you luxuries weren't important to me.'

His gaze fastened upon her face, and there was a subtle defensive shift in his features. 'This isn't over yet, Princess.'

* * *

Karl didn't sit, though he knew Serena expected it. Her words sank into him with the realisation that she was right. He didn't know her at all, but he'd placed her in the same class of every other princess who would fall into hysterics if there was the tiniest flaw in her food.

All of them would have wailed at the prospect of cooking a meal; instead, Serena had only asked that he help her. Her fortitude was like nothing he'd ever seen before.

She stood up from the basket and took his hand. 'For ten minutes, stop being a prince, and just be an ordinary man. Sit and enjoy yourself.'

He guessed she was trying to ease his tension, to break up his mood. But the words only reminded him that he was a nobody now. A man without a throne, without a future.

He pulled his hand back. 'I don't want to stop being a prince, Serena. It's who I am. It's who I've always been.' The words came out harsher than he'd meant, but it was too late to take them back.

Serena returned her attention to the basket and shrugged. 'I only meant…for a few minutes.'

Her confusion was justified, and he realised how

brutish he'd sounded. She didn't know what had happened within his kingdom. And once she did, she'd want nothing more to do with him.

If he had any sort of honour, he'd tell her right now that he was illegitimate and had no claim to any kingdom. He ought to let her go.

But if he did, he'd have to face a life he didn't want.

She stared at him, and he looked away at the sea. 'Forgive me. It's just the…falling out with my father.'

Serena moved beside him, her gloved hand barely brushing against his. She smelled like spring and the rain she'd danced in last night. Though he tried not to stare at the outline of her gown, the buttons drew his eye to the swell of her breasts. He saw the faint moisture upon her skin from their walk, and he had a sudden vision of unfastening her buttons, running his hands over her flesh.

The sudden desire caught him like a fist, and he drew a slight step away.

'What caused the disagreement?' she asked.

The fact that I'm a bastard. And that the queen

was right all those years when she claimed I wasn't her son.

'Nothing within my control,' was all he could tell her. 'Suffice it to say, I'm not the favoured son right now.'

He'd been too young to understand what had happened; only that the queen had gone mad, claiming that he was a changeling prince. She'd hated the very sight of him and he couldn't remember a time when she'd ever shown him any affection. Once, when he was six, he'd drawn a card for her, laboriously printing the letters to wish her a happy birthday. When he'd presented it to her, she'd torn it up and cast the pieces into the fire.

And when he'd met his real mother a fortnight ago, a strange kaleidoscope of memories and tangled visions had resurfaced. He didn't know what was real and what wasn't, but the king's mistress made the queen look like a saint.

'Do you believe a marriage to me will bring you back into your father's good graces? Is that the reason for your haste?'

He didn't miss the tension in her tone, but he admitted the truth. 'Nothing will change the king's opinion of me. Whether I marry you or not.'

Serena's shoulders relaxed a little, and she knelt down, pouring him a cup of wine. When she handed it to him, she offered, 'You're the king's only son. That matters a great deal.'

No, I'm not. I'm a bastard that no one wanted.

Karl drained his cup and sat down beside her. 'He doesn't matter to me any more.'

'Then what does?' She knelt down beside him, her green eyes concerned.

He reached out and untied the ribbon tied beneath her chin. His hands framed her face for a moment as he took off the bonnet and cast it aside. 'I think you know the answer to that.'

Serena didn't move, but she felt the warmth of his bare hands against her skin. He hadn't worn gloves, and the sudden intimacy made her heart race. Karl traced her jawline with his fingers, but though he stared at her, he didn't kiss her.

He hadn't shaved in a few days, and she wondered what the bristle would feel like against her cheeks. Would it be rough? Or would it be soft?

His breath warmed her face, and she stared at his firm mouth, wondering if he would kiss her again. The last kiss had shaken her, sending her world off-balance.

This is part of his game, her mind warned. Now that he'd discovered that the hardships of poverty didn't bother her, he would try another tack.

'You're not going to seduce me,' she said firmly, lifting her chin. She couldn't allow herself to weaken, just because he made her pulse quicken. Her fingers trembled as she retied the ribbon of her bonnet.

'I'm not?' There was a lazy air to his voice, as if he intended a full assault upon her virtue.

Serena sat and reached for a sugar biscuit, pretending as though he hadn't spoken. 'No.'

'What do you suppose ordinary men and women do, when they're alone?' he murmured. 'Especially betrothed couples.' He leaned forward, his hands resting on either side of her. Though he didn't touch her, his physical presence made her nervous.

'Play cards?' she guessed before his mouth moved in to claim hers. Serena could hardly do more than catch a breath, before he laid siege to her defences. She tasted the sweetness of wine on his tongue, and tiny shudders of breathlessness slid beneath her skin.

A slight smile tilted the edge of his mouth as he stared down at her. His hazel eyes were dark with need, and a thousand second thoughts crossed her mind. The pause was giving her the chance to push him away.

'Is that what you want to do?' he ventured. 'Play cards?' His hand moved down to the hem of her skirt. Every inch of her seemed to be on fire, her blood coursing through her veins with an intensity that couldn't be stopped. She couldn't seem to summon up a clear thought, not when he was touching her.

When his hand moved to her ankle, he sent her a chiding look. 'You're not wearing stockings.'

'They—they got wet.'

She shivered, closing her eyes when his hand moved beneath her petticoats, up her bare leg.

Stop him, her conscience ordered. *You don't want this.*

But he was touching her with reverence, as if he couldn't believe she was allowing it. *She* couldn't believe she was allowing it. His mouth returned to hers, and the kiss was softer, coaxing a surrender. She held on to his face, not knowing whether to push him away or pull him closer.

Above the knee, his palm caressed her, and suddenly she grew moist between her legs. She imagined his fingers stroking her with the same gentleness, and heat blossomed inside her as she craved the forbidden touch. When his tongue entered her mouth, she kissed him back, swept away by the tide of shocking sensation. She was drowning, caught up in him.

He doesn't love you. He only wants to wed you because you're a princess.

Karl moved his hand from beneath her petticoats, and when he held her ribs, she had the sudden image of her father's fist striking her. Over and over, the searing pain causing her to cry out.

She broke away from the *fürst,* ordering him, 'Stop. Please.'

Heated tears filled her eyes, as she imagined the way her father would chastise her for such behaviour. She'd behaved like a wanton, ignoring every rule that would protect her virtue.

'I want to go back,' she said, not looking at him. She sat up and drew her knees up, burying her face in her skirt to hide her feelings.

'Go, then.' His voice was flat, and she heard the anger within it. 'I'll join you in a few moments.'

She rose to her feet, her body still heated, her breasts tight against her gown. It was hard to catch her breath, though it had nothing to do with exertion…and everything to do with forbidden desires.

Her steps carried her back to the forest's edge until she realised she'd forgotten the basket. Though she should return for it, she was afraid of coming too close to the *fürst*. His body was tight with tension, and no doubt he would bring it for her.

She began running down the hill, and whether she was fleeing from the prince or from her own fears, she didn't know. The ruined abbey lay just ahead, and the trees blurred as she held on to her skirts.

Her knees buckled with a blast of pain, and she hit the ground hard. Breathless, she tried to get up, only to see a man holding a staff that he'd used to trip her. He grabbed her by the arm, a dark smile upon his face.

'You shouldn't run through the forest alone, Princess. Don't you know there are wolves that prey upon the weak?'

A hard blow struck her skull, and darkness enveloped her.

* * *

Karl watched Serena leave, and he resisted the urge to slam his fist into the stone altar. He'd pushed her too soon, once again. But once he'd tasted her mouth, she'd become an irresistible temptation. He'd let her bewitch him, even knowing that it was unwise to touch her.

She didn't want to wed him; she wanted her freedom. And the only recourse he had left was to convince her that there could be more between them than a political union. He'd meant only to kiss her. But when her hand had come to rest upon his face, he'd been undone by her innocence. No one had ever touched him with affection or paid him any heed. He'd wanted her fingers to be everywhere upon his skin.

You're unworthy of her, his conscience reminded him. *Nothing but a bastard trying to take advantage of an innocent girl and her kingdom.*

And so, he'd let her go. He'd needed a few moments to gather up his wits and calm the raging lust. In the distance, the twisting sea echoed his confused thoughts, battering the shore.

Karl picked up the basket and walked down the path. He looked for a glimpse of the princess, but there was no sign of her. No doubt she'd hastened back to the abbey, wanting to put as much distance between them as possible. He couldn't blame her for that.

But when he reached the ruins, she wasn't there. Not in the hall and not in the kitchen.

'Princess!' he called out. No answer.

His concern grew tighter when he could no longer find her. Had she run away from him? Didn't she know of the danger upon the island? The only reason they were safe at Durin's fortress was because no one knew they were there.

He left the ruins and studied the path. There were footprints in the rain-softened earth, but heavier than Serena's. A cold fear broke through him when he measured the size of the foot and saw that it was only slightly smaller than his own.

He tracked the prints down the hill, and only at the end did he see Samuel lying unconscious where he'd been struck down. Blood trickled across the man's temple, and Karl raced to the man's side, trying to rouse him.

Samuel blinked, groaning as he clutched his head. 'He took her, Your Highness. Tried to stop them—but there were half-a-dozen men.'

Karl let out a curse, blaming himself for leaving Serena alone. He'd known it wasn't safe, and yet, he'd given her a few minutes to herself. That was all his enemy had needed.

But he was going to get her back.

'Who are you?' Serena whispered, clutching her head. There was a rough bandage against it, and the wetness told her that it had been bleeding. Her vision was blurred as she fought to grasp consciousness.

She saw a man whom she guessed to be in his early forties. His face was thin, and a brown beard obscured his features. She'd never seen him before but wondered if he'd been among the men who had attacked the other night.

'To you, Princess, I'm a nobody.' He sat at a table and poured a drink into a wooden cup. Her eyes took in her surroundings, as she tried to discern where she was and how long she'd been here.

She was in a dwelling smaller than her bedchamber, with only a mattress, a fireplace and a single table and chair. Her hands were bound behind her back, as were her feet. In the corner stood a taller man, whose face was dirt-streaked, along with his hands. Possibly a farmer.

Serena struggled to remember how they'd brought her here, but after the blow the bearded man had struck to her face, she couldn't remember much of anything.

A sinking ball of dread formed inside her stomach, but she forced her words to remain calm. 'What do you want from me?'

'You're going home, Princess. Someone wants you there badly enough to pay for your safe return. They're waiting for you across the water.'

Terror clenched inside her. 'Who is waiting?'

The man's smile widened as if he'd confirmed her identity. 'He paid each of us fifty marks to bring you. I'd give you over to the devil himself for that.'

Likely it was *Freiherr* Albert von Meinhardt. The baron would stop at nothing to bring her back, for he craved the king's favour. She couldn't stop the unsettled feelings that swelled up inside, drowning out any hope she might have had.

She lowered her head, closing her eyes. Though she wanted to believe that *Fürst* Karl might come after her, there was little he could do now. Her days of freedom were at an end.

Hours passed, and there was still no sign of the prince. Serena pressed back the fear, telling herself that Karl would come eventually. He had to, if he expected her to marry him. She bit her lip, trying to silence the chattering of her teeth. She was unbearably cold, now that the weather had shifted once more.

Outside, she could hear the rhythm of the violent waves surging against the sand. Rain slashed through the roof, pouring down on all of them. The storm had returned, transforming into a raging tempest that made it unsafe for a crossing. The men had changed their plans, intending to leave at dawn. Though it had granted her a brief reprieve, she didn't know if the prince could find her in time.

What if they succeeded in bringing her back to the mainland? The paralysing fear swept over her, numbing her mind. She wasn't ready to face her father again. Not so soon.

She studied her surroundings. A fisherman called Jürgen was their leader, and though he'd ordered the other men not to touch her, she saw them eyeing her with interest. Thank heaven, she still had her cloak, and she kept it firmly around her body, hiding every inch from view.

There was only one entrance within the wooden dwelling, and it was heavily guarded. It was late at night now, and though exhaustion threatened to claim her, Serena forced her eyes to remain open.

She might have to rescue herself. It was a reality she didn't want to face, but what other choice did she have?

In the darkness, she could hardly see anything, but she knew the men were armed with guns and knives. Her ropes were too tight to untie, and she fumbled against them, hoping to somehow loosen the knots.

After an hour of trying, her wrists were numb and raw. She was near to tears, and though several men had fallen asleep, it was impossible to steal a knife without waking them. With her bound feet, she couldn't walk or hop, either. When she was first taken captive, they'd stolen her shoes from her, keeping her feet bare to prevent an escape.

Trussed like a Christmas goose, she thought.

Wasn't that just lovely? Her anger and frustration grew stronger as time dragged onwards. How could the prince have just left her? Had he changed his mind and decided to find another bride after all?

You're overreacting, her mind warned. *He'll come.*

And get himself captured in the attempt? Not likely. *Fürst* Karl was not an impulsive man, and likely he'd gone for help. Which was perfectly logical, except that in her foolish mind, she wanted him to charge in, seize control and take her away.

The longer the night dragged on, the more she began to worry that it wouldn't happen. Karl had only two men to help him. How could he possibly do anything against these odds?

He couldn't. She sobered at the conclusion. And here she sat, enduring her captivity instead of using her head to try and escape. Not once had she called out for help, nor even made the attempt to leave. She'd let herself become their victim, without fighting back.

Just as she'd never fought back against her father. Because she was too afraid.

She'd suffered his wrath, obeying him and doing

everything in her power to please him. Even when he'd broken her ribs, she'd done nothing to stop him.

A sudden surge of frustration and rage welled up within her. Why? She didn't deserve any of the wounds inflicted upon her. She'd done nothing wrong, not in all these years.

Blind obedience had given her nothing but bruises to show for it. And now, she had fallen back into her habit of hiding in the shadows.

You can't keep hiding, a voice inside her warned. Her escape from the palace had been the first shaky step, but it wasn't enough. She'd been waiting for someone else to take the lead, to make the decisions.

Not any more.

In the darkness, she stood up, with hands and feet bound. No one moved, nor did the sleeping guards notice her. She couldn't walk very well, but after her efforts to loosen the ropes, there was just enough slack to allow her the smallest fraction of steps. Slowly, with a numb, shuffling movement, she managed to make her way a few feet across the room.

A hand caught her, jerking her backwards until she fell hard upon the ground. 'Don't.'

She didn't recognise which man had spoken, but his words alerted the others. Within seconds, she was forced to the back of the enclosure, fully surrounded.

A bleakness settled over her, and she wondered why she'd bothered to fight back when there were six of them. What chance did she have of gaining her freedom against so many?

Better to try and fail, than not to try at all, her mind advised. And then another idea took root, sinking into her consciousness with possibilities. She waited a few moments, then stood up, deliberately tripping over one of the guards. Her bound hands bumped against his waist.

'Can you not sit still, woman?' he demanded, shoving her back against the hut. 'You'll not get free, no matter what you try.'

Serena hid her face, showing no response. After he let go, she moved her legs forward, using the hem of her gown to conceal the knife she'd unsheathed from his belt.

She remained motionless for a long time, until he turned his attention elsewhere. Though she risked cutting herself with the blade, she didn't care. She would free herself from the ropes and find a way out. Somehow.

One of the guards came near and crouched down behind her. 'Give me the blade,' he warned. Her hands froze behind her, and she dropped the knife, trying to hide it. 'You're doing a poor job of cutting the ropes,' came the whisper at her ear. 'Allow me.'

It was Karl.

A rush of emotions clattered through her mind. Had he been here all along, disguised among the men? How had he done it without being discovered? In the darkness, she couldn't see his face, but she felt the blade cutting through her ropes; first her wrists, then her ankles.

His mouth returned to her ear. 'Keep your hands and feet behind you for now. When you see the signal, I'll grab you and take you to the entrance. We'll make our escape then.'

Before she could ask what signal he meant, he predicted her question and whispered, 'You'll know.'

Though he'd freed her hands, she felt the tingling of blood flowing back through her skin. It hurt worse than she'd thought it would.

The prince remained behind her, and she felt his hands upon her ankles. At first, she winced at the sensation of him touching her bruises. A moment later, he left his hands in place, letting them warm her feet. She held herself motionless, not at all certain she should allow it. But his hands felt good, the barest touch sending heat through her cold skin. The futile wish, that he could take her into his arms and warm her body with his own, crossed her wayward mind.

He protected you, just as he'd said he would.

Something shifted inside her, for she'd not truly believed he'd keep his word. Despite their circumstances, he'd infiltrated the enemy and found a way to keep watch over her. Though they hadn't yet made their escape, he'd given her a reason to hold on to faith.

Serena reached back to touch Karl's hand with her own. In the darkness, no one saw them, and she held his hand with her own in a silent thanks. His presence brought her comfort, knowing that he hadn't abandoned her. And though she couldn't guess what sort of signal would provide the distraction they needed to get away, already she felt better with him here.

She squeezed his hand, and he returned the gesture.

It was then that she smelled smoke. With horror, she understood that someone had set the shelter on fire. Karl grasped her hand and forced her to run while behind them, flames erupted.

Chapter Ten

The fierce heat consumed the small hut, and Karl had no doubt that Durin had used oil to speed up the fire. He took Serena's hand and ran outside with her, while the other men coughed and stumbled from the flames. All around them were armed men, the priest holding his own weapon. As promised, he'd managed to recruit the forces they needed.

When they reached the circle of men, Serena kept close to his side. 'Who are these men?'

'I sent Father Durin to hire men we could trust. I needed help to get you out.' She rubbed her arms, and Karl drew her cloak tighter around her.

'He hasn't forgotten his days as a castle guard, has he?' she predicted in a low voice.

'No. And I trust him,' Karl admitted.

'What will happen to the men who tried to kidnap me?' Serena risked a glance at the men. Father Durin's hired soldiers had surrounded them.

'Until my father's men arrive, they'll remain imprisoned. Bernard and Samuel will bring back forces from Lohenberg within another day or so, and they'll stand trial for their crimes.'

'They needed the money,' she said quietly. 'They were starving.' With a breath, she added, 'Instead of punishing them, I think we should show mercy.'

He reached out and touched the dried blood on her forehead and his gaze grew rigid. 'They hurt you.' *Mercy* wasn't a word in his vocabulary, when it came to those who harmed someone under his protection. Taking a defenceless woman, for any amount of money, was unforgivable.

'Not that badly.' Her eyes met his, the fire reflected within the green. 'For a while, I was afraid you wouldn't find me.'

'I would always find you.' He reached out and took her hand in his. Her palms were cold, her body drawn inward with exhaustion. She needed sleep and warmth right now. With her hand in his, he led her to his waiting horse. 'I'm taking you back to the abbey, since it's closest.'

'Alone?' She looked uneasy about the prospect.

'No, we'll take a few men as escorts. And there will be additional guards within the hour,' he promised. 'Durin will send them, once he's handled the matter of your captors.'

When he boosted her up on the gelding, Karl swung up behind her. 'The three days aren't over yet, Princess.'

She didn't meet his gaze when he held her close, trying to warm her. As they rode away, the air was heavy with smoke.

It was your fault they took her, his conscience taunted. *You never should have left her alone.*

He'd mistakenly believed they were well hidden from their enemies. It had been an error of pride, one he intended to correct with the men he'd hired. Tonight they would have a dozen men guarding the perimeter of the gates, and perhaps in the morning, Bernard would return with supplies from Lohenberg.

As he held on to Serena's waist, his mind plagued him with thoughts of what might have happened to her. She'd been completely at their mercy, and he worried that she hadn't shared everything that had happened.

The horse covered miles of shoreline until they

reached the narrow forest path winding toward the abbey. Serena rested her back against him but didn't speak a word. Only when they reached the gates did Karl dismount and lift her down. Since she wore no shoes, he continued to carry her inside.

'Please, put me down,' she protested.

'Not yet. You haven't any shoes.' He brought her within the large hall with the Gothic windows, before he crossed over to the winding staircase. For a moment, he eyed it, considering what to do.

'If you try to carry me up those narrow stairs, you'll knock my head against the wall,' Serena warned. 'I can walk.'

She was right, and he saw no choice but to let her down. When her bare feet touched the ground, she winced at the cold. Karl followed her up the stairs to the chamber, noticing the abrasions around her ankles from the ropes. And yet, as she walked, she carried herself like the princess she was. Her posture was straight, her hemline gently lifted as she ascended.

But he scented the fear around her and the way she seemed to be holding herself together by the barest thread. He blamed himself that they'd taken her. The injuries were *his* fault for not protecting her well enough. And no matter that they'd achieved a rescue, he couldn't forget his failure.

When she opened the door to her chamber, Karl spied the straw mattress on the floor. He'd forgotten how meagre her accommodations were, for he'd deliberately kept everything austere. He'd meant to provoke her into agreeing to the marriage. Instead, it made him feel like the bastard he was, for treating her like this. She hadn't deserved any of it.

His gaze fixated upon the mattress while his mind went through an ordered list of how to best handle the situation.

'If you'll build me a fire, I'll be comfortable enough,' Serena said. Her expression had *Go Away* firmly written on it.

He wasn't about to extend her suffering for another night. Not when he could offer her something better.

'You're not sleeping on that tonight.'

She sent him a confused look, but followed him outside the chamber, down to the largest chamber where he'd spent the previous night. Karl pointed inside his own room. 'You'll sleep here.' Though the bed was small, at least the coverlet was warm.

Serena turned and stared at him. 'You had a bed last night while I slept on the floor?'

He ignored the question and began preparing a fire in the hearth. From behind him, he heard her approach. 'Answer me, *Fürst* Karl. Did you sleep there?'

'I did.' He stood while the fire struggled to catch hold of the tinder. Behind her pale complexion, he saw the anger rising. There were no excuses for what he'd done, and he didn't bother attempting an explanation. 'I made the wager intending to win. By any means possible.'

Her eyes glittered like shards of ice. 'And you thought that would make me want to marry you?'

'I'm a bastard, Serena.' He admitted the truth, even knowing she wouldn't take it for its true meaning. 'I always have been.'

She stared at him, shaking her head. 'I know you rescued me tonight. And perhaps you think I owe you a debt. But—'

'You're not going to marry me,' he finished. 'And you'd die before considering it, wouldn't you?'

She stared at him in disbelief, as if she couldn't

find the right words to respond. But neither did she deny it.

'I'll sleep in your old chamber tonight,' he informed her. 'In the meantime, I'll bring you something for your wrists and ankles. And food.'

She moved nearer to the fire, huddling as close as she dared. Just as he was about to leave, she admitted, 'Today was yet another reason why I don't want to be a princess any more.'

In her eyes, he saw the downtrodden look, as if she had little hope remaining. There was nothing he could say to convince her otherwise, for she'd already given up. If she wanted nothing more to do with him, so be it.

He left her in search of warm water and bandages for her wrists and ankles. All the while, he tried to convince himself to simply send her away. Let her live her own life, since that was what she wanted.

But she was innocent of the ways of the world. Someone would take advantage of her naivety and exploit her weaknesses.

He tore off a piece of bread from a loaf and slammed it on a tray, along with some wine. The problem was, he didn't want to send her off by herself. Despite her wishes, he wasn't about to return to Lohenberg as a defeated man.

Karl returned to her chamber with a tray he'd arranged, as well as an old pair of Durin's shoes. It wouldn't do much, but it made him feel as if he could make amends for what had happened.

When he entered the room, he found her sitting in the same place. Her hands were clenched around her knees as if she couldn't get warm.

'Here.' He handed her a cup of wine and the bread, not entirely certain how old it was. While she ate and drank, he turned his attention to her feet, lifting the hem of her gown to her ankles.

She froze at the touch of his hands and pulled her feet away. 'You needn't bother. They'll be fine in the morning.'

He ignored her and dipped a cloth in the water, washing away the dried blood from her ankle. She gave a slight gasp at the cold water, but held still. Her feet were dirty, and when he started to wash them, she gasped.

'I'm sorry,' she managed. 'It tickled.' She reached for the cloth from him, but he wouldn't relinquish it yet. Instead, he rested her bare foot upon his knee and washed the top of her foot and ankle, moving down to the sole. Her feet were delicate and bruised, the ankles reddened from where her captors had bound her.

She stared at him in silence, as if she couldn't understand why he was doing this.

'It was my fault they took you,' he said quietly. His hands moved over her other foot, washing the dirt away, and he felt the rise of goose bumps over her skin. 'I won't let it happen again.'

She acknowledged his promise with a nod and said, 'I've stayed here too long. I need to leave in the morning.'

'Not yet. We have our wager to finish.' He handed her the shoes he'd borrowed. They were too large, but she put them on without complaint.

She shook her head. 'Karl, I don't think—'

'You gave your word. Just as I gave mine,' he reminded her. 'One more day, and at the end of it, you'll wed me. Or I'll take you away myself.'

Her gaze turned serious, and she tucked her feet beneath her skirts. 'I never know what to expect from you.' She gripped her hands together, adding, 'You're not like the other princes I've met.'

'Spoiled and arrogant?'

'Not spoiled. But arrogant, sometimes.' From

her tone it almost sounded like a compliment. 'And ruthless.'

Karl reached out to touch the curve of her cheek. He let his hand rest upon her face, staring into her green eyes. 'When I decide I want something, I don't stop until it's mine.'

Her lips parted and she moved her hand on top of his. 'I can't be yours,' she whispered.

'Can't you?' He lowered her hand and dipped his cloth in the water again. Her wrist was abraded from the ropes, and he washed it gently. 'Or are you too afraid of the way I make you feel?'

'I don't feel anything,' she insisted.

'Liar,' He drew his hands to her shoulders, sliding them over her sensitive arms. In the faded light, she allured him with her emerald eyes and her soft lips. 'You weren't pushing me away when I kissed you last night.'

She lowered her gaze, guilt flushing her cheeks. As a distraction, she poured wine into the cup and passed it to him. 'You didn't eat or drink tonight either, did you?'

'Between finding Durin, hiring men and rescuing you?' He lifted the cup and drank from it. 'No.'

She tore off a piece of bread and handed it to

him. He ate, studying her in the light. Her blond hair had fallen around her cheeks, the tousled locks making her look as if she'd just awakened from sleep.

'I caused a lot of trouble by leaving the palace, didn't I?' She stared into the fire, her face disconsolate.

'Marry me, and I'll take you home,' he said. 'I imagine your father would be grateful to see you safe again.'

Immediately, she shook her head. 'I can't.'

'Why? Surely your family would be glad to have you home safely.'

She stared at him for a long moment. 'The night you helped me unlace my corset,' she whispered, 'I know you saw the bruises.'

He gave a slight nod. 'And you wouldn't tell me who was responsible.'

Her gaze grew distant. 'Just after Christmas, he broke my ribs. Because I dared to give him a chess set made of silver instead of gold. Though he thanked me in front of my mother and sister, he punished me later. I never told them.'

A sickening suspicion made the room seem colder. 'Who punished you, Serena?'

She stared into the flames. 'The king.'

He didn't move, didn't speak. The hurt and betrayal on her face made it clear she was telling the truth. Knowing that her father had done this made him want to kill the man. What sort of a monster would inflict beatings upon his own child?

But then, he knew what it was to be hated by the woman who should have loved him, never understanding why he hadn't belonged with the family who had raised him. He understood her pain, for it echoed his own.

'Has it always been this way?' he asked.

She shook her head. 'It started just after our betrothal. When I was little, he hardly paid attention to me. But since then, it doesn't matter what I do or say. It's never proper enough. Sometimes I think he enjoys punishing me.'

'And what of the queen? Does she stand by and allow it to happen?'

'My mother is very ill,' she whispered. 'I didn't tell her at first, because I didn't want to upset her.' Her gaze lowered to her skirt. 'She found out, just before I left. And she agreed that it was right for me to go.'

'What about your sister?'

Serena shook her head. 'I don't know. I've tried to keep it from her, but I suspect she might have found out, since she sent you that letter. Thank goodness, she's been away at boarding school most of the time and he hasn't touched her, so far as I know.'

Karl studied her. 'Are you afraid the king will come after you here?'

'I know he will.' Dread lined her voice, mingled with resignation. 'That's why I was taken tonight. I believe someone from the palace hired men to bring me back.'

'What do you want to do now?'

He stood up, his mind circling with the consequences of her actions. A man who would beat his daughter for no reason at all would find many reasons to justify hurting her. If she returned to the king, she would only suffer more. A seething anger took hold beneath his skin, a cold rage at the thought of anyone harming Serena.

'I won't go back,' she repeated, her voice growing resolute. 'I'm tired of being his victim.'

'You're right,' he said softly. 'You won't go back without me.' He had no qualms about standing up to the king, nor was he afraid of the man.

Serena shook her head. 'After all the time we've spent alone together, he would assume the worst. Nothing good would come of it.'

'Nothing?' he ventured, reaching out to cup her cheek. His thumb edged her mouth, and she caught his meaning.

Her face flushed and she looked away. 'He's the king of Badenstein. No one can touch him or stop him from doing as he wishes.'

It was clear that she believed herself utterly alone, that she had no faith in anyone protecting her. 'So you'll keep running away from him for the rest of your life?'

'I can live a quiet life. It hasn't been so bad these past few days.'

'Is that what you want?'

She stood up in the oversized shoes and walked toward him. 'I want my freedom, above all else.'

'And you think a man as proud as the king of Badenstein will let you go, without sending an army to search for you?'

'Oh, he'll search,' she said, 'but not because he wants me home safely. By running away, I've defied his will. He'll want me back to punish me.'

Karl sent her a hard stare. 'Let him try.' She

started to shake her head, but he caught her hand. 'Face him, Serena. Only then will you have your freedom.'

Her fingers curled in his, as if she sought courage from him. 'I wish I could.'

'How badly do you want to leave?'

'Very. But I don't know if there's any way he'll let me alone. He won't forgive my disobedience.' She raised her eyes to his, and in them, he saw the shadow of her fear. 'There's nothing I can do.'

She wasn't even considering him as a protector. Karl let go of her hand, suddenly seeing the truth. 'You were never going to agree to a wedding, were you? The wager meant nothing.'

She shook her head, and a flush bloomed in her cheeks. 'I couldn't involve you in a war with my father. That wouldn't be fair to you.' Her voice softened and she ventured a sad smile, 'I believe you'll make another princess a perfectly good husband.'

He couldn't listen to her extolling praises that weren't true. 'No. I'm a selfish bastard, and I wanted to wed you for the good of our kingdoms. Nothing more.'

Her expression faltered. 'If you were so selfish, why did you rescue me?'

He ignored the question. 'Everything I did was for my own purposes. I intended to use you.'

In her eyes, he saw the disappointment, the maidenly hope that perhaps there might have been something between them. But he couldn't lie to her any more. She deserved the freedom she wanted, and he deserved whatever misfortune happened to him now.

He started to leave her room when she blocked his path. 'Why did you kiss me, then?' she whispered. 'If you felt nothing at all.'

The softness in her face, and the way she looked at him made him stiffen. If he had to destroy all of her illusions, so be it. 'It was part of my plan to seduce you. If you were expecting my child, your father could do nothing to prevent a marriage between us.' He laid everything bare, knowing that he was only fuelling her hatred. It didn't matter. Better that she should go, well rid of him.

The door closed behind him, and Serena stared at the wood for a long time. So much of what he'd said was brutal and callous. She felt as if she'd taken an imaginary blow to her stomach, for he'd done everything in his power to make her hate him.

Instead, she sat down near the fire, thinking to herself. He'd not slept at all last night, but had gone for help. He'd disguised himself among Jürgen's men and had brought her here safely. Then he'd given up his bed, brought her food and even another pair of shoes.

For a man who claimed to be a selfish bastard, it didn't add up.

He'd said that there'd been a falling out between him and his father. Everything he'd done had been meant to force her into marriage, likely to regain his father's approval. She didn't understand it. Nor did she understand the words he'd thrown at her, behaving as if he were a villain instead of the man who'd saved her.

Without knowing what she was doing, Serena adjusted the oversized shoes and left her chamber. She walked down the hall, but Karl was not in her old room. She held on to the stone walls as she walked down the winding spiral stairs, and there she saw him sitting near the large fireplace. Outside the windows, she saw the flicker of torches.

Karl heard her footsteps and saw the direction of her gaze. 'It's the men we hired. They've returned to guard us tonight.'

'Good,' she murmured, crossing the room. Karl was hunched over near the fire, looking haggard and exhausted. She didn't know what drew her near, but she sensed that everything he'd said was meant to push her away. And she wanted to know why.

She stood in front of him, and he raised his gaze to her with wariness. 'What do you want?'

'I never thanked you for rescuing me.' She took a breath, her heart pounding faster. As she stared at him, he looked angry with her. Even so, she held her ground.

'You've done so. Now go back to your room.' The order had an unexpected sharpness, as if he couldn't bear the sight of her. Her first instinct was to obey, but something rooted her feet in place.

She said nothing, not understanding the tremble of the pulse inside of her. She'd seen a side to Karl that was ruthless and bold. He'd risked his own life for hers, and he'd kept his word to protect her.

Was it possible…that she could face her father's temper and gain her true freedom? Karl was right.

The king would never stop searching for her, for any successful escape was a blow to his pride. He'd forbidden her to leave, and once her father got word of her whereabouts, nothing would stop him from forcing her back.

Face him, Serena. Only then will you have your freedom.

The *fürst* was right; she knew it. But she needed a way of protecting herself from her father's wrath. The king held all the power over her, at no risk to himself. She didn't know what to do.

'Serena, go.' The prince's voice was soft, but within it, she heard the nuance of desire, the magnetic quality that drew her closer. Over the past few days, she'd seen another side to Karl. He was rough and callous on the outside...but he'd been hurt by his family, just as she had.

She didn't want to leave. Not yet. And though her footsteps took her straight into the path of a frustrated man, she no longer cared.

Karl stood up from the chair, and without warning, seized her around the waist. 'You were warned.'

She lost her breath when he cut her off with a fierce kiss. There was nothing polite or calm about it. In his kiss, she tasted hurt and bitterness. He was doing everything in his power to push her away, to give her a reason to run away and hide from him.

She let him unleash the anger upon her mouth, answering it by winding her arms around his neck. At her sudden embrace, he softened the onslaught, sliding his tongue against the seam of her mouth until she opened to him. She surrendered, letting him enter her mouth, and the sensation sent a wave of drowning desire rippling through her. His hands moved down her spine, resting upon her hips. When he pulled her near, she felt his arousal pressing against her.

She reached up to cup his face, and at her touch, he drew back. Hungry eyes stared into hers as if he'd never expected her to respond to him. As if she'd touched him in a place that went deeper than his skin.

His hands moved up her ribs, resting beneath her breasts. She was starting to lose her awareness, unable to grasp all the reasons why this was wrong. His arms came around her, and for a moment, he rested his mouth within her hair. She heard the rapidity of his breath, but he didn't let go.

'I'm no good for you, Serena, and you know it,' he murmured, drawing back. His hazel eyes were darkened with need, and her thoughts were in disarray.

'Is it so wrong, wanting this?' she answered. 'It's just a kiss.' Within it, she'd found the answer she was looking for. He did want her. Everything he'd said about using her seemed impossible to believe.

His hands moved to rest upon her shoulders. 'Go back before I do something we both regret.'

'You wouldn't hurt me,' she whispered. She'd stake her life on it. A part of her craved the affection he offered, for she'd never been treated this way before. He'd claimed her mouth as if she were everything he needed.

His mouth moved to her throat, dropping a kiss on the curve between her neck and shoulder. In a husky voice, he whispered, 'Right now I want to unfasten those buttons, one by one. I want to move my hands over your skin and slide the chemise from your body.'

Her body went soft at his tantalising words, her skin prickling. She felt the touch of his hands upon her bodice, and her nipples went rigid.

Then what? her traitorous body demanded.

Karl moved his thumb to the first button, playing with it slightly. 'I'd bare you to the waist and touch your breasts with my hands.'

Serena's arms came up to cover her chest, and his hands caught hers. Her breathing had quickened, and with his words, she grew more aroused. 'Karl—'

'Then I'd kiss you again,' he interrupted.

She wanted that, to feel the firm caress of his mouth upon hers. Without even realising it, her fingers had gone to touch her lips.

Karl took her hand back. 'Not there, sweet.'

He lowered her fingers, bringing them to touch her own breasts. Serena felt the sudden clench of need, tightening her nipples, sending a hidden ache within.

'There,' he corrected, leaving her with the image of his ravenous mouth upon her breasts, arousing her with his tongue.

Before she could say another word, he left her standing in the hall alone.

Chapter Eleven

'We've heard from Karl at last.' Lady Hannah Chesterfield smiled as she entered the drawing room, holding out a folded letter. 'He's visiting Vertraumen.'

Michael Thorpe, the *fürst* of Lohenberg, rose to greet Hannah, kissing her cheek. 'Is he?' Though he knew she worried about his half brother, he was less trusting. Karl had been the Crown Prince of Lohenberg, and he wasn't the sort of man to turn his back on his birthright—Michael fully expected Karl to fight for the throne.

'Yes. Apparently the island is in trouble.' She detailed Karl's report about crop failures, along with his request for supplies, a household staff and soldiers to help stabilise the government. 'The king has already sent the men, but he wants you to go and inspect the state of affairs on the island.'

Inside his chest, he felt the tightness. The king hadn't given him any duties as the new *fürst* until now. And Michael was well aware of his ignorance. He'd been trained as a soldier, not a prince. He didn't have the first idea of how to be a future king.

This was the first task he'd been given, and he sensed it was a test. His mind tried to assimilate all of the information, seeking the best course of action. Karl had provided a detailed list of the island's problems, along with his suggested solutions.

For that, he was grateful. While he went over each point, he missed Hannah's last remark.

'Don't you think it's romantic?'

He frowned. 'He's starving on the island and you think it's romantic?'

'No.' She closed the door to his study and crossed the room. From the sudden change in her demeanour, he opened his arms, and she sat on his lap. 'Didn't you read his list? He asked for a complete wardrobe for a young woman—gowns and ladies' maids. Since your brother isn't likely to be wearing women's clothing, I presume he has a female guest.'

Michael frowned. 'Who would he have brought with him? He was betrothed to Princess Serena of Badenstein.'

'I don't know, but I'm certain he's not alone,' Hannah breathed with a smile. 'Can't you just imagine it? The two of them, on an island, with no one in the world to interfere? I'd love to spend time with you in a place like that. Perhaps after our wedding.'

She leaned in and kissed him, and Michael tossed the list aside. 'We don't need an island, Hannah.' His hand moved to her ankle, sliding up the glorious silk stockings she was wearing.

'We could go and visit your brother.' She smiled against his mouth and rose from his lap. 'Find out what he's up to.'

Michael took her hand in his, with a full intent of seducing her, when his gaze fell upon a newspaper folded beside the tea service. He let out a foul curse when he saw the headlines.

'What is it?' Hannah asked, following his stare. When she saw the large block letters announcing that the Princess of Badenstein had gone missing, her face paled. 'You don't think Karl would—'

'I wouldn't put it past him. If he seduced her

or married her, they'll have to name him prince consort.' Michael rang for a footman and gave the terse order to pack his belongings.

Hannah's face fell. 'The king of Badenstein would be furious with him.'

'And he could threaten Lohenberg.' Though Michael didn't believe it would cause a war between their countries, neither would it improve their relationship. Karl's fallen status would infuriate the king, if his daughter were involved with a bastard son. 'We need to discover if she's there with him.'

'And if she is?'

'We'll bring her home.'

The following morning, Bernard arrived at the fortress. He bowed low before the prince. 'Your Highness, His Majesty has sent your requested supplies and the household staff. I took the liberty of bringing them to the manor house, but there are guards here awaiting your command.'

'Good. You've done well.'

His footman gave a slight smile and bowed again. 'I will wait with them in the courtyard. Is the princess—?'

'She is with me still,' Karl said. 'I will accompany her back to the house.'

After they departed the abbey and rode along the beach, Serena joined at his side. 'Have I won the wager, then?'

'I will keep my word, as promised.' With a sidelong glance, he saw that she'd cloaked herself from throat to ankle. No doubt she was still wearing the cream-coloured gown backwards. After she returned to the house, the ladies' maids would descend upon her, and she would become a princess once more.

Their three days were at an end.

Karl kept his gaze fixed ahead, his spine straight. He needed time to consider the best options for Serena, but more than that, he needed to determine his own fate. The future stretched out before him like a wasteland, an unknown that kept slipping away from his carefully laid plans. He'd meant to wed a princess, not squander a week of his life.

But Serena had changed everything until he didn't know what to do any more. Last night, he'd spent the hours huddled on a straw pallet, unable to stop thinking of the way her hands had moved through his hair and against his face. She'd provoked him, until he'd kissed her in an effort to drive her away. With her tentative caresses, she'd captured him…making him imagine that she cared about him.

Impossible. She wanted only one thing from him—her freedom. That had always been clear. And although they'd spent a few moments in each other's company that had been more intimate, he understood that she would never want him as her husband. Especially if he admitted that he'd lost his kingdom.

He rode through the countryside, glancing back to ensure she was still there. Her gaze drifted over to the sea, and Karl guessed she was uneasy about her father learning of her whereabouts. Would she want to face the king? Or would she run away again?

When they reached the manor house, Serena found herself surrounded by a dozen maids. Four of them had served the queen at the Royal Palace in Vermisten, Lohenberg. From the appalled expression on their faces, Serena could only imagine how terrible she looked. Her hair hadn't been brushed, and on her feet she wore the oversized leather shoes. Without another word to *Fürst* Karl, she followed them inside.

The scent of food tantalised her, and she took a deep breath, savouring the promise of a good meal. But even as she followed the women upstairs and let them draw a bath, she couldn't let go of the coldness building inside her.

She didn't know how to diminish her father's hold, to force him to let her go. Returning to the palace meant that she was in his arena, subject to his whims. Better to make him come to her here on neutral ground.

Fürst Karl and his guards would keep her safe on the island. She had faith in the prince's protection. Perhaps instead of asking him to help her run away, she should ask him to shield her from her father's vengeance. The king wouldn't harm the royal prince of another country, would he? And once he'd let her go, then she could live quietly somewhere else.

A strange loneliness caught her at the thought. She'd grown accustomed to living with Karl, despite his overbearing ways. He had made her feel safe, in a way she'd never felt before.

As her ladies undressed her, Serena realised that

the dress was looser. She'd grown thinner after the days without good food, and one of the ladies sent for a tray of refreshments.

But it was the hot bath that sent her mind spiralling into heaven itself. The water had been scented with essence of lavender, and she leaned back, allowing another maid to wash her hair.

'Your Highness,' one maid ventured, 'Lady Hannah bid us welcome you and if there is anything you need, you've only to ask.'

'I don't believe I know anyone named Lady Hannah,' Serena said, frowning. 'Is she from Lohenberg?'

'No, Your Highness. She is the daughter of an English Marquess and will marry *Fürst* Michael in another week.' The maid's face brightened as she described the plans for the royal wedding, with arches of lilies and roses, along with dozens of attendants. 'Her dress is the most beautiful ivory silk I've ever seen.'

A creeping suspicion tangled in her stomach. Serena had never heard of a prince named Michael.

'This man, *Fürst* Michael,' she began. 'Is he Karl's brother?'

The maid nodded. Her cheeks flushed as she ventured, 'Your Highness, what are your instructions regarding the possessions of your…husband? The footman Bernard thought, perhaps, the adjoining bedchamber?'

The young woman wouldn't meet her gaze, and Serena hesitated. So much had happened, she knew well enough what it must look like, living alone with Karl. If she told the women to put Karl far away from her, then her reputation would be tarnished. The small lie would benefit both of them.

'Yes, I think it would be best to put his clothing in the next bedchamber,' Serena answered, wishing she could stop herself from flushing red.

'Very good, Your Highness.' The maid curtsied and departed to take care of it. From the excited expressions on their faces, she could tell they were bursting to ask questions about her non-existent wedding. But she would give them no explanation.

She sank deeper into the water, washing herself with the soap they'd given her. The maid's revelation, of another prince, bothered her. No one had told her of a brother, and she didn't doubt that Karl had known about it.

'I wasn't aware that Karl had a younger brother,' she began, waiting for more answers.

The comb stopped moving. '*Fürst* Michael is the true heir to the Lohenberg throne,' the woman said quietly. 'I thought you'd heard the news…that your husband was not the legitimate prince.'

The bathwater suddenly seemed to grow cold. 'No. I wasn't aware.'

He'd lied to her. All this time when he'd claimed he wanted to marry her…it was because he wanted to become a prince again.

Serena's eyes burned, but she would not cry. He'd been telling her the truth, when he'd said he was a bastard who was only using her. She hadn't believed it until now.

Karl stood in the bedchamber that adjoined Princess Serena's. One of her maids had moved his belongings inside. He rubbed the edges of his cheeks, knowing he looked like a man who'd lived among wild animals. A valet awaited his orders, and he bade the man to fetch shaving supplies. Another brought out clean clothing, as well as a basin of water.

While the valet shaved him, his gaze focused

upon the adjoining door. Why had Serena given the order for him to remain nearby? It made little sense at all. From behind the door, he heard the sound of ladies talking to the princess.

And then he heard the telltale splash of her bathing in the tub. His imagination conjured up the image of her smooth skin sliding beneath the water, the slight ripple against her bare breasts.

He grew hard, thinking of her. Right now, he wanted to order everyone out, to throw open the thin door that lay between them.

His valet had said something, but Karl was certain he'd misheard the man. 'What was that?'

'My lord, the cook has asked if you and your wife would prefer salmon or beef for luncheon?'

His wife? Now where had that come from? Had the servants made an assumption of their own?

He tested his theory with a question of his own. 'Who told you of our marriage?'

His valet reddened. 'Her Royal Highness told her ladies of your elopement.'

So that was the reason for the adjoining doors. She'd lied to the servants, in order to protect their reputations.

The bastard within him suddenly had a very interesting idea.

'Leave me,' he ordered his servants, dismissing them with a hand. 'You may tell the cook that we'll dine upon salmon for luncheon.'

Once the men had left his chamber, Karl stepped over to the adjoining door and opened it.

Serena stifled a scream as Karl strode through the doors into her bedchamber. Her ladies stared in shock, and fled like scattering birds when he raised a hand in dismissal.

She sank deeper into the tub, trying to hide as much of herself as possible. 'Why are you here?'

'Why did you tell them we were married?' he countered.

Why didn't you tell me you lost your throne?

Her anger at his deception was brewing hotter, and she struggled to maintain her composure. 'To preserve my reputation. Why did you think?' She kept her voice frigid, not wanting him to draw incorrect conclusions. 'Now, I would be grateful if you would leave and send back my ladies.' She was proud of the way her voice held all the haughtiness of a royal court, revealing none of the nerves creeping beneath her skin.

Karl closed the doors behind him and walked over to her bedchamber door, locking it.

'What are you doing?' she demanded, drawing her knees up in the bath.

'Giving myself privacy with my wife.'

'I am not your wife.' She tightened her grip around her knees and sent him a furious look. 'And you, I understand, are not a prince any more.'

'I told you I was a bastard.'

'In more ways than one.'

She huddled within the cold water, trying to protect herself. Karl drew a chair over and sat beside her. Did he think to take advantage of her? She sent him a hard look. The expression in his eyes was unreadable.

'If you think, for one moment, that I'll allow you to take any liberties at all—'

'Do you want to escape your father or not?'

She did, but not at this cost. Once, she'd asked him to be her protector against her father. Now, that plan was irrevocably shattered. A bastard could never stand against a king.

'What are you suggesting?'

'That we continue the facade you created. Let him believe that we eloped. Then break the ties to your throne if that's your wish, and I'll keep my word to see you safely settled elsewhere.'

'When he finds out you've lost your throne, he'll have you killed.' She dismissed the idea as impractical. 'And if your servants already know, he must be aware of it by now.' Her gaze flickered back to his. 'If you're not a prince, you can't protect me from him.'

'You didn't believe that a few hours ago. And there are many Lohenberg guards here to help us.'

'It won't work,' she admitted softly. 'Not against my father.' Covering herself, she added, 'You should leave the island, for you have no reason to stay and help me.'

His hand grazed the surface of the water. 'Perhaps there's something else I want from you.'

She stiffened and crouched as far away from him as she dared to go. Blood rushed to her face and throughout her body. 'Get out,' she repeated. 'You're trying to intimidate me.'

'No. I'm trying to seduce you.'

He knelt beside the tub, resting both hands on either side of it. She didn't like being cornered and averted her face from him. He dipped his hand into the bathwater, then trailed a few drops down the side of her neck. Goose bumps erupted over her skin, and beneath the surface of the water, her breasts tightened.

'I don't want you,' she whispered.

'No one ever has.' An ironic smile played upon his mouth. 'But bastards don't follow the rules, do they?'

His words sent a flood of heat through her, and he leaned in closer, his breath upon her skin. He was staring at her, his gaze drifting beneath the surface of the water as if he wanted to lift her out and touch every part of her. Her mind tangled up, unable to form the words that would force him away.

'If I were a prince, I wouldn't do this.' He dipped his mouth to hers and kissed her hard. Warmth and melting desire shuddered through her. His hands captured her face, his mouth tantalising her.

'You told them I was your husband,' he whispered against her cheek. 'Is it because you wanted permission to give in to your desires?'

She said nothing, for a secret part of her wondered if it were true. Although the servants would have gossiped about them, she could have maintained her distance. Why did it matter if they had lived together for so many days?

His mouth moved to the damp skin of her throat, and she uncurled her body, her hands moving up to grasp his head. 'This is wrong,' she whispered.

'I don't give a damn.' And this time, he kissed her harder, his tongue mingling with hers. Her body was desperate with unknown feelings, but she wasn't afraid of him hurting her. A part of her knew that he'd never hurt her—he'd only try to bring her to his bed.

Though she wanted to remain the good girl, the princess who was ever obedient, she was weakening against this wickedness. Right now, the water was tormenting her bare skin, sliding over her nakedness. She wanted more, and it occurred to her that she could surrender her innocence to him and no one would think anything of it.

But how could she give in to him when he'd lied to her? She couldn't reconcile the man who had protected her with the man who had deceived her. And yet, she felt herself slipping under his spell, as his hands dipped beneath the surface of the water.

Slowly, he moved his palms over her bare shoulders and down to her breasts. When she felt him cupping them, his thumbs stroking the erect tips of her nipples, her breath grew shaken. Last night, she'd come to him, not understanding why.

'Don't be afraid of me,' he ordered against her throat. 'I'm only going to touch you with my hands and mouth. I won't consummate our…"marriage."'

Serena felt the prim-and-proper princess slipping away as he caressed her nipples. Though she knew she should stop him, the darker side of herself was gaining strength. She'd wanted more from him last night, but he'd turned her away.

Sitting up from the water, she revealed her breasts to him until he obeyed her unspoken command, sliding his heated mouth over the column of her throat. Lower still, his tongue circling her damp flesh.

Did it matter that she was behaving like a wanton? All her life she'd been punished for no reason at all, beaten and broken like a woman who didn't deserve to be loved by a man.

Karl had never touched her with roughness. Nor had he taken anything she hadn't offered. He'd touched her with hands meant to arouse, not to hurt.

And when his mouth closed over her nipple, her hands fisted in his hair, her body quaking as needs coursed through her. She was wet, so deeply aroused, that when his hand moved to touch between her legs, the shocking sensation sent her over the edge. He caressed her folds, sinking two fingers within her. She let out a cry, her head falling back as she shattered against his hand. His mouth suckled against her breast, and though she didn't understand the exhilarating sensations breaking through her, she made no move to stop him.

When at last, he pulled back, his eyes were burning with need.

He said not a word, but returned to his bedchamber, closing the door behind him. Feeling lost and alone, she couldn't stop the tears from breaking free.

Chapter Twelve

Karl walked alongside Father Durin in the fields, stopping to examine the soil. Although it was too soon to plant, the earth was muddy and covered in puddles with poor drainage. He'd used the excursion as a means of clearing his head after the encounter with Serena earlier.

Watching her come apart beneath his hands had affected him worse than he'd imagined it would. Even now, his groin ached, and the suffering was exactly what he deserved. The more his mind tormented him with images of Serena naked in her bath, the more he wanted to return to the manor house and seduce her thoroughly.

He'd taken advantage of her lie to the servants, claiming that they were married. But now that she knew the truth about him, no doubt she hated him for the way he'd used her.

It's nothing less than you deserve, his conscience reminded him. He'd been so centred on regaining a kingdom, he'd ignored all the rules of respectability. He hadn't thought about her needs—only his own.

He still wanted her, even if he couldn't be a prince. And though he'd forced her to kiss him, it hadn't truly been against her will. Her hands had come up to touch his face, almost as if she wanted him, too.

Being with Serena had shifted the ground under his feet. Although he wanted a kingdom, even if he were able to wed another princess, he wouldn't do it any more. The only woman he wanted was Serena.

It seemed he was destined to lose everything he ever cared about. He knew better than to think she would accept a man like him. All he could do was protect her from her father, take her away from the island, and give her the life she wanted.

'The rainfall has been three times as bad this year,' Father Durin was saying. 'But if we start the men digging ditches, we may be able to salvage the crops.'

'Has it always been this way?' Karl bent down

to examine the sodden earth while he tried to recall what he'd read of agricultural drainage.

'No,' the priest answered. 'But so many islanders have left, there aren't enough men for the farming.'

Karl moved out of the fields, staring at the island. Long stretches of sand lined the shore, and the hills rose gradually, offering a breathtaking view of the sea. Although it wasn't the intense blue of the Mediterranean, the rough waves had their own untamed beauty. 'What else is here?'

The priest shrugged. 'Not a great deal. No coal or gold, if that's what you're meaning.'

Karl walked alongside the older man for a time, letting his mind drift. Durin was speaking to him, but he didn't hear a word the priest was saying. He could only stare out at the aggressive waves, wondering if Serena would want anything to do with him after the way he'd touched her. Bastard that he was, he didn't regret it. He'd loved watching her come apart, the water sluicing over her naked skin. He'd wanted more, even knowing he deserved none of it.

In the distance, he saw her surrounded by ladies. They were walking along the grass, and Serena carried a bright yellow parasol. Her gown was white, trimmed with yellow ribbons, and she reminded him of a slice of frosted cake. He knew the moment she spied him, for she stopped walking abruptly. Karl shielded his eyes against the sun and watched her draw closer, trailed by the maids. She hesitated, staring at him as if she were contemplating what to say to him now.

'Someone has to,' Durin repeated. Karl glanced back and waited for him to continue. 'I was asking what you want to do with the men who attempted to kidnap the princess?'

Karl didn't care what happened, so long as they were punished for their crimes.

The priest moved to his side. 'I would suggest that, rather than a prison sentence, you allow them to exchange hard labour in return for a reduction in their punishment.'

'Why? They hurt the princess and might have done worse.'

Serena was holding on to her skirts as she trudged uphill toward him. He saw the determined look in her eyes and wondered what exactly she wanted.

'A great deal of these men can't feed their own

children,' the priest continued. 'I know them, and I believe they regret their actions.'

'Possibly.' It was what Serena had said earlier, but he was less inclined to release her kidnappers.

By now, Serena had nearly reached his side. She slowed her pace at the sight of the priest, but he paid little heed to what Durin was saying. Instead, he was staring at her flushed face and the white gown that covered her from collared throat to the floor-length hem. Her bonnet was tied beneath her chin, and her gloves were spotless. Though she spoke not a word about their bathing interlude, he caught the frown playing about her mouth. The prim-and-proper princess had returned, so it seemed.

'Your Highness, someone has to re-establish the justice system here,' Father Durin was insisting. 'Perhaps your brother, the *fürst*—'

'Are you enjoying your walk, Princess Serena?' he interrupted, cutting off the priest's words.

Serena sent a sharp look toward the priest. 'I was. The weather is much nicer today.' With a nod to her ladies, she bid them stand a short distance away to grant them a private conversation. 'You were saying something about the justice system?'

As she walked alongside the priest, Karl could almost imagine her unspoken chastisement. Although she kept a pleasant tone in her responses to the priest, he could feel her discontent.

'We need intervention from the king,' Father Durin continued. 'The supplies that arrived today will be a good start, but we still need more. For years, our petitions to the king went unanswered.'

'I never saw a single petition,' Karl remarked. 'If they asked for help, we knew nothing of it.'

'It may be that the governor never sent them,' the priest admitted.

'What will you do now?' the princess asked, facing him. When Karl shrugged, she stepped in front of him. 'You cannot ignore what's happening here.'

He turned the question back on her. 'And what do you suggest?'

Serena turned to face the ocean. 'If it were my island, I would gather the townspeople together and have them select representatives to form a council.'

Before he could say another word, she continued, 'Attempting to grow crops upon this island is a waste of time. Let them plant their own gardens if they wish, but it's better to bring in food from the mainland. Allow Lohenberg to sell their supplies here.'

'Forgive me, Your Highness, but how would the people pay for these supplies?' the priest interrupted. 'There is little that the folk here can exchange for food.'

'They could exchange services. Many of the wealthy families would welcome the chance to spend some time on an island.' She described her ideas for cozy cottages lining the sea cliffs. In each dwelling, there would be the finest beds and linens, along with a caretaker, cook and servants.

'It would never work,' Karl argued.

'Not yet. But it would offer employment to many who can no longer farm.' The idea struck him as entirely too fanciful and not practical. But he understood the inspiration. 'Like the escape you were looking for.'

'Yes.' Her gaze turned to the sea, where a few ships bobbed upon the waves.

'You won the wager.' Karl kept his voice low. 'Have you decided where you'll go?'

She shook her head. 'I thought about a Greek

island, or perhaps Italy. But you're right. No matter where I go, they won't stop looking for me.'

Though her complexion was pale, she looked as
though she were trying to be brave. 'If I'm ever to
gain my freedom, I have to face the king.' With a
deep breath, she added, 'I'll stay here until then.'

'I'll help you stand against him.' It was more
than holding up his end of the wager; it was his
desire to avenge her for what she'd suffered.

'No.' She sent him a regal nod. 'Once it's done,
you can escort me to another island. That will be
sufficient. In the meantime, I'll leave you to discuss your plans.' Raising her hand to signal to her
ladies, they returned to the manor house.

Although her tone was cool, he didn't miss the
hurt and anger beneath it. She wanted nothing at
all to do with him, believing that he'd only wanted
her throne. It might have started out that way, but
not any more.

After they'd gone, Karl eyed the priest. 'What
do you think of her idea to revive Vertraumen's
economy? Impractical?'

Father Durin's eyes narrowed and he ignored
the question. 'When are you going to marry her
and stop living a life of sin?'

'When she says yes,' he countered.

The priest gave a heavy sigh of defeat and shrugged. 'The princess's idea holds some merit. There are enough abandoned homes that we might be able to renovate them. With appropriate funds, of course.'

'I'll speak to my father.'

The priest's face grew troubled. 'Will he listen to you, now that you're no longer the heir?'

It was a valid concern. 'Vertraumen is still one of our provinces. I don't believe the king will turn his back on the island.'

'And what of you?' Durin asked. 'Has he turned his back on you?'

Karl sent the priest a dark look. 'He hardly ever noticed me. Even when I was the prince.'

Serena sat within the library, feeling restless. She'd watched the ships arriving on the horizon, and despite her resolution to stay here and face the king, the waiting was pressing down upon her nerves. Even when she retreated to the garden outside, the ladies were there, hovering around her. She took no comfort from them, for it only reminded her of her father's impending arrival.

There had to be some way to occupy her time, or she'd go mad.

She stood up from the lawn and asked one of the ladies, 'Who has been distributing the supplies to the islanders?'

'Bernard and several of the guards,' the woman answered. 'They've been delivering grain for most of the morning.'

The idea of bringing food and supplies to the needy struck her as a more enjoyable way to pass the afternoon. Though there might be some danger, she supposed Karl's guards could keep her safe enough.

Her ladies helped her to change into a gown more appropriate for paying calls within the village. When Bernard returned to load up the wagons, Serena informed him of her intent.

'Your Highness, that would not be wise. Some of the places we've visited are…not fitting for a lady of your station.'

'I'll escort you,' came a baritone voice. She turned and saw Karl standing beside the gate. He rode a black horse, and he held out his hand. 'I think I can protect my own *wife*.' He spoke the words with a hint of mockery. 'Unless you'd rather burrow inside the house?'

She bristled at the implication of her cowardice. 'I'm not afraid to go out. The guards will keep us safe.' She gave an order for Bernard to prepare a horse, as she faced Karl.

'Afraid to ride with me?' he dared her.

She only sent him a chilled look. 'No. But there might not be enough room for me with your arrogance in the way.' After straightening the ribbon beneath her chin, she awaited her own horse.

It was back-breaking work, hauling sacks of grain. Princess Serena had attempted to speak with the wives and children, offering words of comfort while Karl helped Bernard to unload the wagon. His footman had protested, saying that it wasn't right for him to join in on the labour.

He'd ignored the man, needing the physical relief from being around Serena. The scent of her hair, the delicate beauty only reminded him of her bare skin and the way she'd responded to him. He wanted her in a way that went beyond the desire to join their bodies. If he could entice her, unravel her until she craved no other man but him…it still wouldn't be enough.

They reached the last house, and it was growing dark. The sun grazed the edges of the sea, casting shades of purple and red across the sky. Karl led his horse up to the pathway, but there were no lights inside the tiny hut. He suspected it was one of the abandoned cottages and when they entered, the dwelling was dusty and barren. His first instinct was to leave, but once he spied a tiny cupboard against the wall, a sudden memory swept through him.

Darkness surrounded him, the air thick and heavy. His small hands had pressed against the door while the suffocating fear consumed him. He'd sobbed for hours without any understanding of why he was there. Only the knowledge that if he dared to push the door open, a worse punishment awaited him.

It was a recurring dream he'd had. And now, Karl recognized it for what it was—a faded memory from his past.

'We should go,' Serena said, starting to leave. 'No one has lived here for years.'

Karl ignored her and walked over to the cupboard, opening it slowly. It was just large enough for a small boy to fit inside. The stifling dusty air of the house evoked pieces of the past he'd forgotten.

Until three weeks ago, when he'd seen the woman who was his real mother.

Serena's footsteps came up behind him, and she stared at the cupboard, not understanding. 'What is it?'

He was about to say 'Nothing,' when another memory flooded through him. A sharp pain, ripping through the back of his leg. Revulsion shuddered through him, and his scar held a phantom itch.

Serena returned to the front door, closing it. When they were alone, she took his hand. 'Tell me.'

He shrugged, not knowing how to answer. The visions were blurred, and he hardly knew what was real and what was not.

'The cupboard reminded me of a dream I had once,' he said quietly. 'I was locked inside, and though I cried for hours, I couldn't get out.' Karl drew in another breath, and the musty odour of the abandoned house seemed to push back the years. 'It was a nightmare I had often.'

'Many children are afraid of the dark,' she said.

'No. It was a memory of my past.' He let go of her hand and went to close the cupboard door. 'I saw her a few weeks ago. My real mother.'

The madness in the woman's eyes bothered him still. Though she was hardly more than a stranger to him, her face had haunted those nightmares. 'She locked me up when I was little. And she did this to me.'

He raised the leg of his trousers, revealing the reddened scar. 'I remember screaming from the pain. She must have done it with a knife, when I was two or three. To make it possible to switch Michael and me.'

Serena's face paled. 'How dreadful. I can't believe any mother would do such a thing to her son.'

His jaw tightened at the memory of her. 'She never regretted what she did. I was never any son to her—just a means of getting closer to the king.'

'In a way, I suppose she did you a favour,' Serena said, returning to his side. 'She sent you to a better place to live, where no one would hurt you.'

'Perhaps.' It was true that he'd been safer there.

But he'd never felt part of the palace life. He remembered little of his early days there, only the feeling that he'd never really belonged. 'But others were suspicious. They called me the Changeling Prince, when I was younger. I never understood why until a fortnight ago.'

'Do you think the king suspected?'

'No. He accepted me as his son, but it made the queen furious. She wanted nothing to do with me.' Karl let out a bitter laugh. 'All those years, I was so confused, not knowing why she despised me. I thought, if I followed their rules and became the perfect son, it would be enough. But as soon as Michael came to Lohenberg, they couldn't get rid of me fast enough.' He steeled himself and shut the cupboard. 'It doesn't matter any more.'

She was watching him with eyes filled with sympathy. 'Don't you want to go home?'

'To a place where the people believe I was responsible for the deception?' He shook his head. 'I was three when it happened, Serena. I don't remember a damned thing about the switch. But they blame me for it.' His expression hardened into a tight shield. 'You're not the only one who wants an escape.'

* * *

Beneath Karl's coldness, Serena saw the pain of a young boy who had never been loved. She was grateful that she'd had her own mother and sister, despite her father's abuse.

But Karl had no one.

He strode toward the door, but she blocked his way. A tension knotted in his stance, a physical manifestation of his frustration. 'We're leaving, Serena.'

'Not yet,' she whispered. She clenched her hands together, her emotions tangled in a maelstrom of uncertainty. 'You said that you were using me to gain a throne. Was that all there was between us?' She wanted to believe that there was more, after all the time they'd spent together.

Her throat closed up as Karl's face remained impassive. His hazel eyes gave nothing away, and his face resembled stone. 'You're better off without a man like me, Princess.'

Chapter Thirteen

Serena began pacing across his bedchamber, her thoughts in turmoil. Though she'd told herself that she'd been right all along, that Karl had only used her, it felt like he'd lied. There was more that he hadn't said, a hovering sense that he *did* want her, even without a kingdom. He'd offered to stand by her side when she faced her father.

She didn't know what to think of that.

A knock came at the door and her ladies entered. Serena sat at her dressing table while the ladies helped her out of her gown and brushed her hair. They offered to stay with her or read aloud, but she dismissed them for the night.

One of the ladies sent her a secretive smile. 'Your Highness, forgive me for saying so, but I think your elopement was the most romantic tale I've ever heard.' She let out a sigh and offered,

'Even if he's no longer the crown prince, *Fürst* Karl is wonderfully handsome.'

Serena gave a nod of agreement. Karl wasn't handsome in the traditional sense, but there was a rugged quality to him, of a man who wasn't entirely as refined as the princes she was used to. He broke the rules and did as he pleased.

He was also unbearably stubborn and refused to listen to reason. Her mind grew numb as she imagined her father's guards arriving, seizing Karl, and imprisoning him for what he'd done. They might even execute him.

She closed her eyes at the thought. Though she was angry about the way he'd used her, she didn't want him to die. In spite of his misguided actions, she had seen glimpses of a good man.

No, she could never ask him to stand by her side and face the king. He had to leave now, before the men reached Vertraumen.

Serena signalled to one of her ladies-in-waiting. 'Please send for the…prince,' she finished, unwilling to call him her husband. 'I would like to speak with him.'

The woman bobbed a curtsy, but it was nearly a quarter of an hour before Karl returned to her chamber. His face was damp, and she caught the faint spiciness of the soap he'd used. Serena dismissed her women, leaving them alone.

'You summoned me, Your Highness?' Karl said, in a mocking tone.

He wasn't going to make this easy for her. But she needed to confront him, before she sent him away.

'I want you to leave the island in the morning. You shouldn't be here when my father arrives.'

Karl crossed the room, his hazel eyes boring into hers. He came close, as if daring her to hold her ground. 'I'm not the obedient sort, am I?'

Her heartbeat quickened at his closeness, and she forced herself to stare at the woven carpet. 'I thought I should warn you.'

'And leave you alone to face his wrath?' There was disbelief in his voice, and he reached out with one hand to cup her cheek. 'You can't do it alone.'

She pushed his hand away. 'He might hurt me, but he'll kill you.'

'I don't run from a fight.' He bent his face against hers, his breath warming her throat. 'Why did you really summon me to your bedchamber, Serena?'

She shuddered when his mouth kissed her pulse.

His hands moved over the soft linen of her night-dress, loosening the ties. 'Was there something else you wanted?'

'Just—just to ask you to leave Vertraumen.'

His hands moved down her sides, reaching between her arms to slide against the curve of her breast, down her ribs, to her waist. He'd removed his coat earlier and the shirt he wore held the dampness of water. He pulled her hips close, and she felt the length of his arousal nestled against her. 'And that's all?'

At the closeness of his body against hers, she felt a strange aching. It reminded her of the sensations she'd felt when he'd touched her in the bath. And she knew that the longer she allowed him to stay, the more dangerous he was.

She closed her eyes and forced herself to push him back. 'That's all.'

In the morning, Karl sat inside the study with a map of Vertraumen unrolled before him. He wrote down lists of island assets as well as the liabilities. The organised lines calmed him as he made a second list of ideas for improvements. If they could devise a method of draining off the excess water from the fields and collecting it for other uses, it might be a way to improve the agriculture. Though he agreed with Serena that the majority of food needed to come from the mainland, it was never wise for an island to be entirely reliant on others.

The sound of footsteps approaching broke through his reverie. He saw Serena standing near the door to the library. She wore a blue tarlatan dress with a fringed shawl and white gloves. Her hair was tucked in a neat arrangement, her blond hair intricately braided around the chignon.

'I don't understand why you won't leave the island,' she began.

'Because I don't like being told what to do?' Because hell would freeze over before he'd allow her to face more of her father's physical wrath. He fully intended to stand between Serena and the king.

'I'm only trying to help,' she said. 'Why can't you be reasonable?'

'Because you're asking me to be a coward. And that's not the sort of man I am.'

Her troubled green eyes met his, as if she were searching for a way to convince him. Karl turned his attention back to the map. 'Is that all you wanted?'

'No. I thought I would return to the village today and speak with Frau Bauherzen.' She walked back into the hall, where her ladies held out her red cloak and bonnet. 'While I await my father's men, I'd like to know what else may be done to help the islanders.'

'You're not going alone,' he warned, standing from his desk and following her.

Serena accepted her bonnet from one of the ladies and stood still while another tied the ribbons. Already she was slipping back into the role of a princess, letting others perform the tasks she was not expected to do. 'I'll take several of the guardsmen with me.'

He didn't know if it was naivety on her part or pure stubbornness, but she wasn't leaving the house again. 'No. You'll stay here.'

'And do what? Organise the linens?'

'Read and drink cups of chocolate,' he suggested.

'In other words, behave like a princess.'

'No. Like a lady.' He raised an eyebrow at her

and spoke in front of the servants. 'As my wife, I believe it is your duty to obey me.'

Her face flamed, for she seemed to have forgotten about their fictional marriage. He could almost see the wheels turning in her head as she formulated her own argument.

'I am…' She paused, reconsidering her argument. 'I believe we should talk further, my lord.' Without waiting for his reply, she returned to the study. The colour in her cheeks and the clench in her jaw meant she had more than a few words to say to him.

When she closed the door behind her, he crossed his arms. 'Why are you so eager to leave the house?'

'If I keep waiting here…for *him,* I'll go mad. I have to be useful somehow.'

'I'll go with you, then.'

'It seems a waste of your time while I speak with a dressmaker. Shouldn't you continue the work you've been doing?' She crossed over to the desk, studying the map he'd laid out of the island. She skimmed over his notes, her face turning serious as she absorbed his ideas.

'What will you do about all of the people who

have gone from Vertraumen?' she asked. 'How will you bring them back?'

'Their families can write to them. Once we've brought opportunities for the existing families, I imagine many will return.'

'Have you thought more about my idea to make the island a place for the wealthy to spend their holidays?'

He hadn't, but he sat down across from her, letting her spin off her ideas. When she spoke of cottages along the sea coast, her face grew animated, her green eyes lit up with excitement. 'It would give the women a way of bringing in coins, not just the men. They could cook and clean for the guests, and—'

'Who would watch over their children?'

'They could take turns,' she offered. 'Or perhaps the older women could look after the little ones. It could work, Karl. I know it could.'

He studied her. 'It will take a great deal of time to build the houses. Most would be unwilling to live in small cottages.'

'The cottages could be kept for the servants. We could build grander houses for the guests.'

'And who would pay for the houses?' he asked.

'I'm a bastard, remember? I haven't the funds for it.'

'Your brother does.'

He said nothing for a time, but took out a piece of paper and handed it to her. 'Write down your ideas.'

A hesitant smile crossed her face. 'You mean, you'll think about it?'

He nodded. 'And after you've left the island, I'll know what your wishes were.'

A shadow crossed her face at that, as if she no longer wanted to leave. 'You're truly going to stay here, then?'

He saw little alternative, since he had no desire to return to the empty house he owned near the borders. Turning his attention back to the map, he added, 'I do know how to care for a country or a province, even if it's no longer my right.'

She picked up the paper and reached for a pen, pulling up a chair on the opposite side of his desk. For the next few minutes, she wrote out lists, her hand moving steadily across the paper. Perfectly formed letters emerged from her pen, and as she bent over the paper, she pressed her lips together in thought.

Karl found himself wishing that one of her tightly pinned locks of hair might fall loose against her face so he'd have an excuse to touch her. What on earth had made him ever believe he could seize a creature like this and force her to wed him? Even if his plan had succeeded, she'd have grown to hate him for it. Perhaps it was best that none of it had come to pass. And he didn't lose sight of the irony, that she'd lied to the servants about a marriage, in order to maintain appearances.

A lie that did neither of them any good, for in spite of her ruined status, the princess would never bend the manners she'd been brought up with.

She set down her pen, her gaze discerning. 'What are you thinking about?'

'What makes you think the king will let you go?' he asked softly. 'You're his heir, his eldest daughter. Do you think words will convince him?'

'I don't know. I've never stood up to him before.' Her lips tightened together with apprehension. 'I want to believe that he does love me, despite everything. And perhaps he'll want me to be happy.'

'You're naive if you believe that.'

'Do you have a better idea?'

Karl stood and went to her side of the desk, leaning back against it. 'Marry me. And your father won't be able to touch you.' He had no intention of stepping aside, letting her surrender to the king. He intended to confront the man and make him pay for Serena's years of suffering.

She shook her head. 'I can't make you into a prince. You know that.'

'But I can take you away from the island. As your husband it would be my right to protect you.' He reached out and touched a lock of her hair, pulling it free of the chignon to satisfy his desire.

'You said I was better off without you.'

'There's no doubt of that.' He crossed his arms. 'It's your choice.'

She remained quiet, thinking to herself. When she met his gaze at last, she shook her head. 'If I wed you, he would find a way to punish us both. It wouldn't solve anything.'

'Then you've already given up.'

'No, I haven't,' she snapped. She pushed back the chair and paced across the room. 'Don't you think I'm tired of being controlled by him? If you truly were a prince, perhaps I would marry you. But you're not. Without any power against the king, you're just another man standing in his way. He would destroy you, and I can't let that happen.'

Her words were like a double-edged sword. *You're just another man.* It was true, that he had no power against a king. He wasn't a prince with political ties or alliances to stand against Baden-stein. But it was her last words that struck the hardest: *I can't let that happen.*

She cared. This wasn't about her father or escaping her life as a princess. She was trying to shield him. And he couldn't understand why or what he should do about it.

He knew he was supposed to say something, to reassure her. But inside, he felt like a stumbling adolescent.

'I—I should go,' Serena whispered. She looked upset, and she tucked the wayward strand of hair behind her ear.

'I'm escorting you,' he reminded her. 'Along with my father's soldiers.' He opened the door to the study. 'You'll go nowhere alone.'

When they left the manor house, surrounded by Bernard and the guards, Serena was surprised that Karl chose a carriage. As they drove toward the village, her chest tightened, thinking of his marriage proposal this morning. Part of her wished she could have said yes, though she knew it would have only complicated matters.

Was it because she wanted to let him shield her from the king? Or was it because she wanted to be with him? Karl wasn't going to leave her, no matter how dangerous the circumstances or what she said to him. With him, she would always be safe. And his steadfast courage had slipped past the defences of her heart.

Above them, the sun shone down and the sea had quieted somewhat, lapping against the shoreline. She held her parasol in one hand, while her ladies followed behind on their own horses.

Her mind drifted back to the problem of her father. Should she threaten to raise a scandal with the newspapers, revealing her abuse? Although it would give her a small bit of leverage, it would cause severe political damage. Undermining the king would harm her country.

Or she could seek refuge with the Lohenberg royal family. *König* Sweyn had the army of protection she needed. If she could gain permission to cross the borders and live there quietly, perhaps that would work.

Her gaze fixed upon the horizon and the sweeping waves of the sea, fuelled by her desire to leave, and the fervent wish to break free of her father. Her mind mulled over potential solutions, and out of the corner of her eye, she studied Karl. In the days they'd spent together at the abbey, she'd been little more than a serving girl. It had been backbreaking work, but she'd revelled in the freedom from palace life. She still wanted that.

But even more, she wanted *him,* even as arrogant and stubborn as he was. It was completely illogical, for he'd behaved like a rogue who tempted her in his wicked ways.

Karl murmured another order to one of his guards, something she couldn't hear. He gave the man a pouch of coins, and the rider disappeared toward the shoreline.

'What was that for?' she asked.

'Nothing. Just some arrangements that needed to be made.'

She didn't question him further, and he ordered the driver to take them through the village until they stopped at the edge of the beach. Karl disembarked from the carriage and assisted Serena. When her ladies and the footmen began to follow, he lifted a hand to stop them.

She sent him a grateful look, and they walked along the sandy edge of the water. It was peaceful, and Karl took her gloved hand in his. Though it felt nice to feel his hand upon hers, she was well aware of how improper it was. Beneath her breath, she murmured, 'You don't need to hold my hand for appearance's sake.'

'It's not for appearance's sake.' He gripped her fingers tighter and they stopped midway along the beach. Karl reached down to pick up a shell for her. When he pressed it into her hand, she couldn't take her eyes from him.

His cheek bones were honed, his face quite handsome, and his mouth…she remembered all too well the feel of his lips upon hers. And the way he'd touched her, making her feel so wanton.

Beneath her skin, a sudden heat prickled through her. She didn't know what to think of it, or how to respond. Quickly, she turned away, shielding her eyes against the sun.

And there, on horseback, she spied Gerlach Feldmann, captain of her father's guards. Her heart nearly stopped at the sight of him. Was he alone? Was her father already here? Sickened at the thought, Serena took a step backwards and nearly stumbled. The raw fear rippled through her, tearing down all of her earlier thoughts that perhaps it might be all right.

But then, Karl's arm came around her waist and he followed the direction of her stare. 'He was there, the day I abducted you. He's one of your father's guards, isn't he?'

Chapter Fourteen

Karl recognized the rider as one of Serena's original escorts. It was the guard who had held a spear to his side. Before he could pursue the man, he saw his half brother approaching from the opposite side of the beach, with a dozen Lohenberg guards flanking him.

A flash of resentment flooded through him, and he muttered a curse. Why was Michael here? To set the island to rights, in case Karl couldn't do so? Whatever the reason, he doubted if the prince's visit was a favourable one.

Michael's eyes narrowed when he spied the princess, and Karl met the accusatory stare with no remorse whatsoever. 'Go back to the manor house,' he ordered Serena. 'My brother is here, and I should welcome him.'

'Shouldn't I greet *Fürst* Michael, as well?' she asked.

'Another time, perhaps.' Given that Karl had kidnapped a princess and stolen her away to an island, he could feel his brother's fury from here. 'Return to the manor house with my guards.' Serena appeared reluctant, but she obeyed his orders, accompanied by his guards.

Karl stood his ground while Michael approached with his horsemen. Though he was at a height disadvantage while Michael was mounted, he didn't move a muscle until the *fürst* drew his horse to a stop.

'You went to the kingdom of Badenstein and stole their crown princess,' Michael began without prelude.

'Yes.' No reason to deny it. He'd taken the princess away, ruined her reputation, and forced her to work like a servant. All for his own gain.

'Were you trying to start a war between our two countries?' the prince demanded. 'Everyone has been searching for her. And you dared to dishonour her.'

'Are you going to imprison me?' he said calmly.

Michael dismounted from his horse, and strode

forward. 'I should.' He strode along the beach, glancing back in an unspoken order for Karl to follow. When they were out of earshot, his brother continued, 'Did you marry her, like the servants claim? Were you that stupid?'

'She refused to wed me,' Karl answered. It wasn't surprising, given all that he'd done to her.

'I don't know which is worse,' Michael admitted. 'What do you think will happen to her now? You've ruined her. The world will believe that you took her into your bed, whether you did or not.'

'I didn't.'

'By kidnapping her, you've drawn the king into this. Her father could rightfully demand your head. And we'd have to give it to him or risk war.'

He could feel his brother's blistering anger, and he deserved it. He *had* taken Serena to this island. He'd fully intended to wed her, seizing control of a title he didn't deserve. And right now, when he looked back at his actions, he realised what a fool he'd been.

'She ran away,' he told Michael, 'because her father was beating her. Weeks ago, he broke her ribs. And on the day she left, he left bruises along her side and tried to strangle her.'

No woman should endure that, princess or not.

His brother's face sobered as he considered what Karl had told him. 'What are you going to do now?'

'Protect her,' was all he could say. The purchase he'd arranged this morning would help somewhat, if Serena chose to avail of it. 'If someone threatened Hannah—'

'I'd kill the man. With no remorse at all.'

'Much as I'd like to, I can't kill a king,' Karl said. Even if he wanted to, he knew better than to risk threatening so powerful a man. All he could do was help Serena to disappear.

'Do you love her?' Michael asked. He stopped walking along the beach and stared at the water, which was starting to grow rougher. In the distance, clouds rolled across the sea.

'It doesn't matter, does it?' Karl could give no answer, for he didn't know what love was. The only thing he understood was power and the lack of it. He was playing a dangerous game with the king's daughter, one that might result in surrendering his life. He didn't plan on martyring himself. But neither would he let any harm come to her.

'You want me to leave her,' he predicted, meeting his brother's gaze. 'Let her father come for her.'

'If you fight against a king, I can't protect you.'

'Can't you?' He stared at Michael's fury. 'You know I won't abandon her to him. Her father might kill her after she dared to flee.'

'I don't believe that.'

'I've seen her bruises.'

His brother's eyes narrowed. 'And where were those…bruises?'

Karl knew what he was implying. 'The servants believe that we married in secret. For her sake, I'd suggest you uphold the lie.'

Michael struggled to regain control of his temper. 'You took advantage of a princess, dishonouring her for your own use.'

'Yes.' He made no denial of what he'd done. 'And I won't walk away from her when she has to face her father.'

When she reached the house, Serena saw a stunningly beautiful dark-haired woman waiting. Dressed in an emerald gown trimmed with lace, the woman sent her a blinding smile.

'You must be Princess Serena.' The woman

dropped into a curtsy. 'I am Hannah Chesterfield. *Fürst* Michael is to be my husband in the next week.' With a soft laugh, she added, 'I imagine my mother is ready to send an army after me. I'm supposed to be worrying about fittings and wedding details at the moment.'

Serena returned the greeting, and Hannah continued a stream of cheerful conversation as she led her into the dining room. 'I hope you don't mind, but I've already arranged a meal for us,' the young woman said. 'I thought we could talk and get to know one another better. You *are* coming to the wedding, aren't you?'

Serena didn't know how to answer. 'I'm certain my father will go. I don't know if my sister and I will be permitted to attend.' It was as close to the truth as she could manage.

Hannah's smile turned forced. 'Oh. Well, I do hope you can.' She drew her inside the dining room and gestured for Serena to sit opposite her. 'There's so much I've been wanting to ask you.' Within moments, a servant brought in the first course, a lobster bisque with a dollop of cream floating in the centre. While the footman ladled out the soup, Hannah said, 'I've heard that you and Karl wed in secret.'

A pang of regret settled inside her, but Serena managed a nod. Though she hated lying to the prince's intended bride, neither could she admit that she'd lived alone with Karl for the past week. 'No one knew of our wedding,' she said.

Because it never happened.

Hannah studied her carefully, as if she were trying to read the truth. 'There's more to Karl than most people would see. He might appear arrogant and rude, but beneath it all, he's a good man. He saved my life once.'

Serena's eyes filled up with tears. It was true, and though she believed it was best for Karl to go on and leave her here to face her father alone, she knew it would never happen. He wasn't the sort of man to turn from a fight.

She left her soup spoon beside the bowl, unable to bring herself to eat. Inside, she felt sickened. Though her father's guard, Captain Feldmann, had disappeared, she knew what his presence meant. She had less than a day before her father arrived. Or, at least his men, if the king couldn't be bothered to come.

'You're crying,' Hannah said suddenly. 'Is everything all right?'

Serena could only shake her head. She folded her napkin and left the table, her stomach in knots. Hannah followed her, but Serena didn't want to reveal her problems to a stranger. It wasn't her way to confide secrets, and she took a moment, trying to gather her thoughts up.

'I'm sorry if I said anything to upset you,' Hannah said quietly. 'I made Michael bring me with him, because I thought you might want some female companionship. And perhaps we could…be friends.'

Serena swiped at her tears, trying to gather her composure.

'Would you like to spend some time together?' Hannah offered gently. 'Perhaps we could visit the village?'

The young woman meant well, and it might be a good chance for her to understand what had happened to Karl and the kingdom of Lohenberg. 'All right.'

Within the hour, both women were inside Frau Bauherzen's shop. Serena could tell from Hannah's strained expression that the fabric choices were nothing like she'd expected. Though the dressmaker was skilled enough with patterns and designs, most of the materials were little more than muslin and tarlatan. There was also black bombazine and a full array of mourning clothes.

Hannah came alongside her and said, 'It's not quite what I had imagined.'

'If you could arrange for fabric from Lohenberg to be sold here, it would help,' Serena suggested. 'The selection is quite limited.'

Hannah gave a nod. 'I'll mention it to Michael. Something should be done.' She moved in closer, lifting a length of white muslin. Lowering her voice to a whisper, she murmured, 'Am I correct in presuming that you and Karl did not wed one another, as the servants believe?'

Serena kept her gaze downcast, but gave a single nod. Inside, she felt such confusion. It was her fault that the servants believed the lie. Though it had given them a false air of respectability, she didn't know what to do about it now.

A gloved hand touched hers, and she saw Hannah's solemn expression. 'Do you love him?'

'I don't know,' was all she could whisper. How

was she to understand what love was? Everything about Karl confused her. He'd lost his kingdom, and though he'd wanted to regain it through a hasty marriage, the choice had always been hers. Not once had he forced her to bend to his will; he'd only coaxed her into feelings she didn't understand.

'If he were to leave you, and you'd never see him again, how would that make you feel?' Hannah asked.

Serena could give no answer, for it would be as if someone had cut her in half. She could only meet Hannah's gaze, letting her see the emptiness in her heart.

'Karl can't stay with me,' she said at last. 'If he remains here, my father will kill him for what he's done. He has to leave, but he won't.'

Hannah squeezed her hand. 'If you want to be with him, I'll do what I can to help you.'

'I don't know what he wants from me,' she whispered. 'Even if I did wed him, he could never be prince consort.'

Hannah pretended to study a length of lace. 'If he's still here, I don't think he cares about your throne any more, Princess Serena.'

Her face flushed at the thought, for she suspected it was true. Every time he'd kissed her, she'd fallen beneath the spell of temptation. But it bothered her that Karl seemed so detached, almost as if he didn't want to love her.

'I need him to be safe,' she said.

'I'll make sure of it.' Hannah set down the lace and regarded her. 'Although he is no longer heir to the throne of Lohenberg, he and Michael are still half brothers. And I owe Karl a favour, after what he did for me.'

The shopkeeper cleared her throat. '*Meine Damen,* is there anything I can help you with? Anything you would like to purchase…?' Her voice trailed off hopefully, and Serena glanced at Hannah.

Hannah intervened with excuses to leave and thanked the dressmaker. She took Serena's hand and let her outside. The footman Bernard was waiting, and he escorted them toward the waiting curricle. But before Serena could climb inside, she saw Captain Feldmann standing at the end of the street. He was waiting to speak with her.

'Bernard, I—need a moment,' she finished.

'Please take Lady Hannah back to the manor house.'

'My orders are to remain with you at all times, Your Highness,' the footman protested.

'Then wait for me here. I'll only be a moment.'

She walked along the side of the street until she reached Captain Feldmann. Her driver Samuel drew the curricle close, though he allowed her a little space for a private conversation. Bernard sat with Lady Hannah, a revolver in his hand.

'You know why I have come,' the captain said.

Serena's heartbeat quickened, and she glanced behind at Hannah and her footman. 'Is my father here?'

'They're a few hours behind me.' His expression turned grim. 'You've no choice but to return, Princess.'

She shook her head. 'I'm not going back to Badenstein. You know what it was like for me.'

The captain stared at her. '*Freiherr* Albert von Meinhardt imprisoned my wife and son after I let you go. If you don't return of your own free will, they'll suffer for it. And I won't let that happen.' His hand moved beneath his coat, revealing a concealed revolver.

A sinking feeling settled into her stomach. She could hardly believe that the *freiherr* would make such a vicious move, to capture an innocent woman and child. But it was clear that Captain Feldmann would do anything on their behalf.

'If you take me against my will, the *freiherr* still might keep them captive,' she warned.

'If you go back willingly, you might help them.' The desperation upon his face reminded her that it was her fault they'd been taken. She was torn on what to do, but the captain wasn't thinking clearly right now. He was thinking only of his family.

'Come with me,' he ordered, reaching for the weapon.

No. Although she sympathised with the man's plight, she wasn't going to go with him without a fight.

'Bernard!' she called out, as she gripped her skirts and fled toward the carriage.

The footman drew his weapon, aiming it at the captain. A second later, Karl emerged from the street, closing in behind Feldmann until he was surrounded on both sides.

'Leave the princess alone,' Karl demanded.

Captain Feldmann retreated. 'I came to warn

her, not to harm her. Her father's men will be here soon.'

Serena moved to stand behind Karl. 'I'm not going back to the palace, Captain Feldmann. But if you help us, I'll do everything I can to free your wife and son.'

The man didn't move, but his posture tensed. 'They're all I have.'

Serena touched Karl's shoulders, and murmured, 'Let him go.'

'He tried to take you against your will.' Karl's voice revealed his reluctance.

'He asked me to go with him,' Serena corrected. 'But he never laid a hand upon me.'

She needed an ally against her father's men. If the worst happened, Captain Feldmann was her best hope.

'Please,' she whispered, leaning in to his shoulder.

'Bernard, take his weapon,' Karl ordered. The captain stood still while the footman removed it from his coat.

Karl stepped back, keeping his arm across her as protection. Without another word, the guard disappeared into the streets. For a while, Serena worried that he might pursue the captain, but he remained in place.

When it appeared safe again, Karl signalled Samuel to bring the carriage forward. 'Is everything all right?' Lady Hannah asked, leaning forward anxiously.

Karl kissed her hand in greeting, and bid her welcome to the island. Though Serena knew it was a customary gesture, the flush on Hannah's face sent an unexpected jealousy flaring through her.

'I want you to return to the manor,' Karl ordered, motioning for Bernard to go with them. 'I'll bring Serena back with me.'

After the curricle was gone, Karl took Serena's hand and led her to his waiting horse. Her complexion was pale, as if a silent terror had numbed her mind and body. 'Are you certain you want to face your father? Or do you want to leave?'

'I'm going to stay.' She squared her shoulders, gripping her hands together. 'I have to confront him, but you cannot stay with me.'

'Try and stop me.' He lifted her onto his horse, swinging up behind. Her skin was cold, but she didn't move away when he brought his arms around her, to the reins.

'I don't want anything to happen to you,' she admitted, so softly he wondered if he'd heard her right. A strange tightness formed inside him, and it seemed impossible that she should care about him, not after everything he'd done.

'Don't waste a thought over me,' he said, guiding the horse along the water's edge. He urged the animal into a swift canter, holding Serena close.

'Where are we going?'

His answer was to draw the horse to a stop. 'Look there.'

In the distance, several ships emerged upon the horizon. He knew she was searching for her father and his men, and the worry on her face made him keep his silence. For a long time, they simply stood there, overlooking the sea. The sun had grown warm, and it glittered against the waves.

Karl caught her in his arms and held her tight. She smelled of flowers and sunlight, and he reassured her, 'I'll keep you safe. You have my vow.'

'And yourself,' she said. 'Promise me.'

He made no reply, but tilted her face up to kiss

her. The words she'd spoken earlier washed over him. *I don't want anything to happen to you.*

No one had ever said that to him before. Never had anyone cared about him, and when Serena kissed him back, he met her mouth, showing her without words what he felt. It didn't matter what happened to him now. All that mattered was protecting her. And he would…no matter what the cost to himself.

A heaviness settled over him, and he fought to keep his kiss gentle, not letting her see the apprehension he was hiding. When her arms came around his neck, she held him close. 'Everything would be different, if I weren't a princess,' she murmured.

'What do you mean?' He didn't let her go, but breathed in the scent of her hair, keeping her body pressed against his.

'I might have married you,' she said, lifting her face to his. 'If you were the sort of man who could love me.'

He framed her face, sliding his hands down to her shoulders. 'How much time do we have left?'

'Perhaps hours, if we're fortunate.'

He rested his hands at her waist. 'I arranged a

gift for you today,' he said. 'I suppose now would be the best time to give it to you.'

She studied him, but shook her head. 'I don't need any gifts, Karl.'

'This one is different. It may not be something you want, but…' he took her hand in his '…it may help you, once this is finished.'

'I don't understand.'

'Let me show you.'

Chapter Fifteen

'You're not going to drown me, are you?' Serena held on to the sides of the sailboat, while the wind battered her bonnet. The skies were grey, and the dark waters of the North Sea appeared more grim than inviting.

'I've sailed before, but it's been a few years.' He pulled at one of the ropes, adjusting the canvas sail and tying it off. 'If we do capsize, we'll die together.'

'That's not reassuring.' When another wave tossed the boat, she lurched forward, landing on her knees. 'Was this meant to be romantic?'

Karl reached out to help her up. 'The boat is yours. If it's your wish, I'll take you anywhere you want to go.'

He meant it. This was his way of offering to help her, if she no longer wished to face her father.

Deep inside, her heart softened at his gesture. 'I know this…journey of ours never turned out the way it should have,' she said. Sadness clung to her heart as she saw the stoic expression on his face. 'I want you to go back to Lohenberg. Create the life you were meant to have. Perhaps you could be an ambassador.' The role would suit him, for he could be the voice of the king better than anyone.

Karl edged his way closer and reached around her waist for another rope. 'That's not the life I want.'

His hazel eyes held a steadiness and a sudden flash of anger. 'There's something else I want now.' Within his expression, she saw a man who wasn't going to let her go. A man bent upon possessing her.

'What is it?'

His mouth came close, resting above hers. 'I want to watch you dancing in the rain until your gown is wet against your skin.' He kissed her throat, his hands sliding over her shoulders. 'I want to smash hazelnuts with rocks and hear your laughter.'

When his arms closed around her, Serena released the tears gathering. 'We had that, only a few days ago.'

His hand passed over her tears, wiping the dampness away, then kissing her cheeks. 'I want it back. And I want you to leave with me now.'

'I wish I could give you my kingdom,' she murmured, resting her head against his chest.

'I don't need it any more.'

Another gust of wind struck the boat, and Karl adjusted the sails, bringing them closer to the shoreline. Serena realised it was a more isolated part of the island, one she'd never seen before.

The bottom of the boat struck sand, and Karl disembarked, his legs sloshing through the frigid water. He hauled the vessel closer and lowered the sails, anchoring it. Grassy hills stretched from the sand, lined with occasional boulders of limestone. There were no houses or people, as far as she could see. They were alone here, and as he guided her up the hill, she revelled in the freedom.

'Norway lies over there,' he told her, pointing out toward the sea. 'Or Sweden, if you'd prefer it.'

Though she understood his offer to take her away was sincere, she couldn't accept it. 'He would only follow me there. I need to face him, Karl.'

'Then I'm not leaving your side.'

She stared at him, understanding that he would be caught up in her father's fury and suffer for it. Or there would be fighting between the Lohenberg guards and her father's soldiers. Her rebellion would cause men to be wounded or some might die.

She took a deep breath, knowing that the only way she could protect any of them was to surrender herself and go back to Badenstein. Her father's greatest weakness was his pride, and she could irrevocably damage it by publicly admitting her desire for freedom, abdicating the throne. The king would have no choice but to let her go, particularly if she threatened to expose his punishments and create a scandal.

She didn't doubt that he would strike her again. But she could endure the pain if it meant fighting for her freedom. And when she'd cut the ties to her country, she might find a way to be with Karl.

'Why did you bring me here?' she whispered.

'To give you a choice. I didn't want you to be taken against your will.'

He led her to sit down upon the hill, and he

joined her, staring out at the dark gray water. She untied her bonnet, setting it aside.

Today would be their last afternoon together for a long time. Perhaps forever, if her plan didn't work. The thought was like a jagged blade slicing her heart open, for Karl would always be the man who had shown her courage, who had taught her how to live without fear. She couldn't find the words to show him the way she felt. But before she ventured back into the lion's den, she wanted a precious memory for herself. Something that would let him know what he meant to her.

The sunlight spilled over the hills, warming her skin. One by one, Serena removed the pins in her hair, placing them inside the bonnet for safekeeping. Her hair slid over her shoulders, and Karl was watching her with unguarded need. As if he were savouring the very sight of her.

When she turned to him, she admitted, 'I wish I could have married you.'

'Then we'll do it now. Right here.'

Serena smiled at him, and he took her hands, staring into her eyes. 'I, Karl Ludwig Eduard von Lohenberg, take you—'

She saw the hooded desire in his face, and the

last barrier in her heart crumbled away. 'Serena Louisa Alexandra von Badenstein,' she finished.

'To be my wife.'

Tears filled up her eyes, but she repeated the vow of marriage. It wasn't legal, and there were no witnesses. In the eyes of the world, they weren't married.

But she understood the unspoken meaning behind his words. They were a promise, to love and protect her.

When Karl bent to kiss her, his mouth was warm, demanding her surrender as he took her lips with his. She returned the kiss, seeking the forbidden tremors that he evoked within her body. Every part of her opened to him, knowing that his touch would never seek to hurt her.

She guided his hands to the back of her gown, placing his fingers against the buttons. 'Help me with these, Karl.'

His mouth pressed to hers, his heated breath melting through her. 'You don't know what you're asking of me.'

'I'm asking you to love me. In this time we have left together.'

In his eyes, she saw the dark resolve and he

swore, 'This isn't finished between us, Serena. I'm not letting you go.'

She gave him no answer, distracting him with her kiss. She didn't care if she was throwing herself at him. This was their time together. A time when she would do as she wanted, not what she ought to do.

Her kiss provoked him, and when his tongue slid against hers, she opened to him. Serena felt the buttons falling away, revealing her chemise and corset. Karl broke away, his breathing deep, his eyes burning into hers.

Against her shoulders, she felt the heat of his hands. 'Don't stop,' she breathed. Beneath her fingertips, she could feel his pulse pounding. She sent him a tentative smile, so afraid he would turn her away. 'You're quite good at taking things apart. Perhaps you should try it out with me.'

Karl had never before seen a more beautiful female body. And it wasn't because Serena was perfect. Her breasts were full, her skin pale and smooth. But when she lay back upon the grass, she stole the breath from his lungs.

Though he'd once believed he couldn't live as a

common man, he could with her. If it meant waking up in her arms, watching her smile…he was willing to live in rags.

He understood that she was planning to face the wrath of her father. And despite her insistence that he leave her, there was nothing she could say to make him go. He would protect her, no matter what the risk.

'You're so quiet,' she said. 'Was I wrong in… asking this of you?'

He lay beside her, both of them resting upon a bed made of their clothing. Reaching out to her shoulder, he palmed the bare skin, moving down her arm to her hip. 'No.' He followed the path of his hand, moving his mouth over her skin. 'I'm taking the time to memorise you.'

The wind rippled through the grass, tightening her nipples. He saw the gooseflesh rising over her skin, and he tried to shield her body from the cool air. With her body beneath him, he could feel the softness of her curves, and he wanted her so badly, his hands were practically shaking.

'In my mind, I've been with you a thousand times.' He moved his mouth to the dip of her waist, his fingers spreading upward to caress her breasts.

'I've touched you everywhere. I've discovered your most secret places.' With that, he moved his hand between her legs, dipping his fingers against the cleft of her body. She gasped, her hands coming up to touch his shoulders.

To be with this woman, to take her body with his, was a gift he was almost afraid to accept. Though he wanted her badly, he didn't want to hurt her.

She never took her eyes from him, though her cheeks flushed at the sight of his nudity. He stroked her hip, moving down her thigh. He explored her body, searching for the places that would arouse her. With his mouth and hands, he tried to show her what she meant to him.

She shivered and he covered her body with his own, gently coaxing her legs open. It brought his shaft up against her silken hair, and the sensation made him want to open her, to slide deep within her body and find the fulfilment they both wanted.

'Don't be afraid,' he said, stealing a kiss from her.

'I know you won't hurt me,' she answered. Her trust made him all the more determined to bring her nothing but the deepest pleasure.

Serena's arms came around him, pressing her sweet breasts against him. When he lowered his mouth to taste her nipple, she trembled and opened her legs a little wider. As an experiment, he moved his erection against her centre, watching her response. Her fingers dug into his hair and she let out a soft moan.

'Do you think this is what our wedding night might have been like, if I'd married you a week ago?' she whispered, moving her hands down his back. The unexpected touch speared through him, making him want her more.

'No.' He moved to the side, facing her with a wicked smile. 'We would have been in a bed, instead of out in the open where anyone could see us.'

A flush came over her. 'Do you think anyone will?'

He stroked her stomach, down to the dark blond curls between her legs, and parted her thighs. 'I don't care if they do. They'll only see me pleasuring you.'

She closed her eyes at the touch of his hand, her breasts tightening. He felt the wetness of her desire against his fingers, and as he deepened the touch, caressing her intimately, her hands dug into his shoulders.

'Karl,' she murmured, her eyes opening. He slid a finger inside her, and her expression grew more intense. 'These days I spent with you… I'll never forget them. You made me happy.'

Her admission seemed to transform Karl from gentle into a man bent upon arousing her. The fierce need in his eyes only darkened as he stimulated her flesh. She could feel herself stretching, rising higher as her body responded to him. But she didn't want him to focus everything on her. Against her hip, she felt the rigid softness of his arousal.

She'd never touched a naked man before, but she wanted to know if she could awaken the same feelings inside him. Slowly, she reached for him, curling her hand around his shaft.

He inhaled, his hand stilling upon her. 'Serena—'

She dragged her hand over him, squeezing gently and found her own sense of power when he closed his eyes, drinking in her touch.

'Am I hurting you?'

'No, but you're making it difficult to think clearly.'

She pressed him back against the grass, marvelling at the strength of his body. Karl had lean, strong arms and a tapered waist. His powerful thighs were muscled from riding, and she sat against him, her hands over his chest. 'I want to touch you.'

He made no argument, as she lowered her mouth to his, kissing him while her palms moved across his body. There was a reddish scar from where the bullet had grazed him, days ago, and she avoided it so as not to hurt him. Lowering her mouth, she kissed his stomach, drawing closer to his manhood.

When she touched it again, his eyes closed, his hands clenching against the grass. She stroked the head of him, sliding down his shaft while he grasped her hips.

He guided her up, her knees around his waist, until his thickness was poised at her entrance. With his fingers, he teased her, dipping against her wetness until she started to move her own hand upon him. He guided her, showing her how to stroke him in a rhythm while he pressed against her body. The erotic sensations started to clench within her, and when he raised up to take her breast in his mouth, the blunt head of his shaft hovered at her entrance.

She felt him slide inside an inch, and she held steady, watching him. Karl didn't move, waiting for her response. Carefully, she withdrew, and then sank against him a little more. It was tight, but her body welcomed the feel of him. The thickness stretched her, but it was an arousal that touched her deep inside.

Karl brought his hands up to touch her hooded flesh while he held steady inside her. 'Wait,' he breathed, keeping her poised with only the head of him inside her. He stroked her intimately, while his tongue laved the tight nipple. Serena felt her body growing languid, the arousal penetrating deeper. His rhythmic caresses started to take hold of her, and she began trembling as he rubbed her flesh. The motion pulled him deeper inside, and she gasped as the tightness seared through her, sheathing him fully.

'Don't move,' he warned, rolling her to her back and easing back. 'I want this to be better for you.'

He continued the rhythmic circular motion, and

she pulled back, arching hard as the sensations deepened. 'Karl,' she breathed, not understanding what he was doing. But he held back, tormenting her, until she instinctively moved against him, forcing him to penetrate her in shallow thrusts.

'Look at me,' he ordered, and she forced herself to open her eyes. He stared at her, and said, 'You're the best thing that ever happened to me, Serena. Worth more than any kingdom on this earth.'

A dark, punishing heat kept driving her harder, and she couldn't control her breathing from coming in quick gasps. He lifted her hips, suckling against her aroused nipples while his hand worked her below. She cried out, pushing back against him, but he kept up the rhythm until his caress exploded through her in a pulsing storm of release. The pleasure tore through her as he penetrated her fully, her body clenching his silken shaft.

As he entered and withdrew, she held him close, feeling him fill up her heart as well as her body. She'd fallen in love with Karl, and it made her all the more determined to keep him safe.

With their bodies joined, he pushed her past the brink once more, until she gasped with the pleasure of it. She revelled in the broken wildness of him as he thrust against her and at last surrendered to his own desire. He lay on top of her, their bodies damp with perspiration.

He held her tightly, his mouth against her ear. 'I'll not let them take you away,' he swore. 'No matter what happens.'

She didn't let him see the tears forming inside her. For if anything happened to him, she couldn't forgive herself.

When they arrived back at the manor house, Karl kept Serena's hand in his. Within moments, dozens of soldiers emerged from the surrounding hills, riding toward the house.

He stopped walking, his hand tightening around hers. He saw the masked fear upon her face, and although she'd pinned her hair back beneath her bonnet, her face remained flushed from their lovemaking.

Serena gripped his hand and took a breath. 'I'm going to speak to my father, if he's here.' Her face was unnaturally pale, her eyes troubled.

A bad feeling snaked into his gut. He didn't know what she intended to do, but he was going to remain at her side, no matter what. 'Don't make a choice you're going to regret.' He leaned in and kissed her softly, trying to remind her of what there was between them.

Although she kissed him back, he sensed surrender in her demeanour. 'My choice has nothing to do with what I want. Only what I have to do.'

'Fight for the life you want,' he urged. 'And I'll fight with you.'

She sent him a sad smile. 'I am fighting. But in my own way.'

From the misery in her eyes, he knew exactly what she was planning. 'You can't return with him. He'll only hurt you.'

'Sometimes defeating your enemy means walking into the fire.' She touched his cheek, and he lowered his forehead to hers. 'I'm going to publicly announce my abdication. If the entire kingdom knows my wishes, he'll have no choice but to let me go.'

'Do you think I'd let you put yourself in danger like that?' His hands moved down to caress the pulse at her throat. 'He tried to strangle you.'

Serena took his hands in hers, looking steadily into his eyes. 'I won't let myself be afraid of him any more. If you care for me at all, you'll trust me to slay my own dragons.' With one last kiss, she pleaded, 'Stay away. And I'll come to Lohenberg, as soon as I can.'

She stepped out of his arms and continued walking toward the house. Did she believe he would stand by and let her leave? That he would act like a coward and let her return to a king who had broken her ribs and nearly killed her?

Clearly, she didn't know him at all.

Chapter Sixteen

The king was already inside the manor house, and *Fürst* Michael and his fiancée Lady Hannah were entertaining him in the parlour. A sick feeling rose up inside Serena at the sight of her father, but she quelled it. If she remained polite and obedient, it might not go too badly. Against the far wall, she spied Captain Feldmann. The look on the man's face held dissatisfaction, as if he hadn't wanted to perform this duty.

As soon as he caught sight of Serena, the king rose to his feet and opened his arms. 'My daughter, I am glad to see you are safe and unharmed.'

She went into the embrace, playing the role he wanted before the prince of Lohenberg. But as his arms came around her, his fingers dug into her shoulders in a tight warning to say nothing.

Even so, she met the stare of *Fürst* Michael,

whose face was grim. His gaze drifted toward the door, and Serena discreetly shook her head. So long as Karl remained absent, she might be able to leave without her father being the wiser.

The king released her from his false embrace and took her left wrist in his hand. 'I've ordered your belongings packed and placed within my coach. We will travel together back to Badenstein.'

'Yes, Father,' she said, feeling the uncomfortable grip of his hand. For the benefit of the *fürst* and Lady Hannah, she added, 'I didn't expect you to come all this way from Sardinia. I meant to return home in another day or so.' His fingers curled so harshly around her wrist, she knew the skin would bruise within minutes.

'You should come to Lohenberg instead of returning to Badenstein,' Michael offered. 'Our wedding will take place next week, and it would be a great disappointment if you did not attend. We would like to offer your family the hospitality of the palace for the next few days.'

The *fürst*'s suggestion was an offer of sanctuary that gave her hope. 'How very kind of you.' She ventured a smile, but her father's expression remained angry.

'That won't be necessary.' He motioned for his servants to move toward the door. 'After what happened with the former prince, you must understand why my daughter cannot show her face in Lohenberg. She was ruined by your brother, and amends must be made.'

'They could still marry,' the *fürst* suggested. 'Karl has been granted an honorary title and estates by our father. He will be an advisor to both myself and the king.'

Her father didn't smile. 'A marriage between my daughter and Karl would be inappropriate. I will send emissaries to Lohenberg with my instructions regarding compensation for the abduction of my daughter.'

'I wasn't abducted,' Serena insisted, but her father's eyes darkened in a warning to remain silent.

The king ignored her words. 'I've arranged for another betrothal between the princess and *Freiherr* Albert von Meinhardt. Given her…conduct with the former prince of Lohenberg, an immediate wedding will be necessary to quiet the gossip.' He offered an apologetic smile to the *fürst,* but Serena didn't miss the threat beneath it. 'I presume I can rely upon you to handle the dissolution of her former betrothal with discretion. Unless you believe it necessary that we bring formal charges against your brother.'

Fürst Michael simply stared at the king and spoke not a word. Inside, Serena was so very cold, she could hardly breathe. Her corset was laced tightly, and she felt dizziness hovering on the edges of her consciousness. Another marriage, so soon?

It shouldn't have surprised her. No doubt this had been the *freiherr*'s proposition, as soon as he'd gotten word of Karl's illegitimacy. Serena disliked the older man, who was little more than her father's pawn. She supposed the man was trying to ingratiate himself with the king.

With a slight push toward her ladies, her father bade Serena, 'Prepare yourself for the journey.'

Lady Hannah tried to follow, but Serena shook her head. She couldn't bear the kindness right now, or she would burst into tears. If she was with strangers and other servants, she could hold her fragile feelings together.

As the ladies dressed her in a travelling gown, Serena couldn't stop thinking of the afternoon she'd spent in Karl's arms. The merest brush of fabric against her sensitive skin evoked memories of his body upon hers.

Don't think of it, she warned herself. Otherwise she would start crying and never stop. She didn't regret making love with him for a single moment. The intimacy they'd shared was something she would bind up inside her heart, holding it close.

'Are you ready, Your Highness?' one of the women asked, and Serena nodded her agreement. Though it was growing dark, she understood that her father would waste no more time in bringing her home.

One of the ladies picked up the blue gown and asked, 'Shall I pack this in the last trunk?'

Serena nodded. Although the gown had grass stains upon it, she didn't care. It was something she would keep for always.

Her mind blurred when they went downstairs and she said her goodbyes to the *fürst* and Lady Hannah. 'I'll write to you,' Serena told her. 'And perhaps we'll see each other soon.'

Lady Hannah exchanged a look with Michael. 'You are always welcome.'

'Take her to the coach,' her father ordered. Captain Feldmann moved behind her, while three foot-man escorted her outside.

Serena took a moment to look around the is-land, casting a longing look toward the shoreline. Though it felt as if she were surrendering to her father, it wasn't that at all. Until she returned to the palace, she had to feign obedience. She'd made many mistakes, but it was time to mend those she could. And that meant weathering the storm that lay ahead.

When she stared out at the horses and coaches, she caught a glimpse of movement near the back of the garden wall. Karl stood there, staring at her. The fierce look on his face spoke of a man who had no intention of remaining in the shadows.

Her courage faltered, and she sent him a silent plea not to interfere. She could endure her father's disapproval and whatever lay ahead, so long as she knew Karl was safe.

'You Highness?' the footman prompted, and she forced her gaze back to the coach. She walked away, trying not to steal another glimpse of Karl.

After the footmen opened the door to the wait-ing coach and helped her inside, Serena rested her head against the small window, steeling her courage. She didn't believe that Karl would stay hidden, and it worried her, not knowing what he would do. She'd almost believed she'd find him hidden inside the coach, just as he'd done when he took her from the palace.

She closed her eyes, taking a breath for the strength she needed. Though she didn't know how long it would take her to break free from Badenstein, she promised herself that she would do everything possible to manage it.

Within a few minutes more, the door opened to the coach, and the footman helped her father inside. As soon as the king settled across from her, his clenched fist shot toward her. Serena tried to avoid the blow, but pain exploded in her face. With both hands, she tried to shield herself.

'Stupid girl,' he growled. 'Did you believe you could run away with your lover and not get caught?'

She said nothing, but neither did she look at him. Instead, she kept her arms over her face, shaken that he'd caught her unaware. The horses began to pull the coach forward, and though her father was cursing and blustering about all the reasons why she'd drawn shame upon herself, she ignored him, letting his words flow over her like meaningless air.

Within another minute, the coach lurched and swayed. A heavy cracking noise resounded, and Serena reached for the door, just as it flew open.

Karl moved inside and pointed a loaded revolver at her father. 'Get out of the coach, Serena.'

'What are you doing?' she whispered, stunned that he would attempt such a thing.

His strong arm encircled her waist while he pulled her free from the coach. 'Kidnapping you again.' Karl set her down, and Serena was shocked to realise that he'd dismantled the wheels. The entire front of the coach was resting on the ground, while the back end was elevated.

When he saw the reddened mark on her cheek from where the king had struck her, his anger turned thunderous. 'You aren't going to take her back,' he informed the king. 'After what you've done to her, I wouldn't mind pulling this trigger.'

Whether or not Karl knew it, the king's men were already encircling them.

She closed her eyes, knowing he'd just sentenced himself to death. Karl couldn't possibly outrun or fight the three dozen guards her father had brought with him. And an ember of fury smoldered inside of her.

Didn't he understand that she'd been trying to save him? The tears broke free, for he'd ruined everything. 'Why would you do this?' she choked out, as he backed away from the coach, holding her hand.

'Because you wanted me,' he said against her ear. 'When no one else did. My family didn't give a damn what happened to me when they learned who I really was. But you were willing to sacrifice yourself for me.'

His hand came up to her cheek, touching the tears away. 'Me. A bastard unworthy of the ground you walk on.'

She saw the guards closing in, and he murmured, 'My horse is waiting by the back garden. If you run, right now, I'll hold them off. Bernard can take you in the boat, away from the island.'

'You'll die,' she whispered, and the burning anger kindled higher. She was seething with it, barely containing her temper.

'It doesn't matter,' he said quietly. 'Not if you're safe.'

'Stop it. Just stop it!' Her voice rose higher, and she seized the revolver from his hand. It was heavy, but the weight of her rage spurred her on. 'Does no one here believe I have the ability to think for myself?' She cocked the weapon and aimed it at the guards. 'My own father believes I'm nothing but a helpless pawn, to be used as he sees fit. And you—' She whirled, the revolver still in her hand. 'You don't trust me to solve my own problems.'

He raised his hands, wary of her weapon. 'I was trying to save you.'

'Perhaps I don't need saving!' she cried out. 'Did you ever think that I wanted to face him on my own? That I needed to drive out my own demons?'

She could hardly see through her own tears, but she pointed the gun toward the guards. 'I'm in love with you, Karl. And I will not stand by and let you die. I won't do it.'

The stricken look on his face spoke of a man who couldn't believe what he'd heard. She gathered what was left of her composure and ordered, 'You're going to leave me now and return to the house with your brother.' To the soldiers, she demanded, 'And you are going to let him go.'

'Arrest him,' the king commanded. 'Former Lohenberg prince or not, he'll face charges for what he's done.'

Serena gestured with the gun, toward the Lohenberg guards who were arriving with *Fürst* Michael as their leader. 'You'll not raise a hand against him.'

She returned the revolver to Karl, and whispered, 'The days we spent together were among the happiest I ever had. If you love me at all, you'll save your own life so that I may come back to you one day.'

'Don't go with him, Serena,' Karl warned. 'If you leave, he'll never let you go.'

'It's my choice to make,' she said, taking his hand. 'Unless I stay, these men will suffer for my actions. And so will you.' She studied her father's guards and saw the loyalty in their eyes. As she'd hoped, they stepped aside, giving Karl a clear pathway to join his brother. If he took this chance, she could save him.

'Please go,' she whispered, before she left him standing there.

After the princess had departed in a separate coach from her father, Karl turned to face Captain Feldmann. 'I'm not leaving her,' he said.

The man shook his head. 'You don't understand

how much power the king holds. Your life isn't safe if you come to Badenstein.'

Karl stared at the guards. 'You stood back and allowed the king to beat his own daughter. You, who were sworn to protect her.'

'There was nothing we could do,' the captain answered. He ordered his men to follow the king's entourage and cast a final look at Karl. 'The princess wanted you to leave the island. I would suggest that you follow her wishes and return to Lohenberg.'

His brother Michael rode closer, keeping his own guards near. 'Let them go, Karl. I'll talk to our father and see what can be done.'

Karl mounted one of the remaining horses. 'Talking won't save her from the king's fists. I'm going after her.'

Michael urged his horse forward and moved beside him. 'You're not alone in this, Karl. Let us help you.'

His brother's words were an offering he'd never expected. And although Karl held little faith that *König* Sweyn would lift a finger to help him, he understood that his brother was trying to make amends for what had happened.

'Try, then. But know that I'm going to steal the princess away from Badenstein. Or die in the effort.'

After travelling through the night without stopping, Serena arrived back at the palace, feeling broken apart. Her ladies brought her back to her room, and she knew that, come the morning, her father would not hesitate to punish her. She'd humiliated him before his men, and at gunpoint, no less.

She was beginning to wish she'd kept the revolver.

'Is my mother asleep?' she asked her lady-in-waiting Katarina.

'Yes, Your Highness. Shall I awaken her? She'll want to see you.'

'No, it can wait until the morning.' Her mother was ill, and Serena wanted nothing to interrupt her sleep. 'What about my sister?'

'Princess Anna asked me to inform her as soon as you arrived.'

Serena nodded her permission and sat before her dressing table while one of her ladies brushed her hair. Another helped her to undress, and when she was in her nightgown, Anna burst in.

'I can't believe what happened. Oh, Serena.' Anna flung her arms around her, and Serena nodded for her ladies to leave them alone. 'Are you all right? Was it as terrible as I imagine it was?'

Her emotions swelled up inside her, but Serena managed to keep herself from weeping. 'The *fürst* of Lohenberg escorted me. He said you sent him a letter.'

Anna drew back. 'Are you angry with me? I was afraid that you'd be ruined if you went alone.'

'I was angry at the time.'

But I fell in love with him. I spent yesterday in his arms, and I miss him already.

'I heard the news,' Anna said, taking Serena's hands in hers. 'That he was illegitimate. I'm so sorry for putting you in such a position. Father sent word to the king of Lohenberg and severed your betrothal.'

She nodded, her throat growing constricted. 'He told me.'

Anna squeezed her hands. 'Was he…very angry?' The fearful tone in her voice made her suspect that her sister knew more about Serena's beatings than she'd let on.

'He was. But it wasn't too bad,' she admitted.

Anna's shoulders lowered in relief. She embraced Serena and said, 'I'm so glad you're all right.' Her sister sat down in another chair and admitted, 'I sent the prince to you, because I thought he could protect you.'

At the mention of Karl, Serena tensed, praying that he had gone back with his brother. Although she'd seen *Fürst* Michael there with his men, there was no guarantee that Karl had obeyed.

I'm not the obedient sort, he'd told her.

But she needed him to live. She would fight her way free of Badenstein and do everything within her power to go back to him. They could live quietly together, in a house overlooking the sea.

'Did you hear what I said?' Anna repeated.

Serena frowned and shook her head. 'I'm sorry. I was woolgathering.'

'You're to marry *Freiherr* von Meinhardt in three days,' Anna told her. 'Father has already arranged it.'

'So soon?' was all she could say. It didn't matter.

She wasn't about to wed the *freiherr,* and nothing could convince her to say yes.

'It's late,' she told her sister. 'We should get some sleep.'

Anna smiled and embraced her again. 'I'm so glad you're home, Serena. I've missed you.'

After her sister left, Serena climbed into bed, her thoughts in turmoil. Had Captain Feldmann released Karl? Was he safe on Vertraumen? She closed her eyes tightly, trying hard not to think of the days ahead.

Humility had never transformed her father's mood, nor had it protected her from his violent moods. There was little point in trying to be the good daughter, for it had brought her nothing but bruises and heartache.

She refused to think about the morning ahead, focusing her mind upon the time she'd spent in Karl's arms. Never would she forget a moment of it. Her tears dampened her pillow, and it hurt so badly to know that she could never be with him.

In the darkness, she heard her door open. 'Who's there?' she asked, expecting to hear Katarina's voice.

'Who do you think?' came Karl's answer.

Chapter Seventeen

He moved across the room and found her sitting up in bed. Though her face was shadowed, he could hear her hushed breathing.

'What are you doing here? You were supposed to stay on the island,' she whispered fiercely.

'Then who would protect you?' He moved in and rested both hands on either side of her body. The clean scent of her skin held a hint of crushed grass, reminding him of the afternoon they'd spent together. He wanted to lie in her arms this night, no matter what the danger was.

Captain Feldmann had led him to Serena's room, but all else was up to him. If he were caught, Karl knew that there was no escaping the retribution. He didn't care.

Serena had given herself to him, allowing him to love her. No woman had ever wanted him, save this one. He'd walk through a storm of bullets if it meant being with her.

'Did you think I would give up on you that easily?'

'Someone could come in at any time. It's not safe for you here.'

He knew it. But the rush of danger only made him more intent upon seeing her. 'I locked the door when I came in.'

She tried to protest again, but he covered her mouth with his, cutting off her arguments with a kiss. 'I know you don't want me here. But I won't allow him to hurt you again. I'll be damned if I stand by and let it happen.'

'Instead, you'll risk being caught?' Dismay and worry mingled in her voice, even as she pulled him into an embrace.

'You're worth any risk, Serena.' She let out a soft gasp when he lowered his mouth to the soft place between her nape and shoulder. Gooseflesh broke over her, and he grew aware that she was only wearing a thin nightdress. He tasted the pulse of her heartbeat, and promised, 'I'll take you away and no one will see us.'

'And we'll be caught before we even get to the

end of the hall,' she said. 'They'll take you below and lock you away. My father will condemn you to death, no matter what your family might do to interfere.' Her voice quavered, and she insisted, 'You have to go. Let me make my own escape.'

He leaned in and pressed her back against the pillow. 'Don't ask me to abandon you.'

'The way your family did?' she whispered. 'Is that what this is about?'

For a moment, he rested with his face against her hair. She held him close, winding both arms around his neck, and he gripped her hard.

A tightness rose up within him, for how could she ever understand? When she'd admitted that she loved him, it was as if the earth had cracked beneath his feet. If something happened to her, he might as well be dead.

'You're all I have left to fight for, Serena. I don't belong anywhere anymore. Not in Lohenberg. Not here.'

'You belong with me,' she said. 'Just as I belong with you.'

Before he could speak, her hands were moving over him, loosening his shirt. When her palms touched his bare chest, he couldn't stop the crashing wave of desire that started to push away common sense.

'There isn't time for this, Serena,' he protested.

They needed to get away now, while most of the castle was abed. But when she took his hands and moved them beneath her nightgown, to her bare breasts, his mind went blank. She wrapped her legs around his waist, pulling him so close, he lost himself to her.

'Touch me,' she pleaded. 'Let me remember what it was like.'

His brain reminded him that this was foolish, that she ought to be getting dressed and fleeing with him while they could. But he wanted her as badly as she wanted him.

He kissed her, their mouths mingling with heat and the forbidden fear of discovery. His hands moved over her skin, caressing her. Against his better judgement, he raised the hem of her nightgown and exposed her to the waist. Between her legs, he found her wet and swollen.

'Please, Karl,' she begged.

He shut his eyes tightly, trying to gather the control he didn't have. But she moved her hands to his trousers, unfastening the buttons. When her hand moved over his erection, he reached in to touch her womanhood, finding the place of her own arousal.

Knowing that anyone could walk in on them at any time seemed to drive his arousal even harder. But he wanted to make this moment good for her. With his thumb, he pressed against the area of her pleasure, slowly circling as he coaxed her to welcome his intrusion. He kissed her hard, and against her mouth, he demanded, 'I'm not letting you go, Serena. You belong to me, and our kingdoms can go up in flames for all I care.'

Serena took him in her palm, guiding him to her slick entrance. Her breath caught when he settled at her entrance, gently probing.

He bit hard against his lip, tasting blood as he fought to keep from plunging deep inside.

He entered her slowly, feeling her wetness sheathe every inch of his shaft. Lowering his mouth to the curve of her breast, he penetrated until he could go no farther. He held steady, not moving as he raised himself up above her.

'I want every night with you. Every morning.' He began to move, punctuating his words with the rhythm of his thrusts. She arched her back, pressing deeply against him. He could feel her body squeezing his manhood as he entered her. When he increased the tempo, she lost every inhibition, her body trembling as she climbed closer to her release.

Serena was achingly close to her climax, and her nails dug into his back. 'I won't let you die, Karl. I promise I'll come to you. But you have to leave.' She was half sobbing, when he covered her nipple with his mouth, sucking hard while his hand stroked the other breast. 'I love you.'

Karl closed his eyes, never ceasing his rhythmic penetrations. It didn't seem possible that anyone could love him, but he needed her. More than anything else.

He held her close as he continued pumping into her, until she shuddered in her climax. As she came apart, he groaned, releasing his seed inside her.

He lay atop her, still mostly clothed, his body damp with perspiration. She lay motionless, not looking at him. Karl adjusted his clothing, fastening his trousers and turning her over. 'We need to leave, Serena.'

She stood and took him by the hand. With slow steps, she walked with him to the door.

'Do you need help getting dressed?' he asked.

She shook her head. 'I can't go with you at this moment. It would attract too much attention. Let me meet you just before dawn. Wait for me beyond the gates where you first kidnapped me.'

Her voice held an emptiness, as if she were trying to make him leave her behind. He drew her into his arms, holding her close. 'Don't surrender, Serena. Fight for what you want.' His hands threaded through her hair, and he felt the dampness of her tears against his shoulder.

She gripped him hard and whispered, 'I'll come…as soon as I can.'

He didn't believe her. The bleakness in her face held the shadow of tears. 'If you don't, I'll come after you. I swear it on my life.'

At first light, Serena went to visit her mother. Queen Clara looked slightly better than the last time she'd seen her. There was colour in her face, and she was seated in a chair instead of resting in bed. The silvery gown she wore accentuated

Clara's light brown hair, and a light filled up her smile when she laid eyes on Serena.

'I've missed you, *liebe Mutter*,' Serena said, kneeling at her mother's feet and embracing her.

Frail arms came around her shoulders, and Clara touched her cheek. 'I understand you were kidnapped by a prince.'

Serena nodded. 'Anna sent him to protect me, believing that it would save my reputation if anyone learned I was travelling alone. But things… turned out differently.'

Her mother reached out and took her hand. 'You have feelings for this man, don't you?'

Though Serena lowered her head in a *yes,* there were no words she could express. She loved Karl enough that she had to protect him from her father's wrath.

Last night, when he'd come to her room, she'd been both elated and terrified that he was here. Though she'd wanted nothing more than to flee, she knew that *Freiherr* Albert von Meinhardt had positioned two dozen guards all around the palace—men loyal to her father. She didn't know how Karl had managed to get inside her room without being seen, but she knew it was impossible for her to escape a second time. Not without leading him into danger.

Better to love him while he was still alive than to bring about his death from her own selfish wishes.

Clara patted her shoulder. 'I am sorry that you cannot marry him any longer.' Her mouth drew into a taut line. 'But I understand you are to wed *Freiherr* Meinhardt in two days.'

'I won't wed him,' Serena said. She told her mother of the *freiherr*'s decision to imprison Captain Feldmann's wife and child. 'Not a man who would stoop so low.'

Her mother looked aghast. 'What will you do?'

'I'm going to abdicate my throne to Anna.' A quiet resignation filled her up inside, and she felt at peace with the decision. Running away would not solve anything. If she was to live her life as a commoner, she didn't want to be constantly looking over her shoulder for soldiers. She wanted to be free.

And that meant facing the king's fury.

'Serena,' her mother continued, 'your father has ordered you to meet with him, once we've finished talking. Shall I come with you?'

'It would be better if you remained here,' she answered, knowing that her mother was not strong enough to defend her. 'I will face him alone.'

And I won't cower before him, she promised herself. Though she didn't believe that the king would let her go, she was ready to face the worst of his temper. She had her own reason to fight, a reason that was waiting for her beyond the gates.

She rose from her mother's side and nodded to her ladies. 'I will see my father now.'

As they walked down the hallway, Katarina came to her side and offered her hand. Serena took it, and though she wore gloves, her fingers were icy cold.

When they reached the door to her father's study, Serena tried to reach inside for the courage she lacked. She needed to be brave. No matter what happened now, she'd done everything she could to protect Karl.

Her lady-in-waiting curtsied and went to announce her presence to the king.

'Enter,' came her father's voice. Standing to the left of the king was Albert von Meinhardt. The smug look on the *freiherr*'s face left her cold, but she kept her expression neutral.

For a long moment, the king said nothing. He

settled a stack of papers upon his desk and stood. Serena held her ground, but her eyes swept over the room. There was a tea tray resting upon a table, with a single cup and saucer waiting. A small *chaise longue* with a square pillow was nearby, and a low fire burned on the hearth.

'I have made arrangements for your wedding to the *freiherr*,' her father began. 'Though it may not silence the gossip, it is—'

'No,' Serena interrupted. 'I won't marry him.' She sent a pointed look toward the Baron, letting him see her disapproval of what he'd done to bring her back.

The look of rage on her father's face made him rise from his seat. Serena seized the pillow from the *chaise longue* and held it with both arms, in readiness to shield herself.

'I'm giving up my throne,' Serena continued, her hands digging into the pillow. 'And I will leave the palace this day. You will not send any men after me. You are going to let me go.'

'How do you dare to give me orders?' The king advanced upon her, ordering the *freiherr* to leave the room. Von Meinhardt didn't bother trying to defend her, but abandoned her to the king's anger.

Serena backed away, trying to move closer to the door. 'It's clear to me that you hate the very ground I walk upon. I was never the daughter you wanted, and yet, you punished me at every turn. I won't be your victim any longer.'

Though his fists were clenched in readiness to strike her, he didn't. Instead, his voice thickened with venom. 'You aren't worthy to hold a throne. But I won't allow you to cast a scandal over my rule.'

'I'll go quietly,' she said. 'Make Anna your heir.'

'Anna was always going to be my heir,' he countered. 'Not you. Why would I want a bastard daughter to rule over Badenstein?'

The pillow dropped from her hands as his revelation sank in. Was that why he hated her so? Because she wasn't his daughter?

'A bastard?' she repeated, hardly daring to hope it was true. 'What do you mean?'

'I learned of your mother's affair several years ago.' He continued speaking of Clara's indiscretion, but Serena could only feel a widening sense of joy. If the king was not her father, then it made sense why he hated her so. And why he hadn't begun beating her until a few years ago.

'I am glad to hear it,' Serena heard herself saying. 'I would rather have any other father in the world than you.'

His hand raised out to strike her, and the motion blurred. She reached for the tea tray to shield herself from his blow. China shattered, and she was dimly aware of the door slamming against the wall as it flew open.

Karl tore into the room, his hands encircling the king's throat. He sent a look toward Serena. 'You didn't arrive when you were supposed to.'

To King Ruwald he ordered, 'You're going to let her go. She won't endure your abuse any longer.'

But Ruwald suddenly broke free of Karl's grasp and lunged forward. The two men fought, and Serena searched for some way to help him. Before she could do anything, the *freiherr* returned with seven guards. Although Karl struggled hard, the men overpowered him.

'Take him below,' the king ordered. 'I want him in chains.' His reddened face turned murderous as he stared at Serena. 'And as for you…you'll wed von Meinhardt without argument or question. Or I'll have your lover hanged before your eyes.'

She couldn't breathe. As the men dragged Karl

away, she sank to the floor, unable to fill her lungs. Darkness clouded at her consciousness, and when her father left the room, a searing pain ripped her heart in half.

Even though the king hadn't laid a hand upon her.

That night, Serena was resting when the door opened. Queen Clara appeared, surrounded by her own ladies.

'My sweet girl, what has he done?' Clara struggled to walk closer and sat upon the bed, touching Serena's face.

'Is it true?' Her voice cracked as she struggled with the words. 'He said I'm not his daughter. That I am…a bastard.'

Her mother let out a slow breath. 'It's true that I took a lover when he was away, many years ago. I suppose it's no secret that our arranged marriage was not a happy one.'

Her hand stilled upon Serena's shoulder. 'But your blood is royal. Make no mistake of it.'

'Then who is my father?'

The queen's eyes closed. 'Ruwald is still your

father. I was already carrying you inside of me when I took a lover.'

The brutal knowledge cracked apart her feelings, and she wept with her head in her mother's lap. 'I wanted to believe that there was someone else. That I had another father somewhere.'

The queen shook her head. 'Whatever he believes, you are his eldest child. Both of you are legitimate.'

It seemed brutally unfair that she had become her father's victim, because of his false beliefs. The injustice of her suffering made her anger rise higher. She'd done nothing wrong, all her life. And yet, he'd crippled her with fear for so many years.

'I don't want to be his daughter,' she cried. 'I wanted to leave here as a commoner. I wanted to marry Karl. And now, the king has taken him prisoner.' She couldn't bear to call him her father any more.

Clara's lips formed a line, her expression showing dismay. Smoothing a lock of hair, she added, 'I'm sorry for what you've suffered.' Her mother leaned heavily against the bedpost as she stood up. 'No matter what anyone tells you, you have a blood-given right to this throne. Whether your father wishes to believe the truth or not.'

'I don't want it,' she admitted. 'And I'm tired of him trying to control my life.' She felt as if the palace walls were closing in on her, forcing her to wed a man she didn't want, in order to save Karl.

'What can I do?' she asked her mother. 'I won't stand for this.'

The queen held out her hand. 'Do you know, you're one of the few people who still asks for my advice? Most believe that because I am ill, I'm powerless.' She sent her a quiet smile. 'But sometimes appearances can be deceptive. And therein lies a different sort of power.'

Serena sat beside her mother. 'I'm listening.'

The prison walls were cold and damp. Though Karl had tried every means of finding a way out, there was no way to remove the chains without ripping them free of the stone walls.

He was going out of his mind. The captain of the guard, Gerlach Feldmann, had informed him that the princess was going to marry the *Freiherr* von Meinhardt tomorrow afternoon. If she refused, the king would order Karl put to death.

He wanted to believe that she wouldn't do it. That she would tell the king to go to hell, and take the freedom she deserved. If they killed him, what did it matter? Without her, his life wasn't worth much anyway.

Footsteps caught his attention, and he called, 'Who's there?' The sound drew closer, until it stopped before the door of his prison. A hand entered the small space, and he sensed Serena's presence before she spoke. 'It's me.'

Hope poured through him, that she'd come to set him free. Karl took her hand, thanking God that she'd come. 'Are you all right?'

'Yes.' He heard the hesitation in her voice, the tone that something wasn't right.

'Open the door, Serena.'

'I can't. That's not why I'm here.'

He rested his cheek against the thick door, and though she held his hand, he already sensed what she was about to say.

'This isn't goodbye,' he told her. 'You're not going to stand on the other side of that door and tell me you're going to wed another man to save my life.'

'Karl, you don't understand.'

He let go of her hand, curling his fist. 'I understand perfectly.' He wanted to smash his hand through the door, demanding that she stay with him.

'How long did it take you to give up? An hour? Did the king break another rib until you agreed to do as he commanded, while I sat down here in this rotting hole?'

It sickened him, to think of her surrendering. He'd done everything he could, but it wasn't enough. She was going to leave him, and when she'd gone off with the Baron, he'd be left to imagine her lying in another man's bed.

'I didn't give up,' she said quietly. 'But I can see that you're in no mood to listen.'

No. No, he wasn't. His mind was filled up with visions that he couldn't bear to imagine.

'Set me free, Serena. If you truly want to fight for us, get me out of these chains.'

She remained silent. He reached out through the small rectangular opening in the door, hoping to feel her hand in his.

Instead, he heard her footsteps disappearing. He kept his hand outstretched, hoping she would return. At last, he drew it back in, and sat down upon the floor with his back to the wall.

What did you expect? his mind taunted.

Chapter Eighteen

On the day of her wedding, the sun was shining, and it was a warm spring afternoon. Serena's father had arranged for the ceremony to be held within the family chapel, with only the immediate family present, along with a few witnesses. The *Freiherr* von Meinhardt would be waiting for her at the altar, while the bishop gave the wedding Mass.

Serena wore an ivory silk gown, embroidered with a thousand seed pearls. Around her throat rested a choker of diamonds and more pearl teardrops hung at her ears. Last, came the tiara that her grandmother had worn upon her wedding day. It was heavy, but Serena hardly felt the weight of the emeralds and diamonds as her sister adjusted her veil.

Her body and mind were numb as she allowed

them to dress her. She hadn't slept all night, worrying about Karl. Though she'd wanted to reassure him, the fury in his voice when she'd refused to free him had silenced her. She didn't know if her idea would work, and even if she'd released him, she doubted if he would have listened.

No, she could only hope that everything would work out as she and her mother had planned.

The queen sat in a chair watching Serena, a satisfied expression upon her face. 'It's time for the ceremony. Now, behave like the princess you are and prepare for the wedding. All will be well in time. You'll see.'

Her mother departed, leaving her with her ladies. Anna was already dressed and awaiting her at the chapel.

As Serena walked toward the family chapel, surrounded by her ladies-in-waiting, her heart turned from ice into stone. At the thought of her father's fury, a thousand fears rippled through her. What if this didn't work?

Anna walked down the aisle first, carrying a bouquet of spring lilacs tied with ribbons. Serena followed, her hands clenching her own bouquet of white lilies, their deep scent choking her. Her father walked behind her, as was the custom. And yet, she half wondered if he was trying to keep her from fleeing. Her mother sat in the front row, a hopeful look in her eyes.

The bridegroom was kneeling at the altar, his back to the wedding guests. Serena was afraid to look as she knelt by his side.

'You look beautiful,' he murmured, but his voice was not the baron's.

She lifted her eyes to his, fighting to keep her courage.

Don't say a word, Karl's eyes seemed to command.

Serena turned around to glance at the queen and saw her mother's calm, contented smile. It was the greatest act of defiance either of them had ever enacted—to wed the man she wanted, right in front of her father's eyes.

And as she heard Karl's low voice speaking vows before the bishop, followed by her own, she was careful to keep anyone from seeing his face. Rings were exchanged, for the bishop had already blessed them at the altar. The cool band of gold was an intricate band of leaves, and it reminded her of the days they'd spent together in the abbey.

'I told you I hadn't given up,' she murmured beneath her breath.

'Don't be afraid of what happens next,' he answered. 'I love you, Serena.'

When it came time for the kiss of peace, his mouth met hers in a slow kiss that reminded her of all the reasons why she loved him.

Then he turned to face a shocked King Ruwald, along with the rest of the palace witnesses.

'What have you done?' the king demanded. Though his words were directed toward Karl, Serena stepped forward with his hand in hers.

'I've married the man of my choosing,' she answered. 'And you're going to let us go.'

The king's fury was visible on his reddened face, a vein pulsing in his throat. With a signal to his guards, soldiers came forward. Serena tried to grasp her train, and Karl took her by the hand, leading her out the side door of the chapel. Outside, the sunlight nearly blinded her, but Serena ran as fast as she could. Horses awaited them, and Karl lifted her up, before mounting his own stallion.

He sent her a roguish smile. 'Any regrets?'

'None.' With that, she spurred her horse onwards

and rode as fast as she dared. Karl led them down a path that trailed over the hill. When they reached the other side, he pulled his mount to a stop.

Hundreds of soldiers stood armed, with Lohenberg flags flying. She recognised *Fürst* Michael, while behind him was an older man with a greying beard and a shrewd look in his eyes. *König* Sweyn. She recognized the king of Lohenberg in that split moment.

The look in her husband's eyes was one of disbelief and gratefulness.

'I always imagined you'd have a more traditional marriage, Karl,' the king said, by way of greeting.

'So did I.' Karl led Serena forward, bringing her beside the king. When the Badenstein guards emerged over the hillside, the two dozen men stopped short at the sight of the army.

'I sent word to your father and brother, but I never imagined they'd come this fast,' Serena breathed.

Karl reached out and took her hand. 'After I followed you back, Michael and Hannah returned to Lohenberg. He asked our father to intervene.' He pressed the back of her hand to his mouth. 'I didn't know if the king would agree.'

She managed a small smile. 'I'm glad he did. And that our arrangements were successful.'

'You should have told me last night,' he said. 'I thought you were planning to give up.'

'You were so angry with me, you hardly let me speak at all. And there were guards there who were loyal to my father. I couldn't reveal our plan until my mother's servants could free you.' She frowned a moment. 'But I'm not certain what happened to the *freiherr*.'

Karl took her hand in his. 'After we freed his wife and son, Captain Feldmann imprisoned the baron in my place.'

Just what the baron deserved, Serena thought to herself.

'He may need to leave Badenstein after this,' Karl continued. 'Else your father will punish him for the betrayal.'

As if in response to Karl's prediction, the king of Badenstein appeared with his men. Though her father was still dressed in his wedding finery, he looked like a man bent upon revenge. His face was beaded with perspiration, while his ruddy face revealed his fury.

When he moved forward to Serena, he ordered,

'We will have this marriage annulled. I did not give my consent.'

The king of Lohenberg rode forward, his expression calm. 'Ruwald, shall we go somewhere else to discuss this in private?'

'That—that *bastard* just married my daughter!'

'Karl may not be of legitimate birth, but I have recognised him as my son. He and the Princess Serena were betrothed before this, and you agreed to the marriage then.'

With a sudden shift in mood, the king of Lohenberg's voice grew angry. 'But when my son was no longer the heir to the throne, instead of discussing a new negotiation with me, you turned your back on the agreement.'

'I will not have my daughter wedded to a commoner.' Ruwald reached for a handkerchief and swabbed at his forehead. It was as if his rage had manifested itself physically, and he stumbled forward.

Serena urged her horse forward. 'I am proud to be married to Karl. Whether he is a commoner or a prince, it doesn't matter to me.' She bowed to *König* Sweyn, since she could not curtsy on horseback. 'I consider it an honour, and I will gladly pass my claim to the Badenstein throne into Anna's hands.'

'There will be no need for that,' *König* Sweyn responded. 'I have made a different arrangement within my kingdom. Karl will still hold a role of leadership.'

But Serena didn't trust her father to relent. He was clutching his heart, rubbing his arm as if it had gone numb. 'I will not agree to it.'

'Then I will consider your country cut off from mine,' the king of Lohenberg countered. 'We will cease trade between our people. What do you think will happen to your economy? Badenstein is smaller than our country and I assure you, it will have little impact upon us.'

König Sweyn's words seemed to break through to her father. His expression turned pale. 'We will discuss this further. Perhaps…an arrangement may be made.'

'Indeed.' With that, the king directed his soldiers to close in around them as they departed.

Serena held for a moment, as she caught sight of her mother, standing amidst her ladies. 'Wait for me,' she pleaded to Karl.

Instead, he escorted her back, helping her down

from her horse in front of the queen. He dropped to one knee and Clara smiled, raising him up. 'Regardless of what my husband believes, I knew you would make a good husband for Serena.'

'I cannot thank you enough,' Serena whispered, embracing her mother. 'You've given me the most precious gift.'

'And perhaps you'll give me the gift of a grandchild within another year or two,' her mother replied. 'If God grants me that time to live.'

After Serena drew back from her mother, Anna hurried forward and flung herself into her arms. Happy tears filled up her eyes. 'I'm so glad for you, Serena. Truly, I am.'

Serena hugged her sister and promised that she would send for her to visit soon enough. After she finished saying her goodbyes, she cast another look back at her father. His men were supporting him as he walked back to the palace, and defeat did not suit him.

She was so overwhelmed at everything that had happened, she didn't care where Karl was taking her. She was with the man she loved. And that was all that mattered.

* * *

They continued riding for the remainder of the day, until at last they passed the borders of Lohenberg. There, Karl offered his father the hospitality of his home.

'No, thank you,' the king responded. 'We're only a few hours away from the palace. Stay with your bride, and enjoy your wedding night.'

Serena dropped into a curtsy before the king, pressing her forehead to his hand. 'I will forever be grateful to you, Your Majesty.'

König Sweyn appeared pleased. 'I shall expect to see both of you at the nuptials of *Fürst* Michael and Lady Hannah within a few days.' He shook his head as if in disbelief. 'Two weddings within a week. A pity you didn't consult with me sooner, Karl.' A gleam appeared in the king's eyes. 'Or should I say, *Fürst* Karl?'

Serena sent him a startled look. 'I don't understand.'

'I have granted the kingdom of Vertraumen to both of you, as a wedding gift,' *König* Sweyn answered. 'It will still remain a province of Lohenberg, but Karl will rule over the island as their prince. When Michael becomes king, he has agreed to grant Vertraumen its independence, once the province is restored to its previous condition.'

The heaviness in his throat constricted, and Karl bowed before his father. 'Sir. I don't deserve the honour.'

'No, I don't suppose you do. But *she* does.' The king smiled. 'Any woman who can tolerate marriage to you deserves her own kingdom.'

I would lay the world at her feet, if I could. It seemed impossible, that after losing everything, he now possessed wealth beyond price.

'We'll leave you now,' the king pronounced. 'And in the morning, you will bring the princess to the palace. We'll finish the arrangements for Vertraumen at that time.'

When his father had left, Karl embraced his wife. Serena's eyes were shining with joy. 'Even if your father had not restored your title, I would still be happier than any woman in the world. I don't need a prince to know how much I love you.'

'You're everything to me,' he breathed, crushing her close. 'More than any kingdom.'

Epilogue

Karl and Serena walked along the beach with their son Ranier holding their hands. Every few steps, they swung him high while the boy laughed with delight.

Along the edges of Vertraumen were newly built houses, each boasting a small staff and a private beach for the wealthy families who spent their holidays here. It had taken over a year, but the islanders were more than willing to adapt. They'd revitalised the island, making it into an exclusive place where royalty and other wealthy ladies and gentlemen could enjoy a sanctuary with full privacy and no interruptions from the outside world.

And in turn, the people of Vertraumen had enjoyed the profits, becoming a prosperous island kingdom. Karl had formed a council of representatives from all parts of the island, and they held regular sessions to discuss the island's needs. He'd found the people were open to new ideas, and he'd enjoyed bringing mechanical solutions to address their agricultural challenges.

'Have you heard from your mother?' he asked Serena.

She nodded. 'She sent me a letter just this morning. Father still has made almost no recovery from his apoplexy. My mother has tried to assume his duties but...she has asked me to return to Badenstein as Princess Regent.'

'You're still his heir,' Karl said softly. 'Is that what you want?' He knew it would gall the king of Badenstein to no end, if Serena returned to rule over the country. Especially with a bastard husband at her side.

'It won't be easy,' she admitted. 'But if you're with me, it will be all right.'

Just as they reached the manor house, the skies opened, and rain poured down over them. Serena hurried into the house and handed Ranier off to his nurse, with orders for a bath and bed. She kissed her son, but was startled when her husband opened the door and led her back outside.

'What are you doing?' she asked. 'We'll both be soaked.'

Karl took her hand and closed the door, leading her into the garden. As the rain drenched them both, she shrieked when he lifted her into his arms.

Against her ear, he murmured, 'I thought you loved standing in the rain and being foolish.'

She laughed as he lowered her to the ground. 'And I thought you weren't that sort of man.'

'I am when it suits my purpose.'

'What purpose is that?' She lifted her face to the rain, letting it soak through her hair. The water dampened her gown, moulding it to her skin.

'If you're cold and wet, you'll need a hot bath. And then, I'll have to wash every part of you.'

'Will you?' she murmured, pulling him into a fierce kiss. His mouth covered hers, and he tasted both the rain and the promise of a night in her arms. Sending him a wicked smile, Serena added, 'Then I'll need you to help me unbutton my gown.'

Karl took her by the hand and led his wife back into the manor. Although it wasn't a grand palace, it was home in every sense of the word.

And it was everything he'd dreamed it would be.

* * * * *

Mills & Boon® Online

Discover more romance at
www.millsandboon.co.uk

 FREE online reads

 Books up to one month before shops

 Browse our books before you buy

...and much more!

For exclusive competitions and instant updates:

Like us on **facebook.com/millsandboon**

Follow us on **twitter.com/millsandboon**

Join us on **community.millsandboon.co.uk**

Visit us Online | Sign up for our FREE eNewsletter at **www.millsandboon.co.uk**